Reading
BETWEEN
THE
LINES

IN BELOVED OLD TESTAMENT
BIBLE STORIES

PEGGY HOUSTON HENDERSON

WESTBOW
PRESS®
A DIVISION OF THOMAS NELSON
& ZONDERVAN

WestBow Press books may be ordered through booksellers or by contacting:

WestBow Press
A Division of Thomas Nelson & Zondervan
1663 Liberty Drive
Bloomington, IN 47403
www.westbowpress.com
1 (866) 928-1240

ISBN: 978-1-9736-0710-6 (sc)
ISBN: 978-1-9736-0712-0 (hc)
ISBN: 978-1-9736-0711-3 (e)

Library of Congress Control Number: 2017917631

Print information available on the last page.

WestBow Press rev. date: 11/22/2017

DEDICATION

I dedicate this book to the memory of my beloved mother, Myrtle Lewis Houston, who went to be with the Lord on January 17, 1991.

A dedicated Christian and a woman of great faith, she was an encourager and an optimist. When I was discouraged, her words lifted me up. When I was critical, she reminded me to look for, and expect, the best.

My mother loved the Lord, cherished His Word, and fought many battles as a persistent prayer warrior. She taught a Sunday school class of teenage girls, was an active member of her church's Women's Missionary Union as it was called then, and sang in the adult choir. She and my dad enjoyed trips with other Christian senior adults, one of their favorite spots being Ridgecrest Baptist Assembly in the spectacular Blue Ridge Mountains of North Carolina.

I inherited my love of reading from my mother, and writing became an outgrowth of that. I am convinced that if the advantages of today had been available in her time, my mother could have become a writer, herself. As it was, her station in life as a faithful wife of sixty-one years and a devoted mother to four children and loving grandmother to nineteen grandchildren was in her view the highest calling of all.

I am forever thankful for her godly influence. I miss her every day.

ACKNOWLEDGMENTS

There are some special people to whom I want to express heart-felt thanks. They are those who, because of their responses to my first book, *Signposts to Victory*, were an encouragement for me to write another.

First, to retired Army Major Charlie Batson, who purchased the first copy of my first book, thank you. What a needed "feather in my cap" that was! Another church friend, C.R. Salmon, arranged a speaking/book-signing engagement for me with his Lions Club members, an event which proved a boost to my sales. Also, friend Oneta Tally expressed her confidence in me by reserving a dozen copies before she had even read my book and then posting a glowing report on line once she *had* read it. Many other church friends demonstrated their support, as well.

In addition, I am grateful to friend Susie Yeatts, Dolores Moore, niece Daina Wilson, and brother-in-law Cecil who purchased a large number of books to share with friends and family.

Last, and far from least, I appreciate the help of my fellow writing guild members who offer constructive advice and beneficial words of encouragement every time we meet.

To all of these—THANK YOU.

INTRODUCTION

Have you ever wondered what happened *between the lines* in those wonderful Old Testament Bible stories? I mean those which reveal limited information about the characters' lives as a whole.

This seven-part Christian fiction with its historical basis, the Holy Bible, is not intended in any way to alter the purity of the Word of God as it was inspired, recorded, and handed down to us. It is my intention, instead, to fill in some of the spaces by imagining what *could* have happened, what *might* have happened. No one can be sure, of course; but it is interesting, even fun, to visualize the characters, places, and events in their possible entirety.

My hope, my prayer, is that these stories will spark your interest to delve into the lives of these characters even more by reading the entire scriptures from which they come.

Please keep in mind: the Holy Scriptures shall always remain God's Word. The Bible records God's creation of the world, documents the history of His chosen people, provides instruction for wholesome living, and much more. Most important of all, it points us the way, the only way, to salvation through our Lord Jesus Christ.

———◆———

The following stories are based on The NIV Study Bible, Copyright 1985, by The Zondervan Corporation, Grand Rapids, Michigan. The base scriptures from which the stories are taken are listed on the Contents Page. Other scripture references are cited in the notes at the end of the book. Also included in the endnotes are the sources for direct quotations, as well as all researched materials. Paraphrased passages refer to the above translation.

———◆———

Of special interest is the number *seven*. It is significant in the Bible, appearing 735 times. It usually refers to "completeness."[1] Perhaps it is mere chance, or possibly divine direction, but the number of Old Testament stories I chose to explore just happened to be seven. I selected characters whose lives are not covered in the scriptures in as much detail as are some of the others. Another unusual occurrence, not planned at all, is that *every other* story I have included is about a character of the opposite sex. They fell that way when I arranged the sequence of seven stories in chronological order.

I encourage you to enjoy the fascinating accounts of Leah, Aaron, Naomi, Jonathan, Abigail, King Josiah, and Esther. The stories are independent of each other. You may read one, put the book down, and pick it up later to read another.

May you gain a fresh appreciation for these interesting characters found in God's Holy Word.

Contents

Abraham's Family Tree[2]

Terah

Keturah | Hagar | Abraham | Sarah | Nahor | Haran

Milcah | Iscah | Lot

Bethuel

Zimran, Jokshan, Medan, Midian, Ishbak, Shuah | Ishmael | Isaac | Rebekah | Laban

Esau | Jacob | Rachael | Leah

12 Patriarchs + Dinah

Abraham and Sarah

Isaac and Rebekah

Esau

Jacob (Israel)

Leah
Reuben
Simeon
Levi
Judah
Issachar
Zebulun

Rachel
Joseph
Benjamin

Bilhah
Dan
Naphtali

Zilpah
Gad
Asher

12 Tribes of Israel

The Story Of Leah

THE STORY OF LEAH

PREFACE

Generally speaking, people know more about Rachel of the Old Testament than they do about her older sister, Leah. However, even with the deserved attention paid to Rachel, whose son Joseph was instrumental in preserving the remnant of Israel, Leah must be remembered. She bore Jacob six male children, half of his dozen sons who would head the twelve tribes of Israel. She also gave birth to their only daughter, Dinah.

Two of Leah's children, Levi and Judah, were ancestors of Moses and Jesus Christ, respectively.[1] She also had the distinction of being buried with honor in the family cave of Machpelah near Hebron along with Sarah, Abraham, Rebekah, Isaac, and her husband Jacob. Rachel, on the other hand, was buried near Bethlehem as the family traveled from Haran to Canaan.

Most important, though, was Leah's disposition. Though not loved by her husband, and aware of it from the beginning, she remained faithful, steady, and obedient.

We will explore some events surrounding her life that are not recorded but *could* have happened.

The Story of Leah

Background

A busy caravan city, Haran was located in northern Mesopotamia.[2] A man named Terah left his home in Ur of the Chaldeans and went there to live where his son Nahor already resided. He took with him his other son Abraham and daughter-in-law Sarai, along with his grandson Lot whose father had passed away. Shortly after arriving in Haran, Terah died at the age of 205.

Haran became a pause in Abraham's long journey to Canaan where God was leading him. After some time, Abraham continued toward his divine destination, taking his wife Sarai and nephew Lot with him. His brother Nahor and his family remained in Haran.

Two generations after Terah, it was Nahor's son, Bethuel, who gave his daughter Rebekah in marriage to Isaac, Abraham and Sarai's son. In fact, Abraham's servant had traveled all the way from Canaan to Haran for the specific purpose of securing a good wife for Isaac, his master's son of promise. In time, Isaac would do the same for his son Jacob, sending *him* to Haran in search of a wife. It is there where our story of Leah begins.

❖ CHAPTER I ❖

The spring sun sent shafts of light through the sparse trees dotted here and there across the pastureland. Germinated seed pushed tiny stems upward with fresh green leaves, stirring the dormant plants close by from their sleep. The land around Haran was refreshed, ready for a new year.

Nahor's grandson Laban had inherited the family property and had become quite well-known and prosperous. His land stretched as far as the eye could see, populated with the finest breed of cattle one could find. His many sheepfolds, well-stocked with their wooly occupants, resembled large wooden pens blanketed with deep, fluffy snow.

The women of Laban's house flung open wide the windows and inhaled the fresh air as it rushed in. The kitchen soon became busy as Talitha stirred figs in a huge stewing pot while Zilpah prepared dough in a wooden trough at a table nearby. Bilhah, another servant girl, lifted a large pottery urn and headed to the well for water. The morning meal had long since ended, and preparations were already underway for the next. Two of the women had worked for Laban for several years. Talitha, one of these, had been there longer than she cared to remember and knew the master's house better than he did.

Laban was already in the fields overseeing the work of his men servants. His two daughters, Leah and Rachel, up before sunrise, were busy at their own chores. Their mother had died when they were young, leaving them to put into practice the few skills she lived long enough to teach them. Leah, the older of the two girls, was the homemaker. She preferred domestic duties while Rachel, three years younger, loved the outdoors. Rachel relished her role of shepherdess, often dancing along carelessly behind her charges as she guided them to water. No sisters could have been more different. Not only did they have diverse interests, but they also differed in form and demeanor.

Everyone knew Rachel was the beautiful one and did not hesitate to acknowledge it. She had long, abundant raven hair that fell with abandon over her shoulders. Only when her father admonished her did she lift the mass and secure it atop her head. Her big brown eyes were cunning and flirtatious, a feature she often used to her advantage. Being the youngest was another asset she enjoyed, sometimes convincing her father to go along with her whims when he might have known better.

Leah, on the other hand, was more mature in looks and actions. Her serious manner reflected her responsible nature. With Leah, there was no silly play-acting. When there was work to be done, she tackled the task and never complained. In appearance, she was taller than Rachel and had inherited their mother's small, gentle eyes, lighter than Rachel's and devoid of any coquettish tendencies.

Laban's family did not often experience exciting events, unless one counted the elaborate festivities at sheep-shearing time or the occasional wedding of a relative or close friend. That was about to change.

CHAPTER 2

The sun was ready to sink in the orange west when Talitha, busy inside the house, heard Rachel's familiar giggle amid the chatter of the approaching shepherds. She was accustomed to Rachel's high-spirited antics but soon noticed that she was more animated than usual. Talitha opened the door to see what the commotion outside was all about.

"Rachel, why all the excitement?" she yelled.

Almost out of breath as she neared the house, Rachel said, "Someone is coming. Look!" She stopped and turned, pointing toward a stranger walking at a slow pace behind the now well-fed and watered sheep.

"Who is he?" Talitha demanded. Strangers were rarely seen on Laban's place, and she was somewhat concerned.

Rachel came close to Talitha. She took a deep breath, then lowered her voice as she shared her story.

"I went to water Father's sheep, and the other shepherds were already at the well. When I arrived, that man was there. When he saw me, he went over and rolled the stone away from the well opening. He then began watering my flock. Before I could question his identity, he told me he was my cousin, the son of Father's sister, Rebekah. He said he had traveled all the way from his home in Beersheba. Talitha, he kissed me!" She paused to savor the moment before continuing. "I ran ahead of him to warn you. I think he will be staying several days. Oh … his name is Jacob."

Talitha was shocked, yet pleased upon learning the man was a relative. They did not get many overnight guests, and it was exciting. She began thinking about what special foods she and the other servants could prepare. She knew that Leah would be thrilled to add one of her own delicacies, as well. Talitha hurried back inside, eager to announce the news.

Laban came in from the fields and upon hearing Talitha's words, he hurried out to meet his nephew, embraced him, and extended his hospitality. Of course, Laban had no idea that Jacob had fallen in love with his daughter Rachel the moment he saw her at the well; and Jacob was certainly not ready to tell his uncle he had been sent there in search of a wife. Before sending Jacob to Haran, Isaac had made it clear that he must find a wife among their own people, not like Jacob's twin brother Esau who had married three idolatrous women against his parents' wishes.

During the evening meal, Laban introduced Jacob to his three sons as well as his other daughter, Leah, who in her quiet manner moved about helping the servant girls, lifting her eyes now and then to acknowledge Jacob's presence. She could not help noticing that his full attention was on Rachel. It was not surprising to Leah because it was always that way. Even so, she was happy for her sister.

<hr>

After Jacob had been there for a month, not as a mere guest anymore but rather as one of Laban's hired hands, he made his intentions known to his uncle one evening.

"I love your daughter, Rachel," he said, stating his purpose with directness. "I am willing to work for seven years without pay if you will give her to me for my wife."

Not at all surprised by that time, Laban rubbed the beard on his chin, giving the erroneous impression that he must consider the proposal. After a long, intentional pause, he replied, "You are family, Jacob. I would certainly rather she married you than someone else. It is a deal!"

To Jacob's delight, there had been no objection. He loved Rachel so much that he vowed to be patient during the seven-year wait; in fact, because his love was so deep for her, he believed that any sacrifice he had to make would be well worth it. Rachel, on the contrary, was not as forbearing. She questioned her sister Leah about the necessity of their father's decision.

"Our friends never had to wait this long. I don't understand. Jacob has made it clear that he is ready to marry me." She shaped her mouth into a pout. "I'll be an old woman in seven years!" She waited in vain for a response from her sister whose face registered no sympathy.

Disgusted at Leah's seeming lack of concern, Rachel went to a chest near the door and picked up one of the several teraphim in the house. That one, Ishtar, was special to Rachel because it was the goddess of love.[3] She held it close and caressed the human-like head of the stone idol.

Leah crossed the room, turned her sister's hand away from the lifeless figure, and returned it to its place. To divert her sister's attention, she said, "Rachel, Father has his reasons. Just be thankful that Jacob loves you enough to honor their agreement." As Leah spoke the words concerning her father, she wondered if he had come up with the plan in order to get as much work out of Jacob as he could. She felt guilty thinking that way, but she had observed through the years transactions Laban had made that were lacking in total honesty. It pained her to think that this might be such a plan.

The most that Rachel and Jacob saw of each other usually occurred during mealtime. When Rachel voiced her unhappiness to her father, he reminded her that since their mother was gone, leaving him the full responsibility of his daughters, he must enforce stringent rules. In private she scorned his reasoning, knowing full well there was nothing she could do, baby of the family or not.

Jacob saw things differently. Back home, his father Isaac had trained him to be a diligent worker. As a result, he was willing to labor long hours to prove himself worthy of his prize. When he was not caring for herds of cattle, preparing soil for planting, or doing the endless other jobs Laban wanted him to do, his mind was on Rachel. He had never seen such a beautiful woman. In all of Beersheba, there had been none to compare. He wished that his mother and father could see her and get to know her. He was sure they would be more pleased with her than their current daughters-in-law. He dreamed of taking Rachel home with him one day, back to the land of his birth. He had one consolation: *Only seven years. I can do that.*

Day after day, Leah witnessed Rachel's infatuation with her new love. Sometimes when Rachel saw Jacob working with other men near the house, she found an excuse to be outside in his full view. Watching the two as she did, Leah was never convinced that Rachel loved Jacob the way *he* loved *her.* To Leah, it seemed that her sister was merely enjoying a romantic adventure, kept alive by Jacob's flattering attention. As hard as she tried to avoid it, every now and then Leah experienced a passing, wayward fancy of her own. *Rachel is lucky. If I were in her place, I would be a good wife to him. I think Jacob is a good man.*

Little did Leah know how self-fulfilling her musings would become.

CHAPTER 3

The years of service to Laban were long and laborious. Jacob was apart from Rachel most of the time, his living quarters being separate from the main house. He was thankful, though, that his work occupied almost every waking hour, for he was too tired in the evenings to do more than eat and retire for the night. No time for thinking.

Because of the instruction he had received from his father, Jacob was not only a hard worker but also a smart businessman. He devoted his time to improving the quality of Laban's livestock as well as increasing its size. Everything he turned his hand to seemed to prosper, and he came to be recognized around Haran for his keen farming skills.

Although Laban was quite aware of Jacob's contributions, never once did he commend him for all his efforts. He knew the only thing that kept Jacob pushing forward was to gain Rachel's hand; therefore, he decided to enjoy as much work from him as possible in the time agreed upon, a fulfillment of Leah's concerns.

The months slowly turned into years, and at last, the seven years of Jacob's service came to a close. The last few days had been the longest for him. Before going to sleep each night, he had marked the days, and just seeing the lines drawn through the recorded days had kept him sane. Like a runner sprinting toward the prize at the end, he was exhausted, but elated that the victory was close at hand.

After breakfast on the day of his appointed freedom, Jacob was almost breathless as he initiated the conversation with his uncle.

"Laban, I have finished my seven years as we agreed upon. I am ready for Rachel to become my wife." Jacob smiled in eagerness as he awaited Laban's response.

Laban smiled back and said, "Yes, it is time." He sat for a moment, turning over in his mind Jacob's statement. Then with apparent reluctance, he added, "I ... I will host a big wedding feast to celebrate the occasion."

Those words were golden to Jacob, and he rushed out to find Rachel and tell her the good news.

———◆———

The event was festive. Most of Laban's acquaintances, especially the prominent ones, were present at the joyous nuptial celebration. No expense was spared; elegant food and the best wines were in abundance. Totally engaged in the splendor of the occasion, no one present could have imagined the deception that would unfold at the end of the day. That is, no one except Laban.

It was late before the last of the guests departed. Jacob waited with the same patience with which he was well-acquainted, as Rachel with Leah's help prepared for her wedding night. Meanwhile, Talitha kept Jacob busy rearranging items that had been displaced during the celebration. The two of them had no idea what was going on beyond the wall.

Unannounced, Laban entered his daughters' room and explained what would for them become a tale of woe.

"This may be hard for you to understand, girls." He looked from one to the other. "I am short of help. It is almost harvest time, and I must keep Jacob here longer. He is the best worker I've ever had. There is only one way he will agree to remain here. He has already begun talking about returning to his father's home as soon as he weds you, Rachel." Laban avoided eye contact with Leah as he announced, "Now I must do what is necessary to prolong that event."

Taken by surprise, Leah and Rachel froze in place as they stared at Laban, afraid of what he might say next. What frightened them most was that they knew whatever he said, they were obligated to obey.

Laban began. "Leah, you must wear the veil prepared for Rachel. Cover yourself completely. Jacob will come to *you*, expecting your sister."

The strong, finalizing words of their father shook Rachel so much that she swayed, turning pale. Leah reached out to steady her sister.

"I cannot believe you are doing this, Father," Rachel said, barely above a whisper. Standing erect again and regaining her voice, she continued. "I cannot wait longer. I have waited all these years!" If she had not been her father's youngest, and his apparent "pet," she would not have had the courage to say what she did.

"You will do as I say, Rachel," he replied, not to be deterred. "You, Leah, ready yourself for your new husband!"

His flippant manner disturbed them both. They looked at each other, too stunned to utter a complaint, for they knew that in their culture the father was obeyed without question.

Without anyone else knowing, Laban directed Rachel to another part of the house, leaving Leah to ponder what she had just heard. As many times as she had observed Jacob and wondered what it would be like as his wife, Leah felt sorry for her sister. She would never have wanted the evening to end that way. Leah's premonition about her father had come true. It was of no consequence; her father had spoken, and it was the law.

<hr />

The following morning when the sun showered the room with its brilliance, Jacob discovered Laban's deception. There was Leah beside him, not his beloved Rachel. He had no desire to hurt Leah, yet his anger against Laban burned like a fire out of control. He immediately went to find him.

"Laban, why have you done this thing? I have worked hard all these years for Rachel—all in vain!"

The explanation Laban gave his nephew would have been hard for anyone to accept, least of all believe.

"Jacob, you may not be aware of our customs here. The youngest daughter cannot be given before the oldest. I will do this, provided you agree. Live out the rest of the week with Leah. Then I will give you Rachel if you promise to work another seven years."

Jacob was crestfallen. His heart sank. *Seven more years? How can I do that?* But, when he considered further, he wondered how he could *not* do it. He had come to know Laban quite well. He knew it would do no good to ask him why he had not told him all that before. Jacob had never been in such a situation. If he stayed longer, his parents Isaac and Rebekah might think he had met with some disaster and would never return. In addition, how could he trust Rachel's father who had already lied to him? He was caught in an evil web of trickery. He wanted to see Rachel and talk with her about what had transpired. That, too, was in Laban's hands as all decisions seemed to be.

Jacob decided he would finish out the week as Laban said. At least, then he would have Rachel as his own even if he had to remain in Haran much longer than he had planned.

As a gift to Leah, Laban gave her Zilpah to be her maidservant. Jacob would not learn until much later the consequences of having so many women enter his life. He only knew that he loved Rachel and would do whatever was necessary to have her as his wife.

———◆———

Leah's week of having Jacob for her husband was not pleasant. She knew that he did not love her; if so, he would have chosen her in the beginning. Another blow to her heart was knowing that Jacob slept with her that week only because it was part of the agreement. Neither her facial expressions nor her verbal responses to him were offensive; still, before she closed her eyes each night, she wished somehow it could be different, for she loved Jacob with all her heart.

During that week, Rachel's behavior toward Leah changed, inflicting more pain. She began to interpret Leah's innate, strong personality as a declaration of triumph. After all, Rachel had temporarily lost Jacob to an older woman, one she knew could not match *her* in beauty. The fact that it was her sister engendered more jealousy in Rachel than if it had been someone else. Each morning she had to encounter Leah leaving her bedroom after a night with the one she had expected to be *her* husband. Rachel's envy soon bore bitterness.

Leah avoided her sister as much as she could. They did not, of course, share a room anymore, so that made it somewhat easier. Mealtime was different. It became uncomfortable for the whole family as they sat with long faces while pretending all was well. It was not, especially for the two sisters. Leah wanted the week to end. At least Rachel would be happier despite the fact that it was not what she had planned. Leah knew from the start that she, herself, would become Jacob's *other* wife, yet expected to bear him children. That was just the way it was and she would accept it.

Talitha became Leah's only confidante. When things seemed unbearable, Leah sought support from the one she had known for many years, more a friend than a servant. She always chose private times when Rachel was outdoors and Zilpah and Bilhah were too busy to notice.

"I don't want to burden you, Talitha, and it isn't fair for you to choose sides. I just need a word of encouragement." The solemn, earnest expression in Leah's gentle eyes saddened Talitha. She touched Leah's shoulder to show her concern.

"Don't pay Rachel any mind. We all know she is a pampered, spoiled girl, and she is plenty old enough to know better."

"I know, Talitha. It's just that I remember how close we were before Jacob arrived. I miss our talks at night and the fun we once shared. After Mother died, we clung to each other. Besides you, Talitha, there was no one. Father was always busy."

"I have a feeling, Leah, that this is all going to work out. You are much too kind and forgiving not to be rewarded someday. You'll see." She gave Leah a warm embrace and went back to her work.

Leah watched her friend, now up in years, going about her usual duties with calm resignation. Her movements lacked the speed of earlier times, but those words just spoken were a soothing balm to Leah's wounded heart. Talitha's comfort would be needed more in future days because of the changes taking place in Laban's household.

As Laban had promised, he gave Rachel to Jacob at the end of the week. As he had done with Leah, he gave Rachel a servant girl, as well. The selected maidservant, Bilhah, had private reservations, though, preferring instead her former household assignments.

CHAPTER 4

"When the Lord saw that Leah was
not loved, he opened her womb,
but Rachel was barren."[4]

In less than a month, Leah became pregnant. Her body grew heavy as her spirit became weak. She had never been sick and had always had a good appetite; nevertheless, the foods she had loved before were now sickening to her. She was often forced to leave the table to expel what little she had ingested.

As her body grew and evidence of a baby became obvious, she believed she was more undesirable than ever. Yet, it was Leah's new appearance that became a visible, blatant source of Rachel's jealousy, and she resorted to nasty remarks.

"None of your clothes fit you now, Leah. Your tunic doesn't even cover you. You may have to stay in bed soon because you don't want others to see you looking like that."

The words burned, yet Leah kept her tongue. As the months passed and she felt the movement of life within her, she had to smile knowing she would soon present Jacob with his first child. *Maybe he will love me then.*

"I think it will be a son, Talitha," she said one morning. "I don't know why I believe it will be so. If it is, I will name him Reuben. That is a good, strong name."

Talitha smiled. She was pleased to see Leah happy after her months of illness.

"I, too, hope it will be a son, Leah. Jacob will be so happy."

What Leah did not share with her servant-friend was that she hoped once the child was born, Jacob would surely love her.

If Leah's childbearing had been a measure of Jacob's love, he would have loved her immensely because after Reuben was born, Leah bore in rapid succession three more sons, Simeon, Levi, and Judah. She could not have known the future significance of two of those births. All she could think about was that all those sons would make Jacob love her. After all, sons indicated a father's strength, and she had borne him four!

<hr />

Being present as Leah gave birth to those sons should have made Rachel happy for her sister. Their family was growing, and Leah had given her four nephews to love. Instead, Rachel's jealousy exploded into anger, and Jacob became the recipient of her rage.

"What is wrong with you, Jacob? Why have I not become pregnant? If you don't give me children, I'll die."

Jacob tried to be understanding of Rachel's barrenness. Regardless of his patience, her constant nagging soon made *him* angry.

"I am not God, Rachel. There is nothing I can do."

His answer did not satisfy her. Like Abraham's wife Sarah had done many years before, Rachel decided to take matters into her own hands. She gave her maidservant, Bilhah, to Jacob to bear children for her. According to the culture of the time, the child would be recognized as Rachel's own. Even when Bilhah gave birth to a son named Dan, it did not placate Rachel. She again gave Bilhah to Jacob, and she conceived another son and named him Naphtali. Then the "Baby War" began!

Even Leah got caught up in the struggle and displayed a side of herself not seen before. Since she had not been pregnant in some time, and thinking her childbearing years might be over, she used the same tactic that Rachel had used. Leah gave *her* maidservant Zilpah to Jacob, and she, as Bilhah had done, bore Jacob two more sons, Gad and Asher. As the years passed, the battle between the sisters went beyond competition; it was bitter and even involved one of Leah's offsprings.

Not to be outdone, Leah sent her first-born, Reuben, into the fields to gather mandrakes for her. It was believed that if a woman ate of the roots of the plant, she would get pregnant.[5] When Rachel saw Reuben with the mandrakes, she demanded that he must give them to *her*. In defense, Leah, for the first time in her life, yelled at Rachel.

"You have already taken my husband and now you want to take my son's mandrakes?"

By that time, Rachel was desperate. She was ready to do anything that promised fertility, just as Jacob had been willing to do anything to gain her as his wife. So, she bargained with Leah.

"If you will give me the mandrakes, Leah, I will give Jacob up tonight, and he can sleep with you."

Leah agreed and informed Jacob of the bizarre arrangement. The plan, as it turned out, worked in reverse, and Leah, not Rachel, conceived and bore Jacob a fifth son, Issachar, and then a sixth son they named Zebulun. Leah followed that with an unexpected surprise. She bore Jacob's only daughter whom they named Dinah. She could have gloated at her successes, for everyone praised her openly, but she chose not to flaunt her enviable station in life. Instead, Leah grieved that she had fallen prey to the ridiculous game they had played; and contrary to what she had believed, bearing him seven children had not made Jacob love her any more than before. To her surprise, she felt sorry for Rachel who had no children of her own. She might have been comforted had she known that in time *that* would change.

CHAPTER 5

As the years in Haran passed, Jacob became even more of a successful farmer and sheep owner while still working in partnership with his father-in-law. He had worked hard and gained for himself large flocks of sheep along with great numbers of goats, camels, and donkeys. Jacob's sons who were old enough to help their father in the fields became an indispensable asset, as did the many servants he had acquired.

Young Dinah, the delight of Jacob's life, blossomed into a pretty young girl who looked more like her Aunt Rachel than her mother Leah. Rachel looked upon Dinah, the "family darling," with envy, not because she lacked admiration for Leah's only daughter, but because she longed for a child of her own before her child-bearing years were spent.

The Lord heard Rachel's lament. While she was no longer a young woman, God looked upon her with favor, opened her womb, and she became pregnant. She felt that her disgrace had finally ended. She gave birth to a son and named him Joseph. She, like Leah, had no way of knowing the divine plans involving any of their children. Only time would reveal the unparalleled part Rachel's son Joseph would play in the survival of the Israelite nation.

Jacob stayed in Haran for twenty years. He had a large family and had become prosperous in his own right. Although life was going well for him and his family, he decided it was time to return to his homeland. It would be a long trip, perhaps a difficult one. Maybe on the way he could even see his brother Esau who lived in Edom. He also dreamed of a joyous reunion with his father and mother, introducing them to his wives and numerous offspring. He now had eleven sons and a daughter. How proud he was.

First, he wanted to get his father-in-law's blessings before he left. After all, he would be taking Laban's daughters and grandchildren a great distance, and he knew their leaving would be painful for him. What Jacob did not know was that Laban, anticipating such an event, had devised another plan to deceive him.

After the evening meal, Jacob presented his plans to Laban, reminding him of how long he had worked for him. His father-in-law was not happy with the news. He begged Jacob to stay. When he realized his entreaties were futile, Laban asked what he could give Jacob.

Jacob had thought of that ahead of time and laid out his request:

> All I ask is that you give me all the animals, goats and sheep alike, that are spotted or speckled for my own, and you may keep all of those that have *no* markings. I think it would be fair to divide them that way. I will continue working for you until all of this can be accomplished. It may take some time.

Laban knew he had prospered greatly due to Jacob's hard work over the past twenty years, but he was not ready to give in so easily. Verbally, he agreed, even while his wicked mind was already planning a scheme to trick Jacob. That same night, he removed all of the streaked or spotted animals that Jacob had asked for and directed his sons to hide them, perhaps sell them. Then he made himself unavailable by traveling a good distance away from Haran.

The next morning when Jacob learned of the deception, he selected only the strong animals from those left behind and placed tree branches with striped bark in their drinking water. When those he had chosen mated, the females produced spotted, speckled offspring, leaving Laban with only the weaker breeds. Laban who had initiated the deceitful plan would soon find himself the victim of similar trickery.

When Leah heard what had happened between Jacob and her father, she was distraught. She found her faithful friend Talitha who was gathering grapes in the vineyard behind the house.

"Talitha, Jacob has not confided in me, but I think he is making plans to leave right away. One of the male servants said that Father and Jacob have been plotting and scheming against each other for several months and now do not even speak."

Talitha lowered her basket of bounty to the ground and wiped the sweat from her forehead with the back of her hand.

"Leah, I have heard the same thing. You know it is no secret that Jacob has wanted to return to his own home for some time now. That is the only way to have peace in this family." She reached for Leah's hand, holding it for several moments before continuing. "I will miss you, dear Leah, but I believe this is the will of Jacob's God. You will do well wherever you are, and your children will be your comfort. I believe in time Jacob will realize what a good wife you are. He will love you, Leah."

Leah's expression reflected surprise that Talitha would say that, that her friend really believed what she had said. Nonetheless, it made her happy. There was hope.

When Jacob's plans were finalized, he called Rachel and Leah together and told them why he had to leave Laban. Without a word of resistance, the two women began gathering what they needed for the long trip. Though Leah could not prevent what she saw her sister doing, she did not approve. Rachel went throughout the house, selecting several of her father's small idols and packing them into her saddle bags. Although she remained silent, Leah was disappointed in her sister's thievery. Jacob had said that one of God's commandments was that one must not steal.

She is stealing from our father. I could never do such a thing. Besides, I want to know more about this God of Jacob's, the one he talks about so much. He says his father Isaac is a believer, as well. Perhaps when we reach Canaan, I, too, can learn more about Him.

While Laban was away conducting business, Jacob loaded his wives and young children on camels and donkeys; and he and his older sons drove their herd of livestock ahead of the others as they all departed Haran, the only home his wives and children had ever known. Laban was unaware they had left.

CHAPTER 6

Jacob's caravan, including a huge drove of animals, his family of seventeen, and a dozen servants, left Haran and crossed the Euphrates River west of Carchimish. After several days, he and his entourage reached the fertile hill country of Gilead and set up camp. It was a safe place, and there was plenty of water.

Three days passed before Laban returned home and discovered that Jacob had left. He was furious. In haste, he summoned his sons and several of his servants, and they left Haran in pursuit of what Laban considered to be his stolen property and his kidnapped family.

———◆———

The next morning as Jacob prepared to break camp and leave the hill country, Leah and Rachel spoke about their father for the first time since leaving Haran.

"Leah, do you think our father has returned home and learned of our leaving?"

Leah had been wondering the same thing. She knew Laban well enough to know that he would be enraged when he did make the discovery.

"He probably has by now, Rachel. If he finds us, there will most certainly be trouble. Don't worry. We are many, and I don't think he could force us to return."

"I hope you're right, Leah. Our father seems to hate Jacob, and I know Jacob does not trust our father anymore." Rachel looked off in the distance, and for the first time in a long time appeared to be deeply grieved. "If Mother were alive, this would not be happening. She would have had a soothing influence on our father." Rachel lowered her head, and Leah feared her sister might cry.

"Rachel, I miss her, too, even though we have only scattered memories of her."

Before she could finish, the two women, as well as the entire camp, heard the dreaded sound of rapid hoof beats in the distance. Soon dust rose above the horizon, beneath which speeding donkeys could be seen drawing near.

"He's coming, Rachel. We must gather our family together."

The two women and their maidservants found the children and hurried them to their tents. The men soon joined them. No one knew what to expect.

Soon Laban, his sons, and menservants arrived at the camp and halted their animals. Anger etched deep lines in Laban's face, now flushed a bright red from the hard riding. He looked first at Jacob, then toward his daughters and grandchildren.

"Why have you done this? What do you mean leaving without telling me? I didn't even get to kiss my family goodbye. I could do you great harm right now if I had not been warned in a dream not to do so." Laban continued with a more important concern of his. "If that were not enough, you have also stolen my idols."

Jacob assured Laban that no one in their company had his gods. "Search our tents; we haven't disassembled them yet. If you wish, search each person. You will not find them here. If you do, I promise you, that person will not live!" If Jacob had known that his beloved Rachel was the thief, he would not have uttered those condemning words.

Laban looked in every tent, turning items this way and that in his quest. He had no idea that his own daughter was the guilty party. When Rachel saw her father in his relentless hunt, she hid the stolen idols under her saddle. Looking on, Leah silently compared her sister's deceit with that of their father who had tricked Jacob into working all those years. Furthermore, she knew that Laban had taken his dishonesty a step further by hiding the animals that rightfully belonged to Jacob. While she could not control her father's behavior, she could easily have divulged Rachel's hiding place and gotten revenge for years of hurt. She did not.

The idols were not found, and Jacob's ire flared because of Laban's harsh words. He again reminded his father-in-law of how hard he had worked for him and the number of years he had spent acquiring his wives. He ended by accusing Laban of his latest acts of trickery.

After much hashing of old hurts and resentments by both men, they at last reached a resolution. In fact, they made a covenant, sealing it by erecting an altar as visible proof of their agreement. Before leaving for his home, Laban issued one last demand.

"Do not ever mistreat my daughters."

After Laban departed and the dust had settled, Jacob and his family packed and continued toward the land of Canaan.

CHAPTER 7

When they reached Mt. Seir in the country of Edom, Jacob took measures to contact his brother Esau whom he had not seen in over two decades. Back then, the two had parted on a bad note.[6] Regardless of the past, Jacob longed to see his brother and effect a reconciliation. He was unsure how Esau might judge his intentions. As a precautionary gesture, Jacob sent out his servants with a message of kindness and good favor for Esau if, or when, they found him. Also, they were to tell Essau all about Jacob's family.

Leah and Rachel for the first time in a long time began to share their common interests in what was occurring. They had discussed their father Laban's threats and deceit, and now they were about to meet their brother-in-law they had only heard about.

"It will be interesting to see our husband's twin brother. I have been told they looked nothing alike when they were young." Leah's light-hearted words revealed how glad she was that lately she and Rachel could talk with each other as two loving, mature women.

"I know," said Rachel. "His brother has red hair. Can you believe that? I bet he has a long red beard, don't you?"

"Probably so, Rachel. Talitha said that even the word 'Edom' means 'red.'[7] I wonder which came first!" The two laughed, something they had not done since Jacob arrived at their father's house.

After some time, the menservants returned and told Jacob that Esau would be coming in the morning with 400 men to meet him halfway. That night as Jacob was alone, he prayed to God for his protection and that of his family. Then an amazing event occurred. God, appearing as an angel, wrestled with Jacob to emphasize that Jacob's struggle was really with Him, not with Esau nor Laban, and that all blessings come from Him, alone. During the encounter which lasted all night, God changed Jacob's name to Israel, a name by which the chosen people of God would be called from that time forward. The encounter left Jacob with a limp as a reminder of his meeting with the Almighty.

The following morning, Jacob began to evaluate his situation before going out to meet his brother. Since he did not know if the meeting with Esau would be cordial or retaliatory, he again chose caution. He selected 550 animals to offer Esau and told his servants to lead them out ahead. Behind them, he placed Bilhah and Zilpah and their children, then Leah and her children, and last of all, Rachel and Joseph. Jacob then went in front of his family to be the first to confront his brother Esau.

Leah was quite aware of the position Jacob had chosen for her and her offspring. They were placed closer to the point of harm than Rachel, Jacob's favorite. She said nothing; all the same, her heart was bruised.

Will he never cease honoring her above me? I have borne him six wonderful sons and a precious daughter, yet that means nothing to him. I don't think Talitha's prediction will come true, not as long as Rachel lives.

Leah did not know that she would live to see her thoughts fulfilled.

———◆———

Jacob and Esau marched toward each other, each unable to predict the outcome. When Jacob spotted his brother, he left his mount, walked forward, and bowed down seven times. Much to his surprise, Esau dismounted, as well, and ran to meet Jacob and hugged him and kissed him. The two men wept for joy. Releasing his hold, Esau asked about all those people he saw. Jacob was proud to introduce his loved ones. He further explained that the animals led by the servants were sent as a gift to him. Esau did not want to take them, saying he had plenty. After Jacob insisted, Esau finally accepted the lavish gift of animals too numerous for him to count.

What a happy reunion the brothers had; they had much to share. When they settled down, Esau revealed some sad news. He told Jacob that their mother Rebekah had died. Somehow word had not reached Jacob or Rebekah's brother Laban. Jacob's joy changed to grief, and his tears expressed great sorrow as well as regret. It was his mother who had helped him gain the birthright from his brother Esau.[8] At the time he was young and close to his mother. As a result, he became a willing party in deceiving his father Isaac. Later, when it pained him to see Rebekah's unhappiness at Esau's choice of wives,[9] he decided then he would never hurt her in that way. Many times in Haran he had wished his mother could know Leah and Rachel, for he knew she would have approved of *them*. Now he had to put all of that aside. He had found his brother, and the meeting had gone well for both of them. Old ills were healed.

The next day Esau and Jacob said their goodbyes. Jacob still had territory to cover before reaching Canaan. Little did he know that an incident involving his daughter, Dinah, would cause them even more delay.

CHAPTER 8

At last, Jacob reached the land of Canaan, stopping near the place where his grandfather Abraham had built an altar many years before. The place was called Shechem, and there Jacob also set up an altar to the Lord. In addition, he purchased a portion of land from a man named Hamor who was a Hivite. He failed to consult God before taking such action and, as a result, the acquisition would prove to be a mistake.

The next day after Jacob's family had settled in their new camp, Dinah, who had grown into a beautiful teenage girl, made a request of her mother Leah.

"I have seen some young people in the area, Mother. May I go out to see if I can meet them? This has been a lonely trip for me. I would like to find someone my age."

Leah sympathized with her daughter. At least, she, herself, had a sister with whom to talk; and now that they were on better terms, it was good to enjoy a pleasant female relationship.

"Yes, Dinah, you may go, but please be careful. We do not know these people, and your father might not approve. Remember, your brothers are close by if you need them."

"I will be watchful, Mother. Thank you." Dinah gave Leah a tight squeeze and she left the tent, happy to be on her own for once.

As Dinah strolled through unfamiliar surroundings, Hamor's son, who had the same name as the town of Shechem, saw her. He had never seen a girl so lovely and wondered why he had not seen her before. With the local girls, he never had trouble making advances. It was obvious this girl was not one of them. He paused for a moment, conjured up the nerve he needed, and then approached her. He even gave a slight bow to show his respect.

"Pardon me. I have not seen you here before. I am Shechem, son of Hamor."

Dinah was somewhat taken aback. She was not accustomed to young men addressing her so openly. Before responding, she took a moment to assess the brash stranger. She remembered her mother's warning to be cautious.

"I am not from this area. My father just yesterday bought some land over there." Dinah shaded her eyes with her hand and pointed east of the town. "We are a large family. I don't know how long we will be here. We are on our way to my grandfather's home. He now lives in Hebron."

A spark of recognition crossed the young man's face. "Oh, so you belong to the man Jacob who purchased the land from *my* father Hamor."

The two smiled at each other, and Dinah began to feel more at ease.

"Yes, Jacob is my father. I don't know that I *belong* to him," she said, with a slight hint of assertiveness.

"I'm sorry. I just meant…." He stopped in the middle of his explanation and stood gazing upon Dinah's beauty. Then he uttered such glorious words of affection, words foreign to her ears, that Dinah was completely captivated by his charm.

Before she was aware of the entanglement that entrapped her, Dinah allowed Shechem to lure her to a spot in a field not far from his home. There he defiled Leah and Jacob's only daughter and left her, hurt and crying, and went on his way.

As soon as she could, Dinah pulled her clothing tightly about her, and physically devastated and emotionally shamed, she made her way back to her mother's tent.

Since there was no hiding her general appearance and her tear-stained face, she explained to her mother what had happened. Leah straightway sent for Jacob and informed him.

When Jacob's sons came in from the fields, he told them what had occurred. They were incensed that Shechem had disgraced their sister, and they began planning their revenge.

In the meantime, when Hamor learned of his son's indiscretion, he and Shechem went to see Jacob and his sons to remedy the situation.

"Men, please understand. This is a terrible thing, but my son loves the girl. He wants her for his wife." Hamor ventured further in order to make the proposition more enticing. He said, "Also, we will be glad to share our daughters with your sons. You can all live here with our people."

"Yes," his son added, "I will pay whatever price you ask. Please let me have her for my wife. I love her, and I want to do the honorable thing."

Honorable? It was at that moment that Jacob's sons put their plan into motion. They agreed to what Hamor and Shechem had suggested—with one exception. If they were to intermarry, the Hivites would have to be circumcised, just as *they* were, to avoid disgrace among Jacob's family. As surprising as such a drastic stipulation was, Hamor, nevertheless, agreed. He convinced all the men of their city to participate in the process, promising that, as a result, they would all get to share in the abundance of livestock and other belongings that Jacob owned.

Three days after all the men of Shechem had been circumcised, two of Dinah's brothers, Simeon and Levi, laid seize to the city and killed all of the males; and with the aid of their brothers, they took everything of value, including the women and children.

Leah stood in the doorway of her tent looking out on her sons' confiscations; strange women and children were everywhere. Dinah came up behind her mother and touched her shoulder. Leah turned, and her sad eyes rested on her sweet daughter.

"My child. Well, obviously you are no longer a child. I am so sorry this thing has happened to you. Who would have imagined that a mere walk into the town would cause such a disaster. I blame myself. I should not have allowed you to go." She swept a stray wisp of hair from her daughter's forehead. "As devastating as it was, Dinah, your brothers should not have taken revenge. They believed it was their duty to right the wrong done to you; nonetheless, your father says that revenge belongs only to God." She paused to change the subject. "It is good we will be leaving here tomorrow for a place called Bethel. We will stop there for a day or two. Your Aunt Rachel cannot travel as far in a day as she once did. As you know, she is with child for a second time, and she will be delivering soon."

CHAPTER 9

Before leaving Shechem, Jacob made all the captured Hivites hand over their false gods, which he buried under an oak tree. He then set out for Bethel where God directed him. When he reached the place where God had appeared to him many years before when he was fleeing from Esau, he built an altar to commemorate the event.

The trip from Shechem to Bethel took its toll on Rachel. She hoped they would stay there longer; it was not to be. Instead, after three days Jacob set out for Bethlehem, hoping thereafter to reach his father's home in Hebron. In spite of his plans, their lives were about to change—again.

On the way, Leah noticed that her sister Rachel had become listless and at times unresponsive. Unable to walk even a short distance, she now rode upon one rested donkey after another. Her pregnancy was responsible for her heaviness, but it was more than that. Leah, having put all past grievances behind her, rode beside her sister with a watchful eye.

"Here. Drink from my water bag," she begged Rachel. "It is cool and will refresh you. Your face is flushed from the heat. Shall I tell Jacob we need to stop as soon as we find a cool place? I think that's a small grove of trees I see in the distance."

Rachel was too weak to reply; she just nodded her head. Leah was worried. She dismounted and ran ahead to find Jacob who was helping his sons prod the herds, now much larger because of their ill-gotten plunder in Shechem.

"Jacob! Jacob!" she called. "I think we must stop when we reach those trees ahead. Rachel is not well. I know about such things, Jacob, and I know she needs a comfortable place to lie down."

Jacob's brow wrinkled, for he loved Rachel with all his being as he had since first he saw her shepherding her father's sheep.

"I will do as you say, Leah. We will be there soon." Jacob began to drive the herds faster, and Leah waited for her own donkey to catch up before continuing her vigil beside Rachel. She assured Rachel that her only child, Joseph, was safe in the company of the older brothers.

Before the large caravan could find a place to stop, Rachel began calling out. It was not for her husband Jacob; she called for her sister.

"Leah, the baby is coming. Please prepare me a place."

Word got to Jacob, and he called a halt beside the road. Several of the women placed blankets in a field of deep grass and prepared a birthing stool. Before long, Rachel's screams could be heard throughout the crowd; some hearers were curious, others concerned. The birth was a difficult one, and Leah again and again wiped her sister's wet forehead during the process.

After what seemed to Leah an eternity, one of the Hivite women with them, who claimed to be a midwife, delivered the baby from Rachel's body and announced, "It's a son ... a fine-looking son."

With what little breath that remained, Rachel whispered, "I will name him Ben-Oni, for it means 'son of my trouble.'"[10]

As another woman took the baby away for cleansing, Leah clasped Rachel's hand. There was nothing Leah could say; the pain in her heart was too great. She knew her sister was dying and was still holding Rachel's hand as she slipped away.

Mourning spread throughout the camp. Jacob knelt beside his beloved Rachel and wept bitterly. After some time, his sons led him away.

◄──◆──►

Rachel was buried there where they had stopped before reaching Bethlehem. Jacob set up a pillar of stone to mark the place. When the period of mourning ended, Jacob held his son for the first time and named him Benjamin, instead, which meant "son of my right hand." He was Jacob's only child born in Canaan.

⟿ CHAPTER 10 ⟾

"A happy heart makes the face cheerful,
but heartache crushes the spirit."[11]

On toward Hebron Jacob and his enlarged family proceeded, stopping late in the day at a place called Migdal Eder. Leah had already endured more heartache than most of the women in her husband's life; that stop burdened her even more. Her own son, her first-born Reuben, went into the tent of Rachel's servant Bilhah, who was also Jacob's concubine, and slept with her.

When the news reached Leah, she fell to her knees in despair. With whom could she share her sorrow? Her only sister was dead, and she did not want to share with Dinah the terrible wrong her brother Reuben had committed. Of course, word was already out. What could Leah do?

It is my husband's place to take action, not me. I am angry with the first child of my womb, but I can do nothing. He is now a grown man.

Pain gripped Leah's heart as she recalled all the events that had occurred since Jacob first came on the scene.

I will put this away as I have done many things before. I am learning of this God Yahweh. He will sustain me through whatever comes. No god of stone can do that. I know it here. Leah pressed her heart. *I cannot see Him, but His presence is real.*

She rose from the floor of the tent and began preparing food for her family which now included Joseph and Benjamin, as well.

At long last, they reached the home of Isaac in Hebron. Jacob found his father very ill. He looked into Isaac's eyes to see if he could get his attention. The moment brought back memories of another time, many years before, when he and his mother Rebekah had tricked Isaac into blessing *him* instead of Esau. Even then Isaac's eyesight had been poor. Now his eyes were vacant; the aged father and grandfather could not see at all. If he recognized his son's voice, it was not evident. Even so, Jacob brought his wife Leah and all his children and introduced them to his father, one by one. Only once did Jacob see a faint smile part Isaac's lips when his grandchildren's names were announced as they paraded before him.

It seemed that Isaac had been waiting for Jacob's return so he could die. The life in his feeble body began ebbing away. A week after arriving in Hebron, Jacob sent Levi and Simeon back to Edom to summon Esau. He knew Isaac's time was short, and Esau needed to be there.

Leah was sad for Jacob, for herself, and for her children. She had hoped to learn much from Isaac, and now that was not to be. At the age of one hundred and eighty, he died before Esau arrived.

Isaac's two sons buried him in the field of Machpelah near Mamre where Isaac had buried his wife Rebekah. It was the piece of land Isaac's father Abraham had purchased many years before, the place where he and his wife Sarah were also entombed.

Even with all that had happened, Jacob decided to remain there at Hebron, for it was the destination he had long sought. He was finally home.

⟶⟰ CHAPTER II ⟰⟵

Leah was a dutiful surrogate mother to Joseph and Benjamin. She treated them as her own children and truly loved them. After all, they were her husband's sons, too. Of the two, Joseph was the dreamer. He was different from his young brother Benjamin. In fact, he was different from all the sons. Perhaps because of Jacob's love for Rachel, he favored Joseph and openly demonstrated it. He even made Joseph a decorative, embroidered robe, perceived by the other sons as a sign of obvious partiality, engendering immense jealousy among them.

Leah was careful not to interfere. It was just not done. However, an incident involving Joseph pushed her to break with tradition somewhat.

One afternoon Joseph came in from the fields telling his father Jacob about a dream he had. He said that in the dream he was in a wheat field where his own sheaf rose upright while his brothers' sheaves bowed down to his. He went further by telling of a second dream in which not only eleven stars bowed down to him; the sun and moon did, as well.

Leah listened as Jacob rebuked Joseph. He asked, "'Will your mother and I and your brothers actually come and bow down to the ground before you?'"[12] The mild reprimand was all Joseph received, and Leah decided she must give Joseph some advice of her own as soon as she had the chance.

The opportunity came the next morning when Joseph came in from his work to get a drink of water. Leah was kneading dough when she saw him enter; she gave the dough one final push with the heel of her hand and turned to face him, waiting a moment to gain his attention.

"Joseph, do you have so little respect for your parents that you would even dream of us bowing down to you? You are our son, not a king!"

Seventeen-year-old Joseph looked at Leah with kindness and said, "I am sorry Aunt Leah. I did not mean to be disrespectful. I have no control over these things, these dreams. They are real to me. I do not know all that they mean. I only know they seem real and I cannot dismiss them from my mind."

"All dreams seem real, Joseph. Even if you mean no harm, telling your brothers such things is not good. You don't want them to hate you." She stopped and pointed to the tall pitcher of water near where she was working. "After you enjoy the refreshing water, go on your way." When he finished, she patted his shoulder as he passed her on his way out to the fields again.

When he was gone, Leah pondered all that Joseph had said. She knew from her own life that God works in strange ways to fulfill His plans. *Can this be something big? Do these dreams mean anything at all?* She could only wonder. Time would reveal that Leah would never witness the importance of the young man's dreams nor the result of the perilous circumstances that would bring it all to pass.

❖

The land on which Isaac had lived was spacious enough for Jacob's large family, as well as all of his animals and accumulated goods. After the land was prepared for planting, he and his sons constructed lodging facilities, including adequate shelters for the Hivites who were still part of their company. The house Jacob built was Leah's first after leaving her father's home in Haran. She was happy to have ample room in which to cook and serve her family. Zilpah and Bilhah had their own dwellings where they provided for the four children they had borne Jacob. It was a good arrangement and all seemed well, that is, until Joseph went missing.

The scene was one of chaos. Jacob's oldest sons had been in the fields working. When they returned, Judah, followed by his brothers, rushed into the house holding a bloody remnant, saying it was Joseph's. They said some wild animal must have torn him apart and carried off his remains and all that was left was a piece of his robe. When Jacob heard their story, he was grief-stricken and could not be comforted. Covered in sackcloth, he mourned for days, refusing to eat. Leah went to Jacob time after time trying to encourage him.

"Maybe it is not what it appears. Joseph could have shed his robe because of the heat, and some animal was attacked and killed there where he left it.

That is possible, Jacob. We just don't know yet. You know Joseph likes to explore. He could have gone off somewhere hunting for birds. Please, my husband, do not be so sad."

Leah's words were in vain. Jacob found no peace in them. She returned to her own room, broken-hearted for Jacob and for his beloved son. She was sorry she had reproved Joseph that day in the kitchen.

As she lay upon her pillow, random thoughts captured her attention. Something about her sons' story did not add up. They had made no mention of seeing any wild animals in the area, not that day or anytime since they had been in Hebron. The bloody fragment the brothers said they found was part of the robe their father had made for Joseph. It was no secret that the sons resented Joseph and often made fun of him. His dreams had stirred fierce anger in them, especially since Joseph seemed to relish telling them the full details. As Leah put the pieces of their story together, she suspected foul play involving Joseph's brothers, and it broke her heart.

Leah, who had never allowed herself the luxury of self-concern, began to feel a burdensome weight, too overwhelming to overcome. Wearisome facts flooded her mind, one after the other: she as Jacob's "other" wife, the struggles with her sister, her father Laban's deceitfulness, Dinah's defilement, Rachel's death, Reuben's sexual exploits, and now Joseph's disappearance. All those things were more than she could bear. An added worry was Jacob's inconsolable bereavement.

Thinking of her beloved Jacob, she rose and went to him. When she saw his weakened condition, she made broth and tried to feed him, telling him he must eat. He groaned in response. After many futile attempts, Leah, disheartened, started back to her room. She had never felt so low. The spark that had always charged her onward was gone. She slowed for a moment and grabbed her left shoulder. She tried to push forward. Before she could reach the door to her room, her legs collapsed and down she went.

Later, it would be said that Leah died of a broken heart. Her life ended in much the same way she lived it daily—in service to others.

What a sorrowful time, for Leah was greatly loved. All the sons, even those not her own, mourned her death for many days. Dinah was devastated and secluded herself in Leah's room, saying she wanted to inhale the sweetness that was her mother. The Hivite women who had been captured by Jacob's sons in Shechem came in groups to express their grief, each one telling a story of Leah's kindness.

Although Jacob was still suffering the loss of Joseph, he, too, wept in loud groans of sorrow beside Leah's body. It is possible he regretted his lack of attention to the one who had stood beside him no matter what happened. He had come to love Leah, but had never expressed it the way he had for Rachel.

It had been only a few months since Jacob and Esau had buried their father Isaac. Now, Jacob and his sons and daughter buried Leah in the same place, the cave of Machpelah near Mamre in the land of Canaan.

In the future, Leah's life would be viewed as meaningful beyond what she could have imagined. Her son Levi would one day be chosen to head the priestly line of God's chosen people, Israel. Her son Judah would be the ancestor of Jesus Christ, the long-awaited Redeemer of the world. What a contribution the modest, weak-eyed, second-place wife of Jacob made without ever knowing it. That is likely the way she would have wanted it.

The Story Of Aaron

THE STORY OF AARON

PREFACE

Much is known about Moses who became the great leader of the Israelite people, leading them from captivity in Egypt to the threshold of the Promised Land. But, it was his brother, Aaron, who became his spokesman to carry out God's plan for his chosen ones.

We will explore Aaron's role in that colossal movement as presented in the Holy Scriptures. In addition, we will speculate as to what might have happened "between the lines," information we do not have for a certainty and can only imagine. The spectacular assistance Aaron provided Moses was certainly noteworthy, but his being chosen as the first priest in the line of Levi was an event that set the standard of future worship for the Israelite Nation for years to come.

Chapter 1

Moses, a Levite, was reared in the household of the pharaoh of Egypt while his fellow-kinsmen were living in bondage there. One day he saw an Egyptian mistreating an Israelite and killed him. He fled to the land of Midian where he lived for forty years. There he took a wife, Zipporah, who bore him two sons, Gershom and Eliezer.

When God's timing was perfect to release His people from their burdens in Egypt and direct them to the land promised years before to Abraham, He chose Moses for the daunting role of leader. Speaking to him from a burning bush near Mount Horeb, God revealed His plan. Moses, overwhelmed, balked at the notion of such a huge undertaking, saying that he was "...slow of speech and tongue."[1] God had an answer. He informed Moses he would provide him help for the mission—his brother Aaron— who was three years older and still living in Egypt. He would become Moses' mouthpiece. According to God's plan, the two brothers must meet in the Sinai Desert.

Nearly two weeks passed before Moses set out with his wife and sons to meet Aaron. It would be a longer trip for his brother traveling from Egypt than for them. Moses was quite familiar with the area where they were to meet because he had often herded his sheep on the eastern side of the desert not far from his home in Midian.

Meantime in Egypt, the land was ruled by a narcissistic pharaoh whose central purpose was to build a vast empire that would exalt him above all those who had come before. Of great concern to him was the rapid growth of the Israelite population in his country. He viewed them as a serious threat to his absolute control. His solution was to subdue them while he had the chance. Therefore, he imposed upon all the men of working age burdens so heavy that they soon became unwilling but helpless vassals. In their dire distress, they did as their ancestors had done many times before: they cried out to God. He heard their pleas and promised to deliver them from their oppression.

At that time, Aaron had no idea of God's visit with Moses at the burning bush. After all, his brother had been gone for forty years. Aaron had heard about him several times from traders who journeyed from Midian to Egypt. Even so, the news was scant, leaving Moses' family wondering how, in fact, he was faring in that distant land.

Like his Israelite relatives and neighbors, Aaron worked hard to provide for his wife and extended family. He had little time to ponder the state of political affairs in Egypt. Most evenings his body was in great pain from bending over for hours, mixing mud with straw and pouring it into wooden forms, one after another, all day long.

One evening after the family meal, Aaron ventured outside to be alone, to enjoy a few moments' respite from the difficulties of the day. The clear night sky showcased a canopy of brilliant stars, twinkling in random rhythm. It was in such a setting that God chose to speak to His servant Aaron.

The voice was unmistakable. Aaron knew for a certainty it was God speaking. The message was brief: *Aaron must become his brother's voice to free their people from Pharaoh's bondage. Aaron must go to the Sinai Desert and meet his brother Moses who would tell him what to do.* That was all.

Aaron was shaken. His first inclination, after regaining a measure of calm, was to tell God he could not do that. He could not just up and leave his family. What would happen if he failed to appear at his job? Yes, living conditions were bad for all the Israelites, but at least it was a life to which they were accustomed. They knew what to expect.

He paused and sighed deeply. He knew better. God's word had always been final, and he had no choice. He was also convinced that God would somehow make a way.

He pondered for a time the message he had received from Almighty God before going back inside to tell his wife, Elisheba. He was not sure how she would respond; nonetheless, she must be told. He faked a smile as he re-entered his home.

Elisheba, busy clearing the table, stopped when she saw Aaron. He asked her to be seated so he could give her some shocking news. That, alone, got her attention. She sat and listened intently as her husband repeated his encounter with Yahweh. She remained attentive as he enumerated all the excuses he had wanted to offer God. Then her countenance changed as the full extent of God's message sank in. Aaron would be going away!

Elisheba was a good wife. All the same, she had reservations about the call even if it *had* come from God. Yes, her children were grown, had children of their own, and did not need her anymore; but she had learned to depend on her husband for so much, not the least of which was his daily counsel and reading of the Holy Scriptures. His work, making bricks for the pharaoh's numerous projects, had become extremely hard, still it provided compensation necessary for their survival. They had somehow managed. What would she do while he was gone? Aaron had never been away from her for more than several hours during his workday. Now she might have to look to others for help, something she had never done. Furthermore, she was getting on in age. While she knew it best to encourage her husband, it was not in her heart to do so.

Early the next morning, Aaron decided to summon his sister Miriam for advice. Along with his wife, he also included his four sons who needed to be informed of this declaration so vital to each one of them. When they were all assembled, Aaron reiterated in detail the event that had transpired the evening before.

Miriam had no qualms about advising her brother. She had always reasoned that she was older and probably wiser. She looked directly at Aaron and began.

"Poor Aaron. You haven't changed much, still unable to make up your mind. Do you remember when we were young children and our father wanted to build small chairs for us. He said you could have a rocker like he was making for me, or a small straight chair. One minute you wanted a rocker; the next minute you wanted a straight chair. Going back and forth finally wore on Father's nerves, and he said you would just have to wait until you were old enough to build your own. That was the final word from our father.

"Your indecision, Aaron, left you empty-handed that day as it did many times thereafter. Don't let that happen now. God has called you. You cannot fail if He is with you. You must go!"

Miriam's words stung Aaron's heart, and it embarrassed him that his sister had to chastise an eighty-three-year-old brother, father, and husband. He had to concede that only Miriam could get away with being so honest with him.

CHAPTER 2

Much had to be done before Aaron departed Egypt for his trip to meet Moses. Elisheba half-heartedly packed food in as many small, individual vessels as she could find, enough to sustain her husband for several days. She included enough for the return trip to Egypt, as well.

As she prepared the supplies, she stopped to thank God for all the food laid out before her on the table. One great blessing the Israelites had enjoyed there in Egypt was the fertile land of Goshen they called home.[2] Over four hundred years before, Jacob's son, Joseph, had found favor in a different pharaoh's eyes and had been given that area of Egypt for his family. There they had prospered and increased in number. There they were able to raise crops that produced an abundance of food, and there they had plenty of grazing land for their animals. Times then were good until later pharaohs came into power who were harsh and unyielding. Even so, the Israelites' one remaining blessing was food, plenty of food.

As time drew near for Aaron's departure, Elisheba begged him to let her accompany him. He refused to even entertain the subject, assuring her he would be fine and that it was much safer for her to remain at home. When her entreaties failed, she said he should at least take a neighbor, someone, with him. Again, he said no, that the two donkeys would be his companions. He laughed at his remark, hoping to lighten the moment, while in his heart he was sincere in thinking: *I must exercise my faith by striking out on my own.*

With the help of his sons, Aaron loaded one of their donkeys with all Elisheba had prepared, including ample blankets and extra clothing. With all readiness complete, Aaron bid his loved ones goodbye as he blessed each of them. It was a sad day. Aaron assured Elisheba and the others that since God had called him, He would surely guide his steps.

Aaron had never been out of Egypt, only to its border once. He knew from traders the best direction to take; still an uneasiness troubled him. Never had he felt so alone, and the donkeys were no help! He had always been surrounded by people, his own people, even when working. Now he was uncertain as to the outcome of this adventure of faith. On the one hand, he knew God would show him the way; on the other hand, he felt utter inadequacy in fulfilling his calling. His sister Miriam was so right.

Despite any misgivings, onward he trod, like a soldier scouting unfamiliar enemy territory. His one consolation was that God was the Commander, directing his every move.

Aaron's journey was long and often difficult. The nights were cold even with warm blankets, and the days were hot. Not one person did he encounter on his way which he determined was a blessing, for he had heard tales of robbers overcoming lone travelers in the desert.

The countless miles allowed Aaron much time to contemplate. *I must not think of my home and family, else I might turn around.* Regardless, unbidden memories of his long ago childhood flooded his mind. At that time, as a means to control the expansion of the prolific Hebrews, Pharaoh had ordered all male Israelite babies must be killed. His brother, Moses, was an infant. Through a sequence of miraculous events, Moses was spared by Pharaoh's daughter who took him to live with her. To others it might have seemed strange that he and Miriam were never jealous of their brother living in the lavish luxury of Pharaoh's palace. Their mother, Jochebed, had reminded them often that it was God's will and that Moses was saved for some great purpose. For many years nothing had come of her prediction. Aaron now believed he was about to see its fulfillment.

The anticipation of seeing his brother after all the years encouraged Aaron and gave him hope. Still, he could not help but wonder: *Will Moses look the same? Will I even recognize him? Surely he will be alone and that won't be a problem.* To put his mind at ease, he reminded himself that the God of Abraham, Isaac, and Jacob was directing his steps and all would be well. He was not to worry.

After twelve long days of uncertain terrain and changing weather, Aaron reached his destination. God had led him to the exact spot where Moses was waiting: Mt. Sinai, a place that would become more significant in the years to come.

Aaron, exhausted as he was, released his hold on the reins of one of the donkeys and ran toward his brother. The two who had not seen each other in forty years greeted each other with a strong embrace. They stepped back in awe of one another. Moses stood tall and strong in his long, striped flax simlah,[3] bleached by the sun the color of the sheep he had herded. His broad, chiseled face, framed by a thick, graying beard, characterized his overall countenance as one wise and resolute. In sharp contrast, Aaron was much thinner than his brother, and his creased face bore evidence of many years of hard labor. His clothing consisted of a light, loosely-woven linen galabeya topped by a long kaftan, indicative of common Egyptian apparel.[4] Moses looked older that Aaron had expected, but good manners dictated that he not mention it. Of more importance than appearance to both of them was what they must discuss concerning God's plans for them. Before that, they wanted to renew their family ties, for much had changed in the past four decades.

"Is your wife Elisheba well, Aaron? And what about your four sons … they were so young when I left Egypt. Are they still there?" Moses threw out one question after another, eager to learn all he could about his distant family.

"Elisheba is fine, as well as our sons who are grown men now, of course. Our sister Miriam is well, too. After all these years, Moses, she still talks of keeping her eyes on you there in the Nile River where our mother had placed you in a little basket to save you from Pharaoh's annihilation of all the male Hebrew children. Only seven years old at the time, she still has a vivid recollection of each minute detail. She was so happy when Pharaoh's daughter found you and took you to live in the palace. Miriam was wise. She was able to convince the princess to allow our mother to nurse you until you were weaned. I was really too young to remember much about it.

"Miriam was worried about my trip here to meet you. The Egyptian officials keep close watch on all our people. Work! Work! Work! That is all they want from us." Aaron stopped abruptly and looked some distance beyond Moses. "Oh, I see you have found a wife, also. Are those your sons standing there?" He pointed to two handsome young men standing by loaded donkeys near their mother.

"Yes," Moses replied. Motioning with his hand, he called out, "Come, Zipporah, and you boys, Gershom and Eliezer. Come meet your uncle Aaron." Moses' sons shook the desert dust from their cloaks and went forward as they were told. They had heard their father mention his brother on many occasions, and they were glad at last to meet him. Zipporah smiled faintly behind the thin veil that covered her face and bowed to honor her husband's only brother.

After much "catching up" on their personal lives, Aaron, after assessing his new-found family, presented a proposal to Moses. He was concerned about Zipporah and their sons accompanying them to Egypt.

"There is much turmoil there, my brother. Your wife and sons are not accustomed to life there as my family and I are. Do not place that burden upon them. It will only bring them trouble. That is not all. The trip back to Egypt may be difficult and could take many days. Please send them back for their own good. As you are well aware, it is not that far back to Midian."

His advice did not sit well with Moses, and it was only after much deliberation that he agreed to send them back to Zipporah's father Jethro in Midian, promising to send for them as soon as his mission in Egypt was completed. Moses asked Jethro's male servant, who had been traveling with them, to escort his family back. After tearful goodbyes were said, Zipporah and their two sons embraced Moses and turned toward home.

Then Aaron and Moses, not knowing the extent of difficulties they would encounter in approaching an inhumane, sinister pharaoh, journeyed westward toward Egypt to fulfill God's purpose in delivering the Israelite people from their bondage. They would walk the entire distance, saving the pack animals for transporting supplies they would need for their trip, many provided generously by Moses' family.

CHAPTER 3

The brothers discussed everything they could think of as they journeyed toward Egypt. Moses told Aaron all about the burning bush that had appeared at the same mountain they had just left. It was there where God had called him to free His people. Aaron knew only that God informed him to travel to the desert to meet Moses and that he would be Moses' spokesman and companion. Aaron did not know what all of that meant. He just knew he trusted God, and he hoped he would prove worthy when the time came. But, he did have questions for Moses.

"What shall we tell the Israelites when they ask who sent us?"

"Moses replied, "God said we must say 'I am' sent us."

Aaron did not want to question God, yet he wondered if that name would also be sufficient for the pharaoh who currently ruled Egypt.

"Remember, Moses. This is not the same pharaoh that Joseph knew, or even the one who reigned while you were there. Can't we just say to the king, 'God Almighty sent us'?" He caught himself and then added, "Oh, that would do no good. They don't believe in our God. If we said that their own god of justice, Mafdet, ordered him to release our people, he might relent.[5] Aaron realized how he was circumventing God's plan with his endless worries. He turned toward his brother and in haste concluded, "We will say whatever God directs!"

The closer they got to Egypt, the more Aaron experienced an internal nagging, a troublesome fear growing from the uncertainty of what the two had been called to do. After all, they were not young—eighty and eighty-three—and the challenges that lay ahead would be difficult for anyone.

"Moses, I'm not sure how we should approach our own people about leaving Egypt. They may think this plan is impossible. Furthermore, they have been in Egypt for 430 years and may not want to leave. That is a problem we must consider."

Moses assured Aaron, "We will call the elders together first and explain all that God instructed me to do. If it then becomes necessary, in order to convince them, we will perform great miracles before them, using our staffs as God directed. Then they will know that God had His hand in this mighty task before us." He added, "Aaron, the deportation of our people is not to be negotiated; it is God's plan, and it will be carried out."

Aaron, not satisfied, continued. "Moses, you don't understand. Our people have multiplied into hundreds of thousands. This is the biggest job anyone could be called upon to accomplish. Are you sure we can do this?"

Exercising as much patience as possible, Moses reminded Aaron that God had spoken to him so clearly at that miraculous flaming bush that could not be extinguished. He had said Aaron was to be the speaker and he, himself, the leader, and that was that!

After many miles, bedding down in make-shift tents at night and suffering recurrent skin-thrashing sand storms by day, the two brothers reached Egypt. They journeyed first to Goshen, the fertile section of Egypt in the northeast that had been awarded to the Israelites during Joseph's time. There Aaron found Elisheba and their sons, and he re-acquainted them with Moses. Next, they went to see their sister Miriam, the oldest of the three. Relieved that her brothers had arrived, she held each one in a firm grasp before leading them to her table.

"Come. You two look famished. We will eat. Then you are to rest." Although their sister was self-willed with a mercurial temperament, her words came as the most comforting thing they had experienced in days. They ate and laughed and enjoyed the pleasures that only a family can provide. Long overdue, the reunion of the three siblings lasted far into the night.

The elders of the various tribes had been apprised of Aaron's trip and the fact that Moses had returned with him. The next day they met with the two brothers. After hearing what Moses and Aaron expected, some of the men voiced strong opposition. They viewed the plan presented to them as staggering and were reluctant to accept it. At that moment, Aaron reached for his staff, as Moses had told him to do, and performed unbelievable signs before them. Finally, he shared all that God had revealed to Moses.

"God has seen your misery, *our* misery, and does not want us to suffer anymore. How could we refuse to follow what God has ordered?" Aaron implored.

The elders' wrangling lessened somewhat, which Aaron interpreted as his having made some headway. After discussions back and forth among themselves, the elders agreed to do as they had been told. Before dismissing them to their own tribes, Aaron ventured a request.

"Oh, one other important thing. Have all the women little by little over the next several weeks collect from the Egyptians any gold and silver that they can, even clothing. We will need those things when we depart this land."

Aaron heard no complaints, and he breathed a sigh of relief. The groundwork for the mission had been laid.

CHAPTER 4

After resting two days from their trip, Aaron told Moses he was ready to accompany him to Pharaoh's palace.

"I think I am prepared to go before the great Thutmose III."[6] Although it served more as a reminder to himself, he added, "You will be my strength, and I will be your voice."

Off they went to Memphis where the pharaoh was presently residing. It took some convincing to get entrance into the palace, but they soon found themselves before the throne of Thutmose III, whose elegant queen sat beside him.

Displaying a distinct air of importance, the colorfully-adorned pharaoh slowly lowered his scepter toward them as a sign of acceptance for them to speak. Aaron boldly stepped forward two full steps to issue his request, bowing ever so slightly.

> This is what the Lord, the God of Israel says:
> 'Let my people go so that they may hold a
> festival to me in the desert.'[7]

Pharaoh rolled his eyes upward; he was not at all impressed. In fact, Aaron's appeal only made him angry. Egypt's ruler turned his attention to Moses.

"The records show that you, Moses, are a criminal escapee. You fled our country after killing one of our citizens."

Before Moses could offer a defense and remind him that it had occurred forty years before, Pharaoh waved his hand to dismiss them.

"Away! Your request has been denied." Two officials whisked Aaron and Moses from the pharaoh's presence.

The presumptuous appearance of the two men infuriated the pharaoh. He would show them! He determined to increase the Israelites' work load. He ordered that they would no longer be supplied the straw necessary to make bricks. As a result, they would have to find and gather their own.

When the Israelites heard of the new, harsher rules, they became angry with Aaron and Moses and blamed them for the additional hardship inflicted upon them.

Now the brothers had to deal with discouragement from their own people. God chose that time to give special instructions to Aaron.

"Yes, Lord. I will go to Pharaoh and perform the miracles you have asked me to do."

So Aaron alone went before Pharaoh and all his officials to ask for the release of his people. He was permitted entrance this time out of curiosity rather than concession. It would be an opportunity to intimidate the lowly Israelite in front of the entire court. Without saying a word, Aaron threw his staff down before them and it turned into a snake. When the court magicians threw their staffs down, producing snakes as well, Aaron's staff swallowed them all. In spite of what he saw, Pharaoh still refused to listen. He was not about to let the Israelites leave his land. They were his best workers, and there were so many of them. Aaron was dismissed again!

<hr />

God then decided to demonstrate His mighty power for all to see. The plagues He planned to unleash upon the Egyptians would be above and beyond anything they had ever seen or would ever see again. They would come to know that He was the Lord God Almighty.

The great Nile River, the lifeline of Egypt, was revered by the Egyptians. They believed that their gods used the river to bring about all occurrences, both good and bad.[8]

God directed Aaron to stretch out his staff across the Nile and strike it. Aaron approached the banks of the river and, lifting his staff, brought it down swiftly upon the water. As soon as he did, the Nile turned to blood, killing all the fish and polluting the drinking water. The Egyptians had to dig wells along the river for sustenance. It mattered not to Pharaoh, at least not outwardly. Contrary to his public pretense, he remained locked within the walls of his palace until the putrid smell that permeated the whole land had subsided. He may have reasoned that was the end of the two Israelites' efforts to convince him. He had no idea there was more to come, much more.

❊ CHAPTER 5 ❊

Aaron returned to Goshen where he and Moses waited for seven days. All of that time, God had his hand of protection over them. Not once did Pharaoh's officials threaten them nor harm them in any way.

Then God issued further instructions to be carried out against the Egyptians.

> Go to Pharaoh and say to him, 'This
> is what the Lord says: let my people
> go.....If you refuse to let them go, I
> will plague your whole country with
> frogs.The Nile will teem with frogs.
> They will come up into your palace
> and your bedroom and onto your bed,
> into the houses of your officials and
> on your people, and into your ovens
> and kneading troughs.'⁹

Aaron, beginning to question God's decision, approached his brother.

"Moses, if the bloody Nile didn't convince Pharaoh, do you honestly believe releasing frogs will?"

It took only one look from Moses. Of course! Frogs were deified by the Egyptians in their worship of the goddess Heqet, whose image was a woman with the head of a frog.¹⁰ Challenging one of Egypt's false beliefs might convince Pharaoh that the Israelites' God was all powerful and that He was the one true God.

"I will do as God has directed," Aaron said, his head not held as high as when he approached his brother.

Casting their fears aside, Aaron and Moses delivered the message to Pharaoh, hoping the threat of such an awful occurrence would soften the heart of Egypt's ruler. It did not. His refusal was even stronger than before. The stubborn leader would have to suffer the consequences.

As the Almighty had ordered, Aaron waved his staff over Egypt's water, and what looked like platoons of frogs came out of the streams and canals and covered the land. They were everywhere. In addition to being a frightful sight, the calamity was viewed as a fearful abomination by the many Egyptians who worshipped the tailless amphibians.[11] Even Pharaoh was affected to the extent that he quickly summoned Aaron and Moses. In desperation, he pleaded with them.

'Pray to the Lord to take the frogs
away from me and my people, and
I will let your people go....'[12]

The brothers agreed, and the frogs disappeared. Regardless of his promise, Pharaoh's heart had become so hardened and his self-pride so strong, that he would not honor his word.

———◆———

For five long months, Aaron stayed busy with the staff God had provided. It would take eight more horrific scenes, all symbols of the Egyptians' pagan beliefs, before Pharaoh would consider allowing the Israelites to leave his country. Had Aaron known *that* at the time, he might have been tempted to abandon his calling. On the other hand, had he seen the burning bush, perhaps his faith would have been as strong as that of Moses. So, honoring his promise, he again took up his staff and with his brother returned to the mission at hand.

Next, Aaron went throughout the land, striking the earth with his staff. The fine, yellow dust instantly became gnats which infested the land. Even Pharaoh's magicians failed to produce anything remotely resembling what Aaron had done, and they had to admit that the Israelites' God had caused this thing to happen. Egyptians throughout the land ran here and there to escape each new horror that descended upon them. Still Pharaoh did not budge. Following the plague of the bloody Nile, the frogs, and the gnats, God's wrath continued with swarms of flies, the deaths of livestock, human boils, and hail stones unlike anything seen before. If that were not enough, devouring hordes of locusts ate everything in sight before a period of darkness covered the land. Every semblance of Egyptian idolatry had been exposed and the Almighty's power had revealed Him to be the one true God; yet the stubborn pride of Egypt's leader persisted. But, despite God's punishment on the Egyptians, He protected His own people and their animals in the land of Goshen.

In spite of Pharaoh's fervent resistance, there would be one plague that would get his attention. Finally. It was the plague on the firstborn.

God's last appeal to Pharaoh through His servants Aaron and Moses was to announce the coming deaths of every firstborn son in Egypt, as well as the firstborn of all the animals, unless he let the people go. One would think that such a pronouncement of judgment would have brought the ruler of the nation to his knees. Again, it did not. Not yet.

It was in the month of Abib, in the spring of the year, that God's word, as foretold, was fulfilled.[13]

> At midnight the Lord struck down all the firstborn in Egypt, from the firstborn of Pharaoh, who sat on the throne, to the firstborn of the prisoner, who was in the dungeon… Pharaoh and all his officials and all the Egyptians got up during the night, and there was loud wailing in Egypt, for there was not a house without someone dead.[14]

But, the firstborn of the Israelites were saved. God had instructed each family to prepare a lamb, which would be called the Passover Lamb. Then they were to apply the blood of the lamb to the sides and tops of their door frames as a sign for God to pass over that household. Thus, all the firstborn of the Israelites were untouched.

In utter helplessness, Pharaoh called for Aaron and Moses and told them to take all their possessions and leave. For some reason, the king asked that they bless him. Perhaps after all that time and all those catastrophes, he came to understand God's own words: "... the Egyptians will know that I am the Lord."[15]

Aaron had to use his staff no longer as an instrument of destruction. Instead, he had to absorb elaborate instructions as God inaugurated the first religious calendar for the Hebrew people.[16] It was significant because in days to come, Aaron would be ordained as the first descendant of Levi to usher in the Levitical priesthood under which his own descendants would conduct the future tabernacle services and later temple worship. This new order began with the Passover Celebration which was always to be a reminder of how God had saved His people and led them out of Egypt.

❈ CHAPTER 6 ❈

What lay ahead for the 600,000 free Israelites, not counting women and children, would be forty years in the wilderness of the Sinai Peninsula. Their lengthy delay would be the result of their disobedience to God's plans. Not only had God freed them from their Egyptian bondage, but He also wanted to plant them in the land promised to them as an everlasting inheritance. First, they must obey, a difficult lesson for what Moses called a "stiff-necked people."

Out of Egypt the massive multitude trekked, carrying food they had hurriedly prepared, the silver and gold they had collected, and the bones of their ancestor Joseph who had requested they be carried back to the land of his birth. Aaron walked beside his brother, holding fast the staff of God that had become a symbol of victory for him as well as for the nation of Israel. If anyone had decided to stay back in Egypt, their absence was not discussed, for this monumental march of humanity that left Egypt strove forward determined and undeterred, at least at the outset, to claim the promise they had heard about for years.

Back in Egypt, nothing had softened the heart of Pharaoh. In spite of his promise to Aaron and Moses, he set out to stop the troublesome Israelites; he should have reconsidered, for God had other plans. The Red Sea opened wide, allowing passage on dry land for His people. Behind them, the pursuing Egyptians perished as the waters covered them, the sea becoming a watery grave.

On the other side, the Israelites were jubilant. Aaron's sister Miriam, tambourine in hand, began to dance and sing, praising her Lord for their deliverance. She was joined by the other women who shared in celebrating the defeat of the Egyptians who had followed them.

Their elation was short-lived. After only three days in the desert with no water, several of the men complained to Aaron. He immediately went to Moses.

"These people are already driving me insane. They keep demanding water and I tell them God will provide when the time is right. They are angry, Moses. What must we do?"

Moses replied that yes, the Lord would sustain them; they must be patient and trust Him. Aaron was not sure that answer would appease the thirsty mob. He relayed the message, anyway.

Sometime later, God directed them to not one but twelve springs at Elim where there was plenty of water for all, and the massive throng of humanity camped there. The fresh, cool water satisfied them for a brief time. Within a month, true to their nature, they had new complaints. While Moses was busy with his "flock" and their many problems, the disgruntled people voiced their concerns again to Aaron.

> 'If only we had died by the Lord's hand in Egypt! There
> we sat around pots of meat and ate all the food we wanted,
> but you brought us out into the desert to starve this entire
> assembly to death.'[17]

Aaron did not know exactly what to tell them. Besides, he was weary of their grumbling. He told them he would find Moses—he would know what to do. After all, it was Moses whom God had called to be the leader of His people. Aaron reasoned within himself that he was called only to be his brother's spokesman. Pushing through the crowds before him, he finally found Moses solving a dispute between two men from the tribe of Dan. When Moses finished, he turned to Aaron.

"Now, what is it, brother? It seems that we solve one problem only to find another." The tight wrinkles on Moses' forehead revealed his dismay.

"It's these stubborn, impatient people! They are never satisfied. They say all the food that each family brought out of Egypt is gone. They are demanding food, food like they had in Egypt."

"That will not happen, Aaron. I will again seek a word from the Lord. Look at what He has done so far. He WILL provide." Moses was right.

Early the next morning, God showered down bread upon the people. It was called Manna. It was white and tasted like honey-flavored wafers. In time it came to be called "Angels' Bread."[18] They were to gather only what they needed for each day except on the sixth day. Then they were to gather enough for two days in order to provide for the Sabbath. Moses, by God's instructions, told Aaron to do something that would be a reminder in the future of God's plentiful, merciful provisions:

> 'Take a jar and put an omer of manna in it. Then place it before the Lord to be kept for the generations to come.'[19]

God supplied even more for His ungrateful, rebellious children. In time he sent an abundance of quail that covered the ground. Time after time, their Constant Protector provided food for them which would continue until they reached the land of Canaan.

It was bad enough that dissension existed *inside* the Israelite camp. After some time, they also encountered serious trouble *outside*. The Amalekites from beyond Canaan came out in full force and attacked the Israelites at a place called Rephidim. Joshua, who had become Moses' stalwart, fearless military commander, went to battle against them. When the Amalekites seemed to be gaining ground, Moses took Aaron and a fellow Israelite, Hur, with him to the top of a hill to survey the struggle. When Moses held up his hands, the Israelites were successful; when he brought his arms down, their opponents gained advantage. Moses' arms grew very weak, holding them above his head while the conflict lasted for hours.

Aaron said, "Help me, Hur. We will move this big rock for Moses to sit on. Then you get on one side of him and I'll get on the other. We will hold up his hands until our men are victorious."

As a result, Joshua and his men won the battle. Many Amalekites were slain while the rest fled.

As the Israelites reached Mt. Sinai after traveling for fifty-two days, Moses sent for his wife and sons. Months earlier, at Aaron's insistence, they had been sent back to their home in Midian. At last, they were reunited with Moses in the desert, along with Jethro who accompanied them.

Aaron, who had at the beginning of their mission objected to Zipporah's presence, was glad now to see her and the rest of the family. He was especially pleased and relieved when he overheard Jethro giving his son-in-law Moses wise counsel.

"Moses, I agree with Jethro completely," Aaron said. "You have been strapped with countless decisions and judgments you've had to make. His advice is just what you need. The job has been too great for one man. As he said, you can appoint judges from each of the tribes to handle the smaller disputes while you reserve the difficult issues for you, alone, to solve."

Moses assured Aaron that he would follow Jethro's sound advice. He had come to realize that in order to deal with those obstinate fellow Israelites, he needed all the help he could get.

CHAPTER 7

While the Israelites were camped near Mount Sinai in the third month after leaving Egypt, God was ready to give His people rules necessary to live by, rules that would set His people apart from all others. The receiving of God's commandments was a Holy occurrence. God informed Moses that he was to go up Mt. Sinai to receive the instructions, and that the people were not to follow. They were to stay below at the foot of the mountain. There was one exception. Aaron was to accompany his brother up Mt. Sinai, not the only time the brothers would be called upon to meet God.

In a huge billow of smoke, God appeared at the top of Mt. Sinai as the whole mountain shook, frightening the Israelites below. One by one God spelled out verbally, for all the people to hear, the Ten Commandments that He wanted them to obey. They would serve as a road map for life, specific rules to keep His people pure, different from any of the people they would encounter. In addition to the ten, God gave Moses many regulations for living that the Israelites would need in their new home. Mostly, they related to one's treatment of his fellowman. Also, God specified how the allotted festivals were to be celebrated, how the sacrifices were to be offered, and of most importance, how to build the elaborate tabernacle according to His explicit instructions. Once it was completed, God promised that as the people traveled, He would guide them as a cloud over the portable tabernacle by day and as a fire by night.

When God finished, Moses went down to the people and reiterated all that he had received. The Israelites, whose emotional pendulum often swung from one extreme to the other, on *that* day said, "Everything the Lord has said we will do." Only time would reveal if they were true to their word.

Again God called Moses to ascend Mt. Sinai. He also asked for Aaron and his four sons, Nadab, Abihu, Eleazar, and Ithamar, to accompany him along with seventy of the elders. They were called there to seal the covenant drawn up between God and the Israelites. God had singled out Aaron and his sons to serve Him as priests to carry out numerous rituals once they erected the tabernacle. Furthermore, Moses was to make priestly garments for the five after which they were to be consecrated for their roles.

Yet again, God told Moses to return to Him to receive the Ten Commandments, this time written on tablets of stone by the finger of God, Himself. Joshua traveled to the mountain with Moses, while Moses, alone, ascended the peak. He was on the mountain for forty days and forty nights while Aaron and Hur were in charge of the people below.

The Israelites grew restless waiting for Moses' return. They began to think maybe he would not return at all. They soon forgot God's parting of the Red Sea and His provisions of water, manna, and quail. They also forgot that He had given them victory over the warring Amalekites. They even forgot that the shoes they wore for years had not worn out. Ungrateful, and disobedient, they wanted a god they could see like they had in Egypt, one they could reach out and touch if they dared.

As usual, they approached Aaron with their demands. Aaron, not the man his brother Moses was, gave in to them. He even wondered, himself, if Moses had met with some kind of disaster. After all, seeing fire and smoke billowing forth from the mountain was frightful enough, not to mention the violent trembling beneath their feet. He believed God might be so angry with His people that He would kill them all.

"Okay," Aaron said. "You men must collect from all the people their gold earrings and bring them to me. I will melt the gold and make an idol for you." The people hastily complied.

Aaron did as he had said, casting the gold into the shape of a calf, and they were satisfied. As he looked at the hideous image, he knew he had done wrong. His mind raced to find a proper appeasement. Finally, he reasoned, *I will build an altar to God in front of the calf. Then I will announce a festival for tomorrow honoring our God.*

The next day the Israelites combined the worship of a Holy God with that of a heinous, forbidden idol while they ate, drank, and danced about wildly. Aware of the blatant idolatry of His people, God sent Moses down the mountain to confront them, adding that He would destroy them because of their corruption. Heart-broken, Moses begged Him to relent. In His great mercy and to honor His servant, God did as Moses asked.

When Moses arrived in camp and beheld the golden calf and the people celebrating, he became angry and threw the stone tablets of laws to the ground, breaking them into a pile of chalky rubble. He then burned and finely ground the gold idol and made the Israelites drink the powdery substance with water. His eyes blazing with rage, he turned to Aaron and asked, "Why?"

Aaron, caught in a tangle of his own doing, chose not to take responsibility for the awful deed. He lied to his brother, at least in part.

> You know how prone these people are to evil. They said to me, 'Make us gods who will go before us. As for this fellow Moses who brought us up out of Egypt, we don't know what has happened to him.' So I told them, 'Whoever has any gold jewelry, take it off.' Then they gave me the gold, and I threw it into the fire, and out came this calf.[20]

If his answer had not been so wicked, Moses might have laughed at such an excuse. Instead, it was a serious matter. Moses appealed to God to forgive them or take *his* own life. God comforted His righteous leader but placed a plague on those who had sinned against Him. Yahweh was a God of justice. The people had to suffer because of their blatant disregard for God's laws, a lesson not yet learned.

Finally, God presented Moses with two new tablets to replace the others and sent him on his way.

✦⋙ CHAPTER 8 ⋘✦

As soon as the Lord had solved one of His children's problems, He had to deal with another. This time it was the sin of jealousy committed by Aaron and Miriam against their brother Moses. Their words were harsh.

> 'Has the Lord spoken only through Moses? Hasn't He also spoken through us?'[21]

"The anger of the Lord burned against them…"[22] because of their attack on his servant Moses. As a result, He punished Miriam with leprosy. It was only after Aaron cried out to his brother to petition God to lift the curse, that God, after seven days of her confinement outside the camp, removed her affliction.

Moses' siblings were not the only ones who displayed their jealousy among the Israelites. A man from the tribe of Levi, as well as some of the Reubenites, resented Aaron's being in control of the priestly duties, and they rose up against Moses. To solve the problem, God instructed Moses to collect a staff from each of the twelve tribes with the name of the tribe's leader written on each one. Aaron's name was on the one representing Levi's tribe. Moses put the staffs in the newly constructed tabernacle, stating that the one that sprouted by the next morning would indicate the person God had chosen as High Priest in charge of all priestly duties. The next day, Aaron's staff had budded and produced almonds. From that time forward, there was no question about who would be the High Priest. God firmly established the priesthood when he said to Aaron, "…only you and your sons may serve as priests in connection with everything at the altar and inside the curtain. I am giving you the service of the priesthood as a gift."[23]

The decision made by God became a crowning glory for the man Aaron. *That* dilemma had been solved. However, his problems, and those of Moses, were not over.

First, Aaron's sons must go through an elaborate ordination service. God had specified basic, stringent regulations concerning the priests' responsibilities in the new tabernacle. Nadab, Aaron's oldest son, was to succeed his father as High Priest when the time came. It would not come to pass because Nadab and Aaron's second-born, Abihu, offered unauthorized fire during the time they were serving, and God struck them down. The Almighty was clear when he had said:

> If you fully obey the Lord your God and carefully follow
> all his commands …the Lord your God will set you high
> above all the nations on earth.[24]

After Aaron's sons died, Moses told him not to mourn by showing outward signs of sorrow. God's rules had not been followed and punishment was necessary. Although Aaron kept his silence before others, he and Elisheba in their private moments wept their share of tears. Aaron's natural regrets as a father crept in.

> Perhaps I should have supervised them more closely.
> They were such vibrant men, though at times somewhat
> stubborn. How we will miss them! Now Eleazar must
> follow me as High Priest, aided by our youngest son,
> Ithamar. I pray they will serve God well and pass forward
> the priesthood that God has established.

———◆———

The Israelites left Mount Sinai and traveled to Kadesh in the Desert of Zin. There Miriam, the sister of Aaron and Moses, died and was buried. At the same time, the people discovered there was no available water for the multitude, and bitter complaints spread throughout the camp. Aaron and Moses were already in anguish over their sister's death, and the cry of their Israelite brothers was almost more than they could bear. With their faces to the ground, they cried out to the Lord as they had done so many times. God heard their distress and told them to *speak* to a huge rock that stood before them and that the waters of Meribah would gush forth. Instead, Moses in his disgust with the people, shouted as he raised his staff and, instead of speaking to the rock, he struck it twice with powerful blows. As God had promised, out came an abundance of water for all the people and their livestock. However, Moses' righteous indignation was ill-spent, for there was a price to pay. Because of their disobedience, God said to Aaron and Moses:

> Because you did not trust in me enough to honor me as holy in the sight of the Israelites, you will not bring this community into the land I give them.[25]

What a disappointment for the brothers who had spent the past four decades of their lives leading a rebellious, stiff-necked people across difficult, alien territories only to arrive at the precipice of the land promised to God's chosen people and not be allowed to enter. It did, without a doubt, re-emphasize the Lord's command which He had tried to instill in them all along. They must obey Him, and He meant it!

When the Israelites left Kadesh, they wanted to pass through the territory of Edom. They sent messages to its king, promising not to harm anyone or anything on the way. After all, the people there were descendants of Esau, brother of Jacob whose name God had changed to Israel. Their appeal fell on deaf ears. They were not allowed passage.

Their next stop was Mt. Hor where Aaron's life-journey would end. God told Aaron that there he would die and the priesthood would be passed on immediately to his son Eleazar. So, Moses had the sad task of taking his brother Aaron and Aaron's son Eleazar up the mountain.

Following God's instructions, Moses removed Aaron's garments and placed them on Eleazar, a momentous occasion—the passing of the priesthood from father to son, a rite which would continue for generations.

Aaron died there on the peak of Mount Hor at the age of 123 years. The Israelites mourned him for thirty days. He had been a servant of the Lord and a faithful, if not perfect, companion to his brother Moses, who died shortly thereafter on Mount Nebo in sight of the Promised Land.

There would be much work to do before the children of Israel could call the land of Canaan their own. Joshua, to whom Moses' mantle of leadership had passed, would prove an apt, worthy military leader. God would give him many victories during the Great Invasion. However, it was Aaron and his prophet-brother Moses who had answered the Almighty's call to free God's chosen people from the throes of Egyptian slavery, guiding them forty years through the wilderness and at last to the edge of their long-sought inheritance, their Promised Land.

The Story Of Naomi

THE STORY OF NAOMI
PREFACE

I n the book of *Ruth*, much is recorded about the young woman for whom the book is named. Ruth did, in fact, become a progenitor of a royal line, including King David, and later the King of Kings, Jesus.

However, little is known about Naomi, who became Ruth's mother-in-law. That Jewish lady suffered great loss and years of uncertainty during the time of Israel's judges. Both her trials and her triumphs are herein explored.

❖—✦ CHAPTER I ✦—❖

"In the days when the judges ruled, there was a famine in the land...."
Ruth: 1:1

"Ouch," she said, lifting her hand quickly from the flat stone surface upon which she was grinding. Naomi could not remember ever pinching her finger before while grinding barley. The smooth, round stone she was using to pulverize the barley seeds formed her fingers to its shape, almost rendering them frozen in place. After raking back and forth for two hours or more, with brief breaks now and then, her strength was spent. She poured the fine meal into one of the large earthenware jars standing on the work table by the wall, saving enough to make porridge for the evening meal and some to make barley cakes the next day. As she sealed the top of the jar by placing a clean small square of fabric over the mouth and on top of that a lump of clay pressed down to a snug fit, her mind slipped back to better times, times when there was plenty of wheat instead of barley, the "poor man's grain."[1] She longed to glimpse again their vineyard that had stretched almost as far as the eye could see, each vine heavy with thick clusters of luscious grapes. She recalled a time, not so long ago, when small trees were aflame with succulent pomegranates, red and ripe for plucking. How she yearned to walk again among the olive trees in the heat of the day and feel the gentle breeze against her warm cheeks. What a treat it would be to stir a leg of mutton in the cooking pot. That was not to be.

The "great famine," as everyone referred to it, had gripped the land. Rain had not come, and the persistent wind was harsh and sifted the dry earth as it swept along toward the east. People were leaving. Their dearest friends, Eldad and Rina, had already left for Egypt to find sustenance just as Jacob and his sons had done hundreds of years before. Naomi, too, entertained the idea, knowing how difficult it would be to leave Bethlehem-Judah, the place of her birth. She and her husband were of the tribe of Judah, and the land had been in their family for many years. Her two sons, Mahlon and Kilion, now in their twenties, were born there, as well; memories of their younger years were rooted in the place of her heritage. Then there was Elimelech. Her husband of thirty years was not a healthy man. At times his breathing was labored and became a great concern to her. She was not even sure he could make a trip, especially a long one. Most days he did what little he could around their home, piddling here and there to convince himself he was still of some use. Naomi came to realize that, out of necessity, she must become the decision-maker, a position she did not relish. Her husband had once been the proud, steadfast pillar of strength for their family.

When she considered leaving their promised land, a pang of guilt convicted her heart. She wondered: *Am I circumventing the beliefs of my people, God's chosen ones? After all, it was Yahweh who planted us here, a fulfillment of His promise years ago to Abraham.*[2] At the same time, she knew that the welfare of her sons, as well as that of her husband, rested with her alone, a responsibility which weighed heavily upon her.

Their sons would return home later in the day, exhausted and dirty after threshing wheat for a neighbor they had only recently met. Maybe then, she reasoned, the family could discuss the idea she had been processing for several days. She decided it would be wise to pick just the right time; Elimelech did not like change. Furthermore, the boys might not be talkative after their hard day's work in the scorching heat.

———◆———

The sun was low in the west by the time the meager evening meal was on the table. Naomi lit a half-melted candle and placed it in the middle. Once seated, the four of them bowed as Elimelech thanked God for the food they had before them and prayed for rain. In unison they recited Joshua's words that had been passed down to them: "… as for me and my household, we will serve the Lord."[3]

As the men were pleasantly enjoying their meal, Naomi spoke.

"Elimelech, I have been thinking. When last I heard, my sister Keila and her husband were doing well in Moab. That isn't as far as Egypt where our friends have gone. I believe, as I think you do, that conditions here are getting worse. People say the famine will last several years, and we have so little food stored away. Also, there are no young women here to become wives for our sons, not to mention that we could all starve to death." She glanced at her sons who could not avoid smiling at the mention of wives.

Sensing she was making progress, she continued. "I have prayed daily, my husband, and I trust God to lead us to a better place. We could live in Moab for a while until things got better here."

The men said not a word. Naomi took that as a positive sign—there were no immediate objections. She smiled as she took her last bite for the night, yet bitter-sweet thoughts swirled inside her head.

———◆———

The next morning as the sun rose again over the thirsty land, Naomi was already busy making barley cakes.[4] With care she mixed the precious grain with water and a small amount of olive oil. She formed the cakes into smooth, even mounds and placed them on a flat tray-like stone, ready for the small oven that jutted from a wall in the courtyard. Crude as it was, Elemelech had constructed it for his wife to make her work easier. She no longer had to use a fire pit behind their home.

The halug Naomi wore was old and a bit faded, but she would never think of wearing her best embroidered tunic on an ordinary day.[5] Without a sound, Elimelech entered the room and stood, admiring her beauty and her industry as she moved barefoot across the cool dirt floor in resolute quietness. When he saw her pause in her work, he drew her aside.

"You are a good woman, Naomi. I have learned to rely on your judgment more than ever. I believe you are blessed with the gift of discernment. Perhaps you are right. We may perish if we remain here. I love our homeland as much as you do, yet I must accept the inevitable. Like those of old, we must go where there is life for us and our sons. I have made my decision. We must sell our home, our land, and what little livestock we have left. I will go today to the marketplace to find a buyer. We must not waste more time."

Naomi had hoped she would be glad to hear those words from her husband. Now that they were uttered, it was all she could do to restrain the tears that she knew would come in due time. Still, she had spoken her mind. Now she must support Elimelech's actions. Deep inside, she wondered whether her influence had come from wisdom or, instead, from selfish disregard for the laws of their God.

CHAPTER 2

The dusty marketplace which a year ago had been teeming with business was barely active when Elimelech arrived. The drought had taken its toll on creatures and land alike, and only those men who were able to sustain a modicum of existence were there. Even so, scales were positioned here and there where grain and skins of wine could be sold or exchanged for other goods. Elimelech approached one acquaintance after another with his proposal, wondering how he could expect anyone to buy anything with times so hard.

His energy, waning with each step, was reaching its peak when he spotted Meshulam, the farmer whose wheat the boys had threshed the day before. Elimelech was thankful *someone* still had grain that needed threshing. Meshulam was a large man with a double-chin, protruding belly, and a heavy, black beard abundant enough for three men. A well-off businessman, he was known to be shrewd in his transactions. *Lord, may he make me a reasonable offer*, Elimelech prayed as he approached the man.

"Peace unto you, Meshulam. My name is Elimelech."

"And unto you, peace, Elimelech."

Deciding to employ some diplomacy, Elimelech added, "Thank you for providing work for my two sons, Mahlon and Kilion. I trust they have been good workers."

"Oh, yes; yes, indeed. They are fine young men and hard workers. Now it is good to meet their father."

The two men bowed slightly to show their respect, Meshulam's long, dark beard collecting particles of dust as a cart passed, pulled by a cantankerous, wayward donkey.

"If I am not intruding upon your time," Elimelech said, "I would like to discuss some business with you." He struggled to keep eye contact with a man who appeared to be restless. He continued, "It is about our ancestral land. I am looking for someone to buy it. It is not producing enough now to support our family, and we have decided to join my wife's kin in Moab. We hope to find things better there." Elimelech could not bring himself to mention his ill health to a man who seemed quite able to take care of himself.

Meshulam scratched the back of his head, surprised at such a decision by a fellow Jew. He motioned Elimelech toward a large, flat rock where they could sit. Once situated, Meshulam got right to the point as one would expect from a man of his standing.

"I could use more land, not that it would be of any use to me now, not until the famine is over. Your property is not far from mine, and it may be just what I need. You do have a good house, do you not?"

Elimelech could not imagine what Meshulam was getting at; still he dared not question the man.

"Yes, it is a nice, good house—built when times were better. It has served us well." Then he added, "If it pleases you to do so, you may come and see."

"I will do that. Today will be gone before my business here is finished. Tomorrow... I will go there in the morning."

Elimelech felt a smile pull at the corners of his mouth. The meeting had not been in vain. He knew Naomi would be pleased.

The two men said their farewells. If Elimelech could have run, he would have sprinted all the way home because his heart told him their prayers were being answered.

Back home, he found Naomi on her knees outside their home, scrubbing clothes on a rough stone, using wood ashes to remove the greasy spots in her men's shirts. In times past she had added bits of fuller's earth, a clay-like soil which attacked the difficult stains.[6] Since its application required additional rinsing, that was a step she now must bypass due to the scarcity of water.

Elimelech approached his wife, leaned forward, and placed his hand gently on the back of her shoulders.

"My wife, my faithful wife of these many years, I have good news."

Somewhat startled, Naomi dropped the linen shirt into a container of what had become precious water, and stood to face her husband.

"Tell me this good news, Elimelech," she said, her eyebrows raised, hopeful yet cautious. Life had taught her to avoid jumping to conclusions ahead of adequate information.

"I think our sons' employer, Meshulam, is interested in buying our land, our home. He sounded most positive. He will be here in the morning to examine the place and make a decision."

Naomi relaxed. There was hope. It *sounded* like good news. Then like the appearance of a sudden storm arriving without warning, the relief fled, and her body became tense. Thoughts of home and family bombarded her one after another. *Our sons. How will they feel about all that is taking place? We are blessed with good, obedient sons who have been brought up to honor us in all things, and I know that will include the selling of our property and moving to a foreign place. Surely it will.*

Tender memories of past days sank into her middle like a sudden illness as she contemplated leaving the place she loved, the place of their ancestors. Her parents, as well as Elimelech's, were entombed nearby, their burial chambers hewn from a huge, soft rock at the end of the field. Family ties had been strong, and leaving would be hard. Naomi wondered if men fell captive to the same feelings as women. She rather doubted it. *I must not think about that now,* she decided. *It must be done. I will be strong.*

She came back to the moment, took a deep breath, and looked hard at her husband who was so proud of the news he had brought. She reached for his hand and clasped it tightly, a gesture of the unity between them no matter what lay ahead. *Would my Elimelech have been this receptive to my suggestions a mere year ago? It is sad to think that his declining health may have affected his mind as well as his body. How I miss his strong shoulder to lean on.*

The following morning as the sun had barely escaped the eastern horizon, Meshulam knocked at their door. Elimelech and Naomi were ready with warm fig cakes and fresh goat's milk on the table. They greeted their guest with the utmost dignity afforded one so respected, and asked him to be seated. After a brief prayer of thanksgiving, Elimelech awaited Meshulam's comments, which came soon, for he was a seasoned businessman who did not waste time.

Yes, he would buy the land if they could agree on a price. His main interest was the house. His daughter, his only daughter and the youngest of eight children, was to be married in the fall following the Feast of Booths.[7] She and her husband would need a home; and since Elimelech's was nearby, it would be just right.

Naomi, assuming her rightful place, arose and busied herself at her loom in another room while the men discussed business. Although Elimelech had always included her in their personal affairs, she knew that it was not the accepted custom and she chose not to denigrate her husband. Besides, there was always work to do, and she now felt pressure to finish the small blanket she had begun weaving days before.

Elimelech walked his prospective buyer through most of the house and into the courtyard. He was proud of the home that he and his sons had built, using the best stones they could find, the weight of which required hours of transporting them to their home site. They had spent hours crushing limestone and mixing it with water to create a strong mortar. Unlike most of their neighbors' homes, their home had four rooms, one of which was above the back part of the house, accessed by outside stairs. It was their sons' room.

Meshulam was impressed. Although he knew the land well, having passed it many times, he had not visited the home before. He was prompt in his assessment. They just needed to agree on a price.

Elimelech, having already decided the amount, told Meshulam what he believed to be a fair price. After all, his buyer would be getting the house, the land, and the few animals remaining except those the family needed for their trip. To Elimelech's surprise, Meshulam did not question the amount, though fully aware of the Jewish right of a kinsman-redeemer.[8] Someday he may have to sell back to the family or a close relative the land he was now buying. That was the way of their people, a right which he understood and accepted. At last, a time for occupation was agreed upon, and Meshulam left.

Naomi rejoined her husband, and the reality of their decision hit them both. She could not avoid the tears, but she wanted to get them over with before the boys returned from work. There was much to do, no time for sadness.

CHAPTER 3

Decisions, decisions, Naomi mused as she sat contemplating what to take and what to leave. She lifted a small pine chest from the hard dirt floor, brushed off its bottom, and placed it on her lap. It had belonged to her mother. She raised the lid and began to finger keepsakes that were much too dear to leave behind. She found a tiny hand-carved animal that Elimelech years ago had fashioned into a toy for their sons. She ran her fingers along the smooth, warm-brown wood, then brought it up and hugged it to her heart. The boys were only a year apart and in their youth had spent hours sharing the small object made from the branch of a poplar tree at the edge of their land. Next she found a gold ring that belonged to her grandmother, purchased from Edomite peddlers on their way back home from Egypt. A square of scarlet wool that had been her mother's lay in the bottom, perhaps meant to be used sometime in a blanket. Spotting her most prized possession, she lifted the filmy, yellowed wedding veil worn at her marriage to Elemelech. The union that had been arranged by their parents, as custom dictated, had grown into a strong love relationship. She could not imagine life without her husband...a good man, faithful and dependable. Naomi paused for one last look before replacing the objects and closing the lid. She knew she would remember that moment for the rest of her life. Such a moment would become a time-marker for later reference. She would someday say, "Yes, I remember holding my mother's chest in my lap and admiring each item inside. That was the day before we left Bethlehem-Judah."

Mahlon and Kilion worked their final day for Meshulam; and while there was still light, they spent the evening helping their father load two donkeys with goods they would need for the trip, as well as things they would need when they settled in Moab. In addition, Elimelech said it would be wise to take along a third donkey for riding when one of them became exhausted. Retaining a semblance of his manly pride, he secretly hoped he would not be the first to need it.

Their father had finalized his business with Meshulam, the date had been set, and now they would be setting out on a journey unknown to them, one which they believed held great promise. Elimelech had spoken often with travelers who passed through Bethlehem on their way eastward, and he had learned that the trip would take seven to ten days. He knew that in his weakened condition, it would be the latter. They would have to walk the entire distance, and the rough terrain would require some climbing from time to time. Traders said that taking the southern route around the Salt Sea was better than the northern one because they could avoid the Jordan River. Emilelech could not reason how that could be a problem as dry as it had been. The Jordan would not be in flood stage. He chose to take their advice, nonetheless, for he doubted his own judgment these days.

His plan was final. They would head south from Bethlehem, go around the Salt Sea, then north to an area near the Arnon River where Naomi's sister lived.[9] There the land was good for farming, and rainfall was plentiful. Elimelech had taught his sons how to cultivate, plant, and harvest the earth, so he was confident they could survive in a new land.

In his private moments Elimelech wondered if starving to death in Judah could be any worse than dying on the way to Moab. He soon learned to put those thoughts to rest, for he had decided his family deserved a chance for a better life. He was willing to face the risks, reminding himself that God would go before them as He had done with the Israelite people for centuries. That assurance gave him great courage.

———◆———

...a man from Bethlehem in Judah, together with his wife
and two sons, went to live for a while in the country of
Moab.[10]

Before daybreak the following day, the four set out. The two donkeys were loaded high and wide with supplies that Naomi had packed into old blankets, binding them with heavy cords. She had included as much feed for the animals as she could, hoping that nature would provide its own feeding spots along the way. In addition, the donkeys would need many rest stops because of their excessive burdens.

There was no looking back. Goodbyes to neighbors and friends were accomplished and a new life awaited them. Any reservations that Elimelech and Naomi might have had about their decision were soon lost when the boys began singing as they led their charges southward along the road. Uncertainty might await them, but they knew that hope also lay ahead when trust was in their hearts.

A mother first of all, always concerned about the safety of her sons, Naomi studied their sandals as they walked on the dry, rocky road. She was glad their leather shoes and those Elimelech wore were in good shape. They were not old and had lots of wear left in them. What a relief to Naomi who was sure the road they now traveled would soon give way to awkward paths and unfamiliar terrain. *Why should I worry? If God maintained our ancestors' shoes for forty years after they left Egypt on their way to the Promised Land, surely He will provide for us for just a few days.*[11] She mentally scolded herself for having doubted for even a moment. She squared her shoulders, raised her head, and strode with renewed courage. Good things were ahead.

◆

The first day went better than expected. Except for stopping to eat small amounts of parched grain and bread followed by frugal cups of water, the family moved at a good pace down the well-worn path. Elimelech had to stop only twice from fatigue, a surprise to Naomi, yet it provided encouragement to face the next day. *Just one day at a time. We can handle that,* she assured herself, not knowing the strength she would need on the next leg of their journey.

CHAPTER 4

The morning of the second day began quite well. The pack animals were refreshed and undertook in obedience their jobs, exhibiting no obstinacy the way they usually did. Traveling south, Elimelech predicted they would make the eastward turn at the end of the Salt Sea in a couple of days and would approach the edge of Moab.[12] As the sun was sinking, they searched for a place to bed down for the night; they did not possess a tent. They had prepared as best they could and relied on God to provide the rest. Before long Mahlon discovered a pleasing thicket and motioned to his father.

"This looks like a good place. It will serve as a cool shelter for the animals, and there is ample foliage for our beds. What do you think?" Mahlon and Kilion always deferred to their father's judgment as a sign of their respect. Elimelech examined the area and pronounced it safe and comfortable. With nightfall approaching, they were hasty in their preparations.

No sooner had they begun to remove blankets from one of the supply donkeys when out of nowhere a wild animal of some sort pounced upon the group from a crest above the camp. Had the donkeys' braying triggered fear in whatever had been hiding in the brush? They did not know. Kilion's sudden scream was more piercing than the vicious growl of the wild dog, displaying its long, shiny teeth between grabs at his leg. His brother Mahlon began pelting the wild thing with large stones while Elimelech grabbed the biggest limbs he could find and made a violent attack of his own. In the meantime, using all the strength within her, Naomi pulled Kilion as far away as she could while the assault on the animal by the other two continued. Blood streamed from a wound in Kilion's leg just above his knee where part of the loose, red simlah he wore was ripped away.[13] In spite of her panic, Naomi recalled where she had put the jar containing the antiseptic she always used. She pulled the small container of olive oil from a bundle, along with a clean cloth, and began applying the deep green, familiar liquid to the injury. By the time she had finished, the other two men had succeeded in killing the tormentor, its battered body lying in a flood of its own blood. At least Elimelech, Naomi, and Mahlon had escaped the vicious animal's attach. Kilion had not been as fortunate.

Elimelech checked his son's leg and was confident that because of Naomi's speedy treatment, Kilion would be fine. He was also aware that wild dogs ran in packs, and he knew what they must do.

"Mahlon, you and I will keep watch during the night, one at a time, while your mother and Kilion try to sleep. In addition to limbs and rocks, we will arm ourselves with knives in case there are others out there awaiting their prey." He reached for one of the supply bags and retrieved two long knives, the blades of which shone as brightly as the wild animal's teeth had.

Naomi insisted that she keep watch, also. Elimelech would not hear of it. Yes, women worked in the fields and did arduous work to keep a family going, but a woman was not equipped to fight off wild animals and he was not going to allow it. She knew it would do no good to insist further, so she proceeded to make their beds in the dense undergrowth praying as she worked. *Father, please take care of Kilion and bring healing to his leg. Wrap us in your protection tonight and give us safe passage into the land to which we go. And God, thank you that it wasn't a lion!*

Naomi's prayer was answered. The only evidence of danger during the night came as ominous howls in the distance. God had delivered them from an event that could have been a catastrophe for all of them. They resolved not to let what had happened hinder them. They would face another day knowing their Maker was watching over them.

The following day proved to be a long one. Kilion was much improved, yet Naomi continued to make frequent stops to tend his wound. Elimelech had begun to require more rest time than usual, and Naomi saw him using his staff more. She wondered how her husband had been able to withstand such an undertaking. She prayed she would not regret her insistence on the move.

At last, they neared the turn of the Salt Sea, a pivot point for the family. Elimelech had almost lost count of the days, and Naomi had informed him their food supply was nearing depletion. As they turned eastward, Elimelech stopped and pointed in the distance where he spotted a large tent with several animals tied close by. He was sure they would find hospitality ahead; travelers could almost always count on that. Closer observation revealed a round of stones, indicating a well. That was even better news because their water was down to a cupful.

Their benefactors saw them coming, and two tall, lanky men, one older than the other, went to meet them. Their greetings were cordial, and Elimelech and Naomi knew they had found friends. Gratefulness filled their hearts and Naomi breathed a sigh. *Thank you again, Lord, for you have provided beyond what we could expect.*

A short, plump woman exited the tent and smiled as she, too, greeted their guests. The older man, the younger one's father, invited Naomi to go inside where, on cue, his wife began preparing a meal, her ample body bouncing about in haste. The five men joined in conversation outside while the two women chatted as women do when their men are out of earshot. Language between them came easy because Naomi learned that they, too, were from Canaan, having left the year before. After discovering a well, they had settled there and gone no further. It had become their temporary home until they could return to Hebron.[14] Knowledge of their new friends' similar departure soothed Naomi's conscience somewhat. Her decision must have been wise, after all.

When the meal was finished, Elimelech and the other three stood and thanked their hosts for their gesture of kindness and the tasty food they had missed since leaving Bethlehem-Judah. The men talked into the evening while the women arranged the sleeping mats. How good it felt to be in a shelter with kind, new friends. Food and rest were always better when shared. The thankful wayfarers knew there was no way they could ever repay the debt. That night was peaceful and stomachs full. If tomorrow brought another difficult day, at least *that* evening they experienced comfort like that of home.

By day eight, Elimelech's family was well into Moab territory. Their water supply had been replenished and their friends had given them food, as well. Reaching a high ridge, they stood in awe, surveying the land spread out before them. As far as their eyes could see, green was everywhere, proof that the area was more productive than the homeland they had left. It was a refreshing picture for the four weary travelers, now aliens in an unfamiliar land.

Needing to cross the Zered River, they began their descent into the valley below.[15] What they finally saw looked more like a stream than a river, so they knew it would not prove an obstacle. After the crossing they planned to follow the valley as far as they could, then climb an escarpment to continue their way to the area near the Arnon River and, hopefully, their new home.

CHAPTER 5

The river, itself, had been easy for the four travelers; but as they reached the top of the cliff on the far side, Kilion dropped to his knees. Pulling the donkeys up the incline had been rigorous, and though perspiration beads dotted Elimelech's and Mahlon's faces and necks, Kilion's countenance was different. His face was ashen, and struggle rippled his forehead. Naomi ran to him as Elimelech grabbed a skin of water strapped to a donkey's side and began splashing it onto Kilion's upper body. Naomi raised his simlah and kethoneth to examine his wound, now several days old.[16] It had almost healed, covered in part by a protective scab. Somewhat relieved, she knelt beside her son.

"Are you just tired, Kilion? What is wrong?" Those were questions a mother must ask.

"I don't know, Mother. I was fine, and then suddenly a weakness overcame me. I think I will be fine. Just let me rest a bit."

"I'll get some bread," Naomi said. "No, nuts. Those will be better," she added. She searched one of the bundles for the jar of wild almonds she had been saving. "They will give you quick strength." It was knowledge her mother had passed on to her. It had to be true. "Here, take," Naomi said, as she handed the container to her son.

Reluctant at first, Kilion finally took a handful of the nuts and began to chew. Before long, he rose to a sitting position on the grassy mound beside the beaten path as color began to return to his face. Naomi passed the nuts to Mahlon and Elimelech, as well, then took some herself, saying it would be good for them all to take a break. They would soon turn north, the final step of their journey, and they would need all the energy they could muster. They had made it that far, their goal was almost in sight, and they were together. Naomi whispered, *Thank you, Lord, for your guidance and watchful eye that is ever before us.*

◆

The village ahead was reminiscent of those seen by past generations entering the Promised Land, that is, according to tales that had been passed down and repeated often by Elimelech's elders. Those ancestors had gazed upon strange places like Gilgal, Jericho, and Ai. What Elimelech's family saw ahead was unfamiliar, too, a town they knew not. They entered it with caution, slow of step, taking it in from one side to the other. What few townspeople they saw were engaged in busy activities and hardly noticed the four. It was not *their* Promised Land, yet a welcome change from the deleterious route they had just traveled.

Their only encounter was a man they met who was guiding a small flock of sheep toward them. His closely cropped beard was red, and his eyes looked straight ahead, trance-like. Elimelech hesitated to interrupt the man, but he needed information. With care, he approached the stranger.

"Peace unto you, my lord," he said, wondering if the fellow would be willing to halt the sheep long enough to reply.

Without looking directly at Elimelech, the man replied, "Unto you, peace as well," He reached out his crook, and in one deft maneuver, surrounded the lead sheep's neck, and the animals stopped.

"What is the name of this town, may I ask?" Elimelech inquired as he bowed in respect.

The stranger's cautious, steely eyes at last made contact. "This is Kir Hareseth.[17] I am on my way home several miles to the south. I have just purchased these," he said, motioning with his head toward the sheep. He hesitated a moment and then his demeanor softened somewhat. "Have you traveled far?"

"Yes, we are from Bethlehem-Judah, west of the Salt Sea. We are seeking a place to call home, at least for a while. My wife's sister and her husband live near the Arnon River."

"You are not far from the Arnon." The man turned and pointed with his free hand toward the north. His sheep remained still as statues. "You might ask others about those you seek. Someone may know them."

"Thank you. May God go with you," Elimelech said. The man lifted his crook, and the sheep began their march again. The four sojourners passed through the town and soon entered rich, lush pastureland. Elimelech turned to Naomi walking behind him.

"Take heart. We will be there soon. Our trip is almost over." He uttered words to encourage, knowing well that it could take days for them to find their relatives. Not as confident as her husband's words indicated, Naomi called on her Ever-Present Help as she always did.

Lord, show us the way. We are weary and need to find Keila and Adnah soon. We thank you for taking us to them.

———◆———

Soon, verdant pastures changed to fertile farmland, and a cluster of small dwellings appeared. They passed one field after another and saw men, boys, and a few women working the land, tilling the soil in readiness for later planting when the winter rains would come. They searched this way and that, perusing each person they passed, looking for a familiar face.

As they rounded the corner of a field lying to the west, there he stood, leaning on a hoe handle, surveying the land. It was Adnah. Elimelech could not believe his eyes as Naomi's eyes flooded with joy, knowing God had directed them to that exact spot. Mahlon and Killion halted their animals and, along with their parents, approached their relative.

Though tanned by the sun and wrinkled by age, Adnah was the most beautiful sight the four had seen since they left home. Sure, the family who had fed them and kept them overnight on the way had been a blessing; but here they had found family, and just knowing that brought blissful rest to their exhausted souls.

Adnah was overcome with the pleasant surprise. He laid aside his implement and embraced each of them. Elimelech pointed westward toward the Salt Sea and quipped to Adnah, "If we could have come straight across, we would have been here long before."

"Yes, I know," said Adnah. The two men laughed. Laughter was good. It meant they had found family after so long a time. Elimelech breathed a long sign of relief as Adnah continued. "Come. We will wait for Keila. She is caring for a sick neighbor-child today. The child's mother will be returning home soon from her day's work in the field, and Keila will come home." He smiled at Naomi. "She will be so happy."

Naomi knew that Keila, older than she, was barren and now well past the child-bearing years. Just the same, her love for children had overflowed into the lives of every young one she met. Her sister's tender devotion to others was something Naomi missed after Keila and her husband moved to Moab. She rushed her tired body along behind Elimelech and Adnah, eager to see her only sister again.

CHAPTER 6

Adnah and Keila's house was clean and adequate, but Naomi could not help comparing it to the home she had left behind, the one where she had spent her happiest days. She realized the memories within its walls would have to remain there until they could return. *We will return.* She believed that with all her heart.

Adnah gave them fresh drinks of cool water as they waited for Keila who did not arrive home until the sun had begun its descent. Keila saw the strange animals tied beside her house. What could that mean? Anything unusual was always reason for concern. With caution she approached the front door. The minute she opened it, Naomi ran to meet her. Surprise. Relief. Joy. The two women stood holding each other until Adnah finally spoke.

"You can let go of each other now. You'll have no breath left in you after all the squeezing!" The men all laughed. The women pulled away and joined in their fun.

Most of the evening was spent with Keila and Adnah catching up on news from the homeland. Later, the men's talk turned to economic matters. Where could the new arrivals find work? Did they know of a place where they could live? Was the Arnon a good place to settle, or should they move on somewhere else?

"There is plenty of work here for Mahlon and Kilion," said Adnah, "You, Elimelech, you need to rest for some time. The journey has been a hard one, and we heard you have been ill. Take your time. We are doing well. You must stay with us until you can get a place of your own. You are family. We will make a way."

Elimelech knew his brother-in-law was sincere. The look on Naomi's face told him it was good news. Yes, they were family, and together they would all make a way. Any reluctance Naomi had felt about her decision diminished. *Surely God is not displeased.*

———◆———

They had been in their new land two weeks. The sons had found work in the field of one of Adnah's friends. Keila was busy teaching Naomi how to weave beautiful baskets to sell at the marketplace in Kir Hareseth. For their craft, the sisters gathered and trimmed grapevines that were in abundance within walking distance. Elimelech, on the other hand, was not well at all. He had developed a severe cough that got worse with each day. Keila made poultices from figs, Terebinth shavings, and ashes.[10] Naomi applied a fresh one to Elimelech's neck every hour. Nothing helped.

"I know what the problem is," Keila declared one evening. "I have seen it before. Elimelech worked the threshing floor for years, even before the two of you were married.[19] The dust has planted itself in his lungs. Some lungs are stronger than others, you know." She pulled Naomi aside and whispered, "There is nothing we can do."

Naomi's heart dropped within her chest. *Not Elimelech, God. He is a good man. He has worked hard, and he has faithfully taught our sons your statutes. If it can be Thy will, make him well again.* Salty wells filled her eyes as she looked at the man she had come to love over the years. She knew that the strong bond which had held them together for so long was slipping away. It pained her more than anything she had ever felt.

In the next few days, they watched Elimelech's condition deteriorate. He would not eat. The cough had changed to a wheeze that was even worse to witness. Adnah, Mahlon, and Kilion worked all day each day, then came home in the evenings and sat by his bed. In their grief, the boys' appetites had left them, as well. Naomi spent hours replenishing cool cloths for her husband's hot forehead; and when it looked like she would drop, Keila took over.

The routine lasted for several days; then Elimelech breathed his last. The wheezing was gone. So was the man they all loved.

Elimelech was buried near a grove of trees in a field in Moab. It was an event Naomi could not have believed was possible. *Am I being punished for leaving our blessed homeland?* She recalled Moses' words passed on to her by her grandfather that they were never to seek peace nor prosperity with the Moabites. It had to do with the treatment God's chosen people had suffered in that land on their journey from Egypt to Canaan.[20] Her sorrow was so great that had she not been a strong woman, she might have given up. There were her boys. Elimelech would want them to take care of their mother, provide for her. She must not worry. They would make it.

CHAPTER 7

Naomi forced herself to stay busy to abate persistent memories of Elimelech. It became her dominant role to manage her relatives' household because Keila was always running here and there wherever an urgency occurred. It might be a sick child, a bereaved widow, or some injury requiring attention. Whatever the need, Keila refused no one. Most of those needing help were Moabites.

Mahlon and Kilion stayed occupied, as well. Their work had been steady until the crops were harvested and winter set in. Then Adnah helped them find work clearing some of their neighbors' fields. Although the land was fertile and productive, the rocks continued to multiply even after what seemed like tons had been removed the year before. The boys would not have believed they would welcome those huge stone intruders. However, it provided them a living, and they were glad. Their extra earnings gave Naomi's sons a plan. They would build their own homes. Their father had taught them building skills and the wisdom to plan ahead. With Adnah's assistance, they acquired a small plot of land and in their spare time began construction. The houses would be small, close to each other, and adequate for each of them and a wife—when the time came. They made it clear that Naomi would be welcome to live with one or the other as she desired. They felt immense satisfaction, for they knew Elimelech would have been proud of them.

In the ensuing months, the two little houses began to take shape. Adnah helped Mahlon and Kilion build furniture pieces, and Naomi and

Keila offered advice when it was requested. In the evenings, the sisters lit their candles and, side by side, resumed their basket-making, a craft for which they had gained coveted notoriety at the marketplace. They took great pains to choose thin grapevines that were pliable for their trade. The larger twigs that they sometimes had to use required overnight soaking to make them flexible, a process which slowed their progress.

The rather mindless work gave them a chance to reminisce about their childhoods, those cherished memories of their blessed land of Judah. They vowed never to forget the stories passed down to them. They remembered their elders saying they must write God's commandments on their foreheads. While some had taken those words to be literal, they believed it meant the heart, a place where the sacred words would remain forever.

Naomi hoped she would someday have grandchildren to teach of the old ways, a desire she could not share with Keila who would never have descendants. As for herself, she often dreamed: *What a joyous gift that would be to hold a precious little one again.* At the same time, she worried that her sons might be influenced to marry Moabite women who would cause them to forsake their godly upbringing.

CHAPTER 8

After spending six years in Moab, Mahlon and Kilion met two young women who were relatives of the farmer in whose fields they had worked. Naomi had feared that would happen. She knew that most Moabites worshipped Chemosh, known by the Jews to be a false god.[21] Keila told her she had met some people there who believed in the one God, the true God. She had to admit, however, that they were Israelites who had migrated to the country because of Israel's drought, and they were few in number. Naomi realized she needed Elimelech's wise counsel now more than ever.

In time, despite Naomi's misgivings, Mahlon and Kilion chose to marry the Moabite women. She wanted to fight their decision, but she had to acknowledge they were grown men, and they had made up their minds. Soon, arrangements were made with the girls' parents and the date was chosen. Naomi had always wanted a daughter. Now she would have two.

> They married Moabite women, one named Orpah and the
> other Ruth.[22]

The weddings in late winter were simple by Israelite standards, taking place in the home of Orpah's parents. Adnah knew a Levite who had followed them to the Arnon, and he enlisted his services. Families and friends celebrated with dancing, wine, and delicacies prepared by the women. Afterwards, the couples went to their homes, one-room mud brick houses, which Mahlon and Kilion had built several years earlier at the edge of the village. They began their new lives together full of hope and dreams for the future as do all young couples in love.

Naomi continued to live with Keila and Adnah at their insistence. She had become proficient at her basket weaving, and she and her sister were proud of the profits they brought home from the sales. As a result, Naomi felt she was contributing to her upkeep. Adnah succeeded in purchasing a plot of land where he could grow his own money crops and plenty of food. He was confident he could sell the property when they were ready to return to Judah. At the same time, Mahlon and Kilion did well, still employed by Adnah's neighbor, Amon. The future looked optimistic for the refugees in spite of their alien status. Life was good.

<hr>

Months turned into years, and before long a decade had passed since Naomi had left Judah. One afternoon when the weather suddenly turned cool and the clouds promised rain, Adnah returned home earlier than usual. He shared the rumors that were spreading among his hired men. A plague of some kind had taken the lives of several of the villagers. No one knew its name or its source. The deadly affliction attacked with little warning; and by the time the victim became aware, it was too late. His news worried the women. They began boiling plants believed from old times to be effective remedies for a host of illnesses. Keila warned Adnah to stay clear of the other workers and to drink only his own water that he carried daily to the field. It was all they knew to do.

Every day a new victim was claimed and fear ravaged the community. It gripped the hearts of mothers everywhere, and Naomi was one of them. She had not seen her sons or daughters-in-law lately, so she decided to walk the distance one evening to pay them a visit. What she found she was not prepared for. At one house and then the other, she found her sons were ill and had been so for three days. They had become infected at the same time after being exposed to a sick fellow-employee. Orpah and Ruth had not informed Naomi because they feared passing the disease on to her.

Naomi was heart-sick. She went from one son's house to the other doing what she could for them. The three women fed them lentil stew with boiled plant extracts, and helped them drink an amber-colored concoction that tasted bad and made them shudder. In vain, the women hoped their suspicions were unfounded, that it was some simple malady that would soon respond to their treatments. In despair, they watched the two men who had been robust and full of life just days before slowly slip into unconsciousness. Naomi prayed as she had for Elimelech: *Our great God. Give ear to our prayers. Renew the life within these our loved ones.* The three women grasped hands, streams of sorrow falling onto their tunics and the sod floor below.

> After they had lived there about ten years, both Mahlon and Kilion also died....[23]

———◆———

Two more burials. Naomi felt that her heart could bear no more. How had she and the wives survived without a single symptom? Even Adnah had escaped unscathed. Why had their medicine worked on them and not her sons? She never questioned God; still she wished it could have been her, instead. What would Orpah and Ruth do? They had no children to fill their days. Where would they go? There were no husbands available for them; most of the victims that the malady had taken had been men. The only good news was that the plague seemed to be in decline. Even with that positive turn, Naomi had never felt more alone in her life. A longing invaded her mind—a longing for home. *What is in Judah for me now? Well, I know that at least good memories are there while none are to be found here in Moab.*

CHAPTER 9

Spring arrived early in Moab, and Naomi knew she must make a change. It would be difficult to tell Keila and Adnah that she must go home. Someone had come with news that rain had been plentiful in Israel for the past two years and crops were thriving again. Naomi's sister and her husband had been good to her, and she would never forget their kindness. They had stood by her during the illnesses and deaths of her husband and sons whom she wished could have been buried in their own country. For certain, nothing had happened the way she had planned.

The decision to leave was hard. For days she had weighed the benefits and dangers. Sometimes the obstacles seemed greater than the advantages. In the end, though, she concluded she was making the right decision even if she did have concerns.

The donkeys she and Elimelech had brought with them had long since died, and she was not sure how she would carry enough supplies for the trip. In spite of the doubts that clouded her thinking, her prayers remained constant. She knew not for certain why such misfortune had been visited upon her; but she knew God was faithful, and she must trust Him.

Naomi loved Ruth and Orpah. They were like daughters to her. It would grieve her to leave them; what a comfort they had been. She decided to go to them, tell them her plans. When she had her belongings packed and all readiness made for the return trip, she paid them a visit.

The news broke their hearts. Without hesitation both decided to go with Naomi and straightway began packing for the trip. Naomi had not expected their response and began speaking against it. She told them how difficult the journey was and how long it would take. Nothing convinced them. They were determined to go. Baggage in tow, they followed her back to Adnah's house. When Naomi realized she could not dissuade them, she gave in.

As always, goodbyes were sad. Keila promised they, too, would return to Israel soon. Her words alleviated the pain somewhat for all of them. Adnah had loaded food, water, and blankets on one of his donkeys which he was happy to give to Naomi. After breakfast the three women left.

When they reached the south side of the village, Naomi stopped and again tried to talk the two into reconsidering. She could not imagine them leaving their families. Her reasoning hit a note of appeal, for Orpah began to cry.

"I want to go back, Naomi," she said, wiping her tears. "I love you, but my mother needs me. I must go back."

Naomi understood and kissed Orpah. She turned to Ruth and said, "You need to go back, too, Ruth. You still have family. They will miss you." She hoped the same approach would influence Ruth, as well.

> But Ruth replied, 'Don't urge me to leave you or to turn
> back from you. Where you go I will go and where you stay
> I will stay. Your people will be my people and your God
> my God.'[24]

She reached out and grasped her mother-in-law's hand. Orpah, still weeping, hugged Naomi and Ruth and scurried back toward the village, back to her own people. The two women watched until Orpah was out of sight, then tugged at their donkey and resumed their journey. The weather was quite cool, but the women's heavy cloaks protected them from the brisk breeze.

"It is good we are going south; the wind is to our backs. That may change after we make the turn of the sea and head north. I'm glad Keila had Adnah pack extra blankets. We may be *wearing* them." Naomi laughed as she spoke. Hearing Ruth quietly laughing, as well, made Naomi glad she had a traveling companion. It made the trip more pleasurable.

—◈—

Nearing the end of the third day, they approached the south end of the Salt Sea. They had walked fast and made better time than Naomi,

Elimelech, and the boys had ten years before. Naomi's heart sank at the thought of her husband. *Poor Elimelech. He had to stop often and rest. I should have known the trip would take its toll on him. I will always miss him, the delight of my life.*

Suddenly, Ruth grabbed Naomi's attention. "What is that I hear? It sounds like hoof beats and someone talking."

The women stopped, and Naomi strained to hear. "Yes," she said. "I hear it, too. Look ahead, just this side of the curve in the path. Aren't those camels? It appears to be a caravan of some sort."

Shortly, the loping dromedaries drew nearer, and their riders began waving when they saw the two women.

Naomi pulled Ruth to the side of the road. "Let me talk to them, Ruth. We can't be sure what they're up to."

Ruth's eyes grew wide. She had never been more than five miles from her home, and the idea of meeting strangers riding camels was foreign to her. She trusted Naomi and remained where she was and asked no questions.

The caravan of ten camels slowed to a stop about six yards from where the women stood. The head camel knelt to the ground, and its rider dismounted. He walked over to Naomi and stood for a moment looking from one woman to the other.

"May I ask where you are going?" the man asked. When the women did not answer, he added, "I am Akenaten. We have come from Egypt on our way to Lower Edom. We are traders who deal in goods of all kinds. We mean you no harm."

When Naomi was sure of his words, she lowered her head ever so slightly and replied to the man.

"I am Naomi. This is my daughter-in-law Ruth. We are on our way to Bethlehem-Judah, my home. Our husbands died in Moab where we have lived for several years. Thank you for your courtesy." Ruth frowned when she heard her mother-in-law divulge so much about them.

The tall, burly Egyptian who distinguished himself as the one in charge continued, "Wait a moment, please. I have supplies that will help you as you continue your trip. You have several more days' travel as you well know." He turned to his camel and removed a satchel bulging with its contents.

He returned and handed the bag to Naomi. "Inside are food, wine, and some special items to make your journey more enjoyable. Realizing the bag was heavy for Naomi to balance, he took it from her; and like the expert that he was in such maneuvers, he attached it to her donkey's side with the existing cords. He bid them goodbye, and he and his men continued down the ruddy road.

"Thank you," Naomi called out to him. "Go with God." She wished he worshipped the same God she did, yet she doubted it, his being from Egypt. She remembered that Egyptians' names often included portions of the names of their false gods. It pained her to recall that Aten was such a god.[25]

At that moment, self-condemnation ascended upon her and almost brought her to her knees. *Here am I, having lived in a forbidden land where they worship false gods, and I am taking a Moabite woman home with me. Am I any different?*

CHAPTER 10

Three more nights sleeping on the damp earth, though wrapped in heavy blankets, was beginning to weary Naomi. She was not the woman of ten years ago. It was not so much the burden of work that had aged her, but rather the heart-rending grief of her losses. Try as she could, the faces of Elimelech and her two sons would not leave her.

She and Ruth were well into Canaan, and home was not more than two days away. That, alone, would have heartened Naomi except for what she discovered at the side of the road.

The women had stopped to refresh themselves and partake again of the delicacies that the kind Egyptian Akenaten had given them. Such elegant fare they had never had before. *No wonder my ancestors in the wilderness wanted to go back to Egypt. The food was so good there.* Naomi smiled to herself, asking God in haste to forgive her for thinking such a thing. *After all,* she mused, *He provided manna from heaven for His people those forty years,*[26] *and all He asked in return was obedience.*

When the two finished their meal, Naomi, of necessity, ventured to the side of the road near a lush thicket. She stopped in her tracks. Lying half-concealed by a large tree branch were the bare remains of what appeared to be some kind of animal. That alone would not have astonished her. What caught her eye near the carcass was a piece of faded, half-rotten cloth, its edges ragged. It was the reddish-colored tint that began to register in her mind. She glanced at her surroundings, turning this way and that. Then it hit her. This had to be the same spot where Kilion was attacked years ago. The ferocious dog had torn her son's outer garment and ripped away a piece of it. She knelt to pick up the remnant, part of it falling away at her touch. She began to weep bitterly. Her wails brought Ruth running to her side.

"What is wrong, Naomi? What has happened?"

Between heavy sobs, Naomi explained all about the tattered piece she pressed to her bosom.

"My heart breaks within me. This place was the beginning of our trouble. Why didn't we turn back? My family would have been saved."

While unaccustomed to speaking to an elder in such a way, Ruth touched Naomi's arm and said, "My mother-in-law, you would not have *me*."

Sorrow mixed with remorse furrowed Naomi's brow. Taking one last look at the place of her discovery, she tucked the decaying bit of fabric into an inner pocket and turned to face Ruth.

"Yes, you are right, my beautiful daughter-in-law," she said, reaching for Ruth's hand. "Please forgive me. The sadness here quite overwhelmed me. You are my joy now, Ruth." Pulling her daughter-in-law back toward the road, she added, "Come."

She put her arm around Ruth, and they continued toward Judah. Their trusty donkey, which they had named Batah,[27] followed faithfully behind. His name was an apt Hebrew description of the loyal companion he had become.

◆

Judah's landscape had changed. New houses of mud and stone came into sight as the two entered Hebron, the previous home of Keila and Adnah. How Naomi wished her sister and brother-in-law were still there. She and Ruth could stop for some cool water and a nice visit. She wondered if her sister would ever return. She and Adnah seemed happy in Moab. Keila always adapted to change better than *she* did.

All of a sudden, a loud call came from behind them, interrupting Naomi's thoughts.

"Naomi! Is that you?" A woman, her long, drab halug skimming the earth, ran to catch up with the women. "Naomi! It *is* you. Don't you remember me? I'm Shira. Your sister Keila was my neighbor."

Naomi studied the woman's face hard. She half-smiled.

"Yes, I do remember you, Shira. My daughter-in-law Ruth and I have traveled alone from Moab. We are exhausted. We should be in Bethlehem sometime tomorrow." She looked down at her tunic and sandals and added, "I'm afraid we are dusty and need to get cleaned up."

There was a time when Naomi would not have hinted for help. Customs that once were significant had somehow lost their importance.

Shira was happy to oblige and led them to her home where she provided bath water, clean clothes, and a warm meal. She insisted that they stay the night, as well. She lived alone with the assistance of her daughter and son-in-law who lived near Tekoa.[28] With their help, she enjoyed a modest existence.

Weary as she was, Naomi listened late into the night to all the news of Judah. In time, sleep overtook the tired women, and they drifted into a much needed respite from their long trip. Tomorrow they would be fresh and ready for the last leg of their journey.

☆ CHAPTER II ☆

"So the two women went on until they came to Bethlehem. When
they arrived [there], the whole town was stirred because of them...."
Ruth 1:19

"Beautiful Bethlehem," Naomi said as they entered the place of her birth and that of her family. Nevertheless, something dear to her heart was missing. Where was the grasp of her husband's hand? Where was the laughter of her two sons? The reality of all that had happened in Moab gripped her in relentless waves of sorrow. The loss of her loved ones became more real now that she was home. Uninvited, grief seized her. The strong front she had faked for Ruth's sake gave way to a torrent of tears.

Word had traveled fast; from this house and that one, old friends came out to meet her, calling, "Naomi! Naomi!"

She wiped her face with her hand and told them not to call her by that name anymore, for God had brought trouble upon her.

"My name now is Mara," she said. The friends who had been happy at Naomi's arrival became sad, too. They knew the name meant "misfortune."

One of the older women, Eliana, ran to Naomi in the road, grasping her arm in urgent appeal.

"Naomi, we have heard of all that happened to you and your family in Moab. Do not be discouraged. God is faithful. Your pain is still raw, Naomi. You will see. In time God will bless your misfortune. He will not forsake you."

Eliana's words stung Naomi's heart, and had she not been drained of all her energy, she would have apologized for her seeming disregard for the

God of their fathers. Instead, her weary eyes spoke of a bitter sorrow one could only know from having experienced it.

"Please come," Eliana's dry, wrinkled face pleaded. "Come to my house. My grandson will feed and take care of your donkey. You and your companion will stay with me until your home is redeemed."

"This is Ruth, Mahlon's wife," Naomi said. She will live with me here in Judah. Thank you for your offer." For a moment, Naomi had forgotten about the Jewish law of kinsman-redeemer that her friend mentioned. Forlorn as she was, the realization struck a chord of hope within her as she and Ruth followed Eliana to her home. The two travelers from across the Salt Sea would find rest for a second night in a real bed.

———◆———

At that time in Canaan, the barley harvest was in progress. The men in the farmlands had finished cutting the ripened grain and awaited the binding process. It was women's work to gather the severed stalks into bundles known as sheaves, readying them for threshing. Naomi recalled many springtimes when she worked alongside other women eating the dust of the fields. Those had been happy times with her young boys following along, learning the ways of farming. At those times she had kept a watchful eye on them, an easy task when they were small. When they grew older, their reins had lengthened as they began the natural struggle to direct their own lives. Now it sickened her to think that she had led them to their deaths in an alien land. It had been her suggestion to go to Moab, a regret she lived with night and day. She had to remind herself that Ruth was the only good that had come from that fateful decision.

Eliana was a kind, generous woman sharing all she had with Ruth and Naomi. As giving as she was, it became obvious by the end of the first week that her food supply was reaching exhaustion, even with the help of her grown grandson who shared her home. Eliana never said a word of complaint. Ruth knew that of the three women, she was the young, healthy one. The obligation fell to her to find some way to contribute to their welfare. She inquired of neighbors where she might find work. They told her of the custom of landowners to leave some of the grain behind when the sheaves were being carried to the threshing floors. It was a Law of Moses that had been passed down from one generation to the next, a practice that guaranteed sustenance for those in need.

Early the following morning, she told Naomi that she would go find work gleaning behind the men who were harvesting the grain in nearby fields. Naomi feared for Ruth's safety, but finally gave her consent with stern warnings.

"Be careful, Ruth. Some of the men may look upon your beauty with evil intent. Servant girls will be in the fields. Stay close to them. You will be safer that way."

"I will be watchful, Naomi. Do not worry. I am strong."

Now Naomi had a relative on her husband's side, from the clan of Elimelech, a man of standing, whose name was Boaz.[29]

It was in the fields belonging to Boaz where Ruth went to glean. Late in the afternoon Boaz came to the field where Ruth had been working all day. Word had arrived that Naomi was back in Judah and had brought her late son's wife, a Moabitess, with her. He wondered if the woman before him was the one of whom he had heard. He knew for certain she was not one of the servant girls.

He approached Ruth, careful not to frighten her.

"Are you Naomi's daughter-in-law?"

Ruth straightened her back and lowered her sack to the ground.

"Yes, I am Ruth. I have come from Moab with Naomi. Mahlon was my husband who died there. I trust you do not mind that I am gleaning the barley here."

"No, no. Of course not. You are welcome here. Stay here in my fields where it is safe. I will tell my men not to harm you. You may come as often as you wish. Please tell Naomi I will try to visit her soon. I hear she is at Eliana's."

Ruth bowed, thankful to meet one so kind. Boaz walked away, his heart heavy knowing a kinsmen was in need when he had so much. Before leaving his workers, he instructed them to pull some grain from the bound bundles and add them to Ruth's sack.

When Ruth returned to Eliana's, tired and wet with moisture after her long day gleaning in the fields of Boaz, Naomi began to question her.

"Where did you find work today, my daughter? It looks like you have done quite well; your sack is full." Ruth opened the sack and pulled wide its opening for Naomi to see.

"His name is Boaz. He was kind to me and gave me much more grain than I had gathered. He encouraged me to return every day until the harvest is over."

Naomi smiled. "Boaz is one of my kinsmen-redeemers, Ruth. I see now that God has blessed you, and me, as well. It is good for you to do as he says. He is a good man, a man of means, and he has no wife."

A plan began to take root in Naomi's mind. Not only did she need to regain her own property, but she also needed to provide for her beloved Ruth.

CHAPTER 12

One evening after Ruth had gleaned a week in Boaz's field, Naomi called her outside Eliana's house to discuss her plan.

"Ruth, it is my duty to do the best I can to provide for you. Our husbands are gone, never to return. I believe God in His goodness will supply our needs. There is something I want you to do. Are you willing?"

"Yes, Naomi. You know I will do whatever you ask. You are my mother now. What would you have me do?"

"Tonight Boaz and all his workers will be at his threshing floor, ready to start the winnowing of the grain tomorrow. This is what I want you to do:

'When he lies down, note the place where he is lying. Then go and uncover his feet and lie down. He will tell you what to do.'[30]

It never occurred to Ruth to question her mother-in-law; the bond she shared with Naomi was strong, yet it could not be fully explained. All she knew was that this woman followed a God that she, herself, had not known before, and she wanted to possess the same faith she had witnessed in Naomi's life. Her God, Yahweh, was unlike the Moabite gods of stone. Naomi's goodness was the result of her devotion to the God of her people. The only flaw she had seen in Naomi was her lingering sorrow, a result of self-blame. She prayed that somehow, some way, she could someday bring joy to her mother-in-law and make her feel whole again.

So, Ruth did as her mother-in-law directed. She went to the threshing floor of Boaz and followed Naomi's instructions. When Boaz discovered someone there at his feet during the night, he was surprised and, because it was dark, asked who she was. When she identified herself, she asked him to join in a custom of the Israelites that Naomi had explained to her: she asked Boaz to spread the corner of his cloak over her, an act known to be a request for marriage. Boaz was shocked that one so young and beautiful would be interested in him, for surely there were younger men far more suitable. He was honored beyond words. Nevertheless, he wanted to make something clear and he needed to do it right then.

The moon that had been hiding behind a cloud peeked out for a moment and Boaz glimpsed Ruth's lovely face. For a second he hesitated before telling her what he knew he must. Being an honorable man, he began.

"Ruth, it is true that I am a kinsman of Elimelech, and by our laws I have a right to marry you and redeem Naomi's land; but I am not the nearest kinsman. Medad is the one who has first rights. I will go to him when morning arrives and present the situation to him. It must be his decision."

As the moon retreated into the cloud's thick veil, Ruth smiled, unseen. She knew that Boaz's words came from one of noble character. No matter what happened, she would be content. She left the threshing floor before full light.

Boaz was restless the next morning as he made plans to find the other relative. In his heart, he could not help hoping that the man would not claim his right. Maybe he would not have the money. Maybe he already had a wife. He knew the man had probably not seen Ruth, so maybe he would not want to take the chance. Boaz would have felt guilty to pray that God would supply one of those excuses; still the idea entered his mind.

> Meanwhile, Boaz went up to the town gate and sat there. When the kinsman-redeemer he had mentioned came along, Boaz said, 'Come over here my friend and sit down.' So he went over and sat down.[31]

To guarantee that the event was witnessed, Boaz gathered ten elders to join them. Then he explained to all of them about Naomi and her daughter-in-law. He then turned to Medad.

"You are a closer relative than I am. It is your right to buy the land ahead of me. My right is second to yours."

Medad pondered all he had heard. It was a good piece of land, and it would be, in his mind, a righteous thing to do. He was about to agree to the offer when Boaz added, "When you buy the land, you must also take as your wife Ruth, the Moabitess, in order to carry on the name of Mahlon, Naomi's elder son."

Medad was quick to change his mind, for he already had a wife and children. "I am sorry, Boaz. You must buy the land yourself."

Boaz had to restrain a smile as he announced to all within hearing that he would buy Naomi's land and take Ruth as his wife. The men had witnessed a great day in Bethlehem, and one by one they congratulated Boaz on his good fortune.

———◆———

Within a month, all transactions had been made concerning Naomi's land, and Boaz became the happy owner. The house that Elimelech and his sons had built was made ready for the marriage of Ruth and Boaz. There was no doubt in anyone's mind that Ruth had become one with the Israelites, embracing their God as her God.

After several months following her marriage, Ruth became pregnant. In time, she delivered a son whom they named Obed. The sorrow that had been a shroud for Naomi disappeared. In its place, the joy of helping care for the young child in her own former home filled her days with gladness and began to melt away the guilt she had felt for so long. She sometimes had a twinge of sadness when she longed to see Mahlon in the face of Obed. The feeling soon passed, for with a thankful heart she claimed Ruth's offspring as her own grandson. She informed her friends to call her Naomi again, for her happiness had returned.

Ruth felt blessed to be a part of the change in her mother-in-law. Her request to God had been answered as she had followed Naomi's wise advice. How could she have known at the time that she, Ruth, once a pagan girl from Moab, would become the great-grandmother of the greatest king Israel would ever know, one "'...after [God's] own heart....'" [32]

...Boaz the father of Obed, Obed the father of Jesse, and Jesse the father of David."[33]

The Story Of Jonathan

THE STORY OF JONATHAN

PREFACE

In the Old Testament book of 1 Samuel, one reads of the loyalty and faithfulness of King Saul's son, Jonathan, especially in his relationship to David who later succeeded Saul as king of Israel.

But, it is refreshing to discover that Jonathan was as human as we are. He did not always obey instructions, even from his own father. The complexities of his personality reveal admirable as well as questionable qualities from his childhood forward.

Another interesting discovery about the man Jonathan is that he was probably as much as twenty-seven years older than David,[1] a fact not expected when we think of the close friendship of the two men.

Very little is known of Jonathan's personal life, in particular his inmost thoughts. The following story is an attempt to piece together in one's imagination what that might have been like.

It would have been easy to concentrate more on the life of David as he was a mighty leader and a man after God's own heart. This story, though, is mostly about Jonathan, the eldest son of King Saul. However, the foregoing two men who influenced Jonathan's life must, of necessity, be included in order to present a full picture of the man Jonathan.

CHAPTER 1

Kyla rushed into the room, rounded the table, and with one hand grabbed the reddish hair of the three-year-old, scattering tiny, freshly-baked fig cakes everywhere. The carob-syrup coating oozed from the child's fingers.[2] Jonathan was caught again, and it always seemed to be the family's servant girl, Kyla, who did the catching.

"You are a spoiled young boy, Jonathan," she lashed out at him. "I told you this morning not to disturb the sweets I had prepared for the evening meal. Will you never learn?"

Kyla released her grip from the youngster's curly locks and turned him to face her. Taking a deep breath, she looked straight into the eyes of her young captive who was still holding a half-eaten delicacy in his hand. His eyes brightened, and his impish half-smile disarmed his captor for the moment. Kyla's angry frown softened, yet she proceeded to chastise her wayward charge.

"When you are given instructions, Jonathan, you must obey. I *should* tell your mother. Now … you must promise me that no more will you take things you have been told to leave alone!"

Jonathan said nothing. When he got the chance, he seized the freedom that his sly cunning had won and escaped Kyla's territory. In a flash, he was gone—outside to find a different venue for his mischief.

Hands on her hips, Kyla stood by the open door, recounting the times the boy had tried her patience. Just the week before, he had stacked whatever items he could find, climbed on top, and attempted to reach a beautiful jar he had spied. His reward was a nasty fall with broken pottery surrounding him. In another incident, Kyla discovered Jonathan pulling his baby brother from his cradle. When scolded, Jonathan said he only wanted to play with "Binny," his name for brother Abinadab. Sometimes his reasoning was quite good, but Kyla was convinced that his errant ways would someday cause him problems. *He looks like his mother Ahinoam, and acts like his father Saul,* she mused, glad her private thoughts were hers alone.

When Jonathan turned four years of age, a third son was born to Saul and Ahinoam named Malki-Shua, followed a year and a half later by a fourth, Ish-Bosheth. Early on, Jonathan disliked "Ishie" as he called him. It was not because Ish-bosheth was the youngest son; there were other reasons. Unusually large for his age, Ish-bosheth often bullied his brothers as they were growing up, especially Jonathan. Once in the heat of an argument, "Ishie" declared, "You may be the oldest, but it is I who will be king of Israel someday." It was only after Jonathan became a grown man that his earlier assessment of Ish-Bosheth made sense to him. The full realization of Saul's youngest son's statement would not come for many years.

As he grew older, Jonathan often invented games for entertainment, that is, when his mother did not have him busy doing chores. He once made a board game hewn from a fallen oak. He used bits of charcoal to mark the squares. For playing pieces he found small, flat rocks with different shapes that represented the "warriors." Jonathan, Abinadab, and Malki-Shua squealed in fierce competition for hours, pretending to be in real combat. Ish-Bosheth was too young to participate, so he developed means of protest. His favorite was to don an improvised crown and strut around his siblings, barking harsh commands. Most of the time, his brothers chose to ignore him and continued playing.

In good weather the three boys romped wildly in the great outdoors they all loved, leaving their young brother "Ishie" in Kyla's care. Jonathan taught Abinadab and Malki-Shua how to make their own arrows and master the bow. Their close union continued until their two sisters were born, a year apart. Things then began to change.

Abinadab took Merab, the older of the two girls, under his wings, while Malki-Shua coddled the baby girl Michal. As a result, Jonathan found himself alone much of the time. Of the six children, Jonathan was the most adventurous, curious, and impulsive, yet there was an inherent tenderness about him. In his early teens, he was quite aggressive while hunting and killing wild game; but, if he saw a small, crippled bird in the field that had perhaps flown the nest too soon, he would gently lift it, take it home, prepare a splint for its leg, and care for it until it was well enough to survive on its own. The duplicity in his personality would follow Jonathan all of his days.

CHAPTER 2

By the time Jonathan reached fifteen years of age, the country of Israel was devoid of leadership. The period of the judges was coming to a close, and the people demanded that the aging Samuel, Israel's final judge who was also a priest and prophet, find them a king. They wanted to be like the nations around them. Samuel objected to their outcries because he knew that God wanted His people to rely on *Him* as their king. In His compassion, God listened to their pleas. He told Samuel to find a man named Saul, an unlikely Benjamite from the smallest of Israel's tribes, and anoint him the first king of Israel.

Saul and his father Kish were successful farmers in Benjamin. When Samuel arrived with his proposal, Saul did not readily accept the offer. Besides, he had a wife and children who depended upon him. The idea overwhelmed him. Simple farm life may have required hard work, but it was not a challenge for him. In contrast, the idea of being ruler of an entire nation, making life-and-death decisions, was far different.

Saul stood head and shoulders above other men and was handsome in every way. Of strong stature, he had the appearance of one certain to be mighty in battle. His personality was a different story. He suffered a serious defect in his makeup: insecurity. A closely related shortcoming was that he was subject to extreme mood swings. The least occurrence, especially one he perceived as a personal threat, often sent him off on a rampage. The next moment he might appear complacent, even docile. Such was the disposition of the one selected to lead God's chosen nation of Israel, and this man was Jonathan's father!

At last, Samuel was able to convince Saul that he was appointed to that high calling by God, and it was not of himself. Wary as he was, Saul accepted the call to the kingship and received Samuel's anointing. He was thirty years old.

———◆———

The life to which they were accustomed changed for Jonathan and his whole family. As king of Israel, Saul set up his headquarters north of Jerusalem in Gibeah, and the family moved into a better, larger dwelling. Farm life ended for the man who believed he would work alongside his father Kish until one of them died. At first it was difficult for Saul to think of himself as royalty. That, too, soon changed.

On one of his trips to Arad, Saul met a lovely young woman named Rizpah. She had escaped there from Mount Seir in Edom where a band of Amorites had invaded her home and inflicted horrible atrocities upon many of the women. Saul took her back with him, provided a place for her in Gibeah, and made her his concubine.

Over time, the new arrangement affected the young man Jonathan. He saw his father's actions as an affront to his former way of life. At least then he had known what to expect even with his father's fluid temperament. On the one hand, Jonathan admired Saul and wanted to emulate his military acumen; on the other hand, he resented his father's bringing Rizpah into their midst. Her presence was a constant source of irritation to his mother Ahinoam. To Jonathan's credit, he did not resent the two sons that eventually resulted from that union. They were, after all, his kin. Also, they filled the void created by Malki-Shua and Abinadab after their sisters were born.

His favorite half-brother, although much younger, was Mephibosheth, for they were much alike. His name meant "exterminator of shame,"[3] and it was a name Jonathan would not forget.

❧ CHAPTER 3 ❧

In the meantime, Jonathan's respect for his father continued to lessen, resulting in a strained relationship between the two men. Sometimes he wished he could be on the battlefield fighting a tangible enemy rather than fighting the unnamed thing inside that was pulling him this way and that. Israel's warring neighbors, the Philistines, who were expanding their territorial pursuits, soon provided Jonathan his wish.

Much to his own surprise, as well as that of his mother, Jonathan received the command to join his father the king in what Saul referred to as a skirmish on the outskirts of Mizpah. Saul's action violated Moses' law which stated that men readied for battle should be at least twenty years of age.[4] Jonathan was only seventeen.

It was Jonathan's first military experience and for him, a milestone. Whether it was because of Saul's dislike for his son or a measure meant to test his son's soldiering ability, he nevertheless assigned Jonathan countless, often unnecessary, rigorous maneuvers. As a result, Jonathan's undeterred resolve was only strengthened to be tough in battle and accomplish his goal to become a seasoned warrior.

While Jonathan's stubbornness and self-will were inherited traits from father Saul, he did learn in part to curb some of his selfish desires. On the contrary, Saul, king of a great nation, never changed his colors.

Since Samuel had been directed by God to anoint Saul as king, he felt divinely urged to test the new king's obedience to God. The Philistine conflict looming on the horizon presented Samuel the opportunity. He made a rule which he asked Saul to follow that would validate his ability to serve as a successful king.

> Before you do battle with anyone, Saul, I want you to go
> to Gilgal and wait there for me to come. Wait seven days.
> I will sacrifice burnt offerings there and then tell you what
> the Lord would have you do against the Philistines.

Not only did Saul fail to follow Samuel's instructions to wait for him at Gilgal, but he also charged ahead and prepared the burnt offerings, himself. That action alone prompted Samuel to prophesy to Saul that someday, because of his disobedience, God would find another king for Israel, one greater than he.

'You acted foolishly...now your kingdom will not endure....'[5]

Turning a deaf ear, Saul continued making reckless military decisions as though he had not been warned. Without seeking godly counsel, he decided to attack the Philistines again. He took 2,000 men of Israel and ordered Jonathan to take an additional thousand from Gibeah. The Israelites' efforts were hopeless before the powerful Philistines that day, and they were forced to hide in caves. It was of no concern to Saul the negative influence he had on young Jonathan.

Soon thereafter, mimicking his father's impulsive behavior, Jonathan struck out with his men; and without orders to do so, they attacked the Philistine outpost at Geba. The next day Jonathan again chose to defy his father, the king. When a detachment of Philistines entered a pass near Micmash, Jonathan, without informing Saul, devised a plan of his own. He enlisted the help of his armor-bearer.

> '.... Come. Let's go over to the Philistine outpost on the
> other side.' His armor-bearer replied, 'Do all that you have
> in mind...I am with you heart and soul.'[6]

The two were able to trick the Philistine soldiers into thinking there were many Israelites mounting the cliff below them. In a surprise attack, Jonathan and his attendant were able to scale the height and kill at least twenty of the Philistines, causing the others to scatter. It was not until later that Saul learned the identity of the ones who had successfully attacked the

Philistine outpost and routed the enemy. Although Saul was often guilty of similar transgressions, he hated Jonathan for his insubordination. His refusal to commend the two men for their bravery added another layer of dissension between him and Jonathan.

Unyielding, both Saul and Jonathan continued to make foolish decisions. Before sending his men into the next battle, Saul forbade the exhausted soldiers to partake of food, not even the plentiful honey available in the woods where they rested. Jonathan was not present when his father made the announcement. It mattered not. When he *did* learn of the abstention, he rebelled anyway.

> I *will* eat this honey. It tastes good and strengthens me for battle. Besides that, my father causes much trouble.

Later, when he learned that Jonathan had broken the faith, Saul sought to kill his own son.

"I ate only a little," Jonathan protested.

In Jonathan's defense, an outcry arose from his fellow-soldiers who recognized his valor in battle. Their fervent stand was the only thing that saved Jonathan that day from his father's wrath.

In the meantime, God directed Samuel to find a successor for Saul, one of His own choosing. The present king's self-glorification had risen to a new level. He had even erected a monument to honor himself on the heights of Carmel. His disobedience and utter defiance of God and His laws had tarnished his kingship. Though it would be several years before the transition would occur, the new king would be a young man from Bethlehem, the youngest of Jesse's sons, a shepherd boy named David.

CHAPTER 4

In due time, Saul and his men returned home from their long struggles. To celebrate their recent victories, King Saul hosted an elaborate banquet. All available servants were called into service. A large tent was erected in Gibeah and carpenters hastily fashioned crude seats inside for all the guests. It would turn out to be the only such celebration Saul would give during his reign.

It was at Saul's lavish event where eighteen-year-old Jonathan met Eliah. There she stood near the opening of the ram-skin shelter, the full moon's glow illuminating her flawless face. It was not acceptable for young people to display in public their attraction to one another; but as the evening progressed it was obvious to onlookers that Jonathan and Eliah were smitten with each other, and nothing would change that.

When Jonathan's mother realized what was happening before her very eyes, she began to investigate the girl's background. She had never seen her among the girls in and around Gibeah. She decided to check with her closest confidante, Kyla, who remained her trusted servant.

"I am not sure," Kyla answered when questioned. "I am told she is from a family of Ammonites who settled close to the Salt Sea. How she came to be here in Gibeah I do not know."

Ahinoam shrieked, "An Ammonite! How can this be? I will speak to Jonathan. This must end, Kyla, and I will see that it does."

When Ahinoam walked away, Kyla whispered below her breath. *May you have luck, Ahinoam. It is known that the fire of love, if fanned, will only flame higher.*

Ahinoam's chance to speak with Jonathan came the following morning as the family meal was finished. She directed the younger children out of the room with a wave of her hand.

"Jonathan, my son, I must speak with you." Ahinoam rose and placed a hand on his shoulder to gain his attention. Before she could continue, Jonathan interrupted.

"Mother, I know what your concerns are. You're worried about the girl. Am I right?"

Somewhat taken aback, Ahinoam paused before she began her attack. "Jonathan, you are an Israelite from the tribe of Benjamin. You know it is the custom of our people, and for good reason, to marry within the tribe. One's inheritance must remain within the clan and be passed on to succeeding generations. You are aware of that, even if you *are* young. Don't let this girl turn your heart away from your upbringing. It must stop NOW. Do you understand, Jonathan?"

Ahinoam lifted Jonathan's chin. She waited.

Removing her hand, Jonathan replied, "Nothing has occurred between us, Mother. We saw each other only last night. Please do not worry."

His words only slightly satisfied Ahinoam. She remembered what it was like to be young, and her heart ached. At the same time, she resolved that she would not let the thing go any further.

Jonathan kept his tongue. He dared not remind his mother that Saul was only fifteen when he, Jonathan, was born, and Ahinoam was somewhat younger.[7]

———◆———

Eliah heard the soft crunch of the dry, scale-like needles in the dense, tamarisk thicket where she hid, a mere earshot from Jonathan's home.

"Is it you, Jonathan?" she called, a nervous uncertainty in her young voice.

"Yes," he replied. "It is I. We don't have long. My father the king is expecting me shortly. He doesn't send for me often, so it must be important."

Eliah spread her heavy shawl on the ground between two of the trees and motioned Jonathan to sit. Her loveliness as on the night Jonathan first saw her stirred the passion within him. His strong morals intact, he determined never to do anything to shame the one before him.

There they sat together. The couple chatted about the usual things that other youth of their day discussed: the constant war threats, their families and friends, their favorite foods, and their dreams of the future. Now and then the moon peeked between the limbs of the evergreens, the same kinds of trees that idolaters worshipped as sacred.[8] Eliah had knowingly picked that spot!

"I am the eldest of my father's sons, next in line to be king of all Israel," Jonathan told Eliah. "That may be a while, but I am prepared and will be ready. Then the one who stands beside me will be Queen of the land."

Eliah's eyes lit up as she dared to speak what entered her mind.

"If it were the two of *us*," she said, "perhaps an alliance could be formed between our two countries, bringing about peaceful times. That would be wonderful for future generations, wouldn't it, Jonathan?"

"I am not sure, Eliah. I have been taught since childhood that we are God's chosen ones who have been warned not to mingle with people of other nations, for we might be influenced to worship their gods. I have been wrestling with these teachings since I met you, Eliah, because you seem to be different."

After an hour of conversation and love words whispered back and forth, Jonathan helped Eliha to her feet. He was uneasy. He wondered if his father's summons involved the subject his mother had already pressed upon him. He hoped not.

"We must go. Will we meet again?" he questioned to elicit her intentions.

"Yes, Jonathan, that is my desire."

Their meeting that evening was the beginning of many. Despite Ahinoam's diligent surveillance, Jonathan was able to evade her watchfulness. The two young people were in love and determined to marry as soon as they could get their parents to agree. As for Ahinoam's consent, it would not be forthcoming. As for Saul, he took limited interest in his children's activities; but he, too, objected to *that* affair. If nothing more, Jonathan was the oldest, and Saul still believed that someday he would succeed him as king. The importance of family lines was one of the few Israelite rules that was important to Saul. They must not marry!

The teenagers' relationship ended less than six months after it had begun. Ahinoam had made life miserable for Jonathan. Her behavior was reminiscent of Isaac's wife Rebecca who, in times of old, had forbidden her son Jacob to marry any of the Canaanite women as his brother Esau had done. Back then Jacob had traveled a great distance to his uncle's home where he gained two wives, not just one. Unlike Jacob, Jonathan would spend his next twenty-five years surrounded by thousands in battle, with not even *one* wife to welcome him home.

✦ CHAPTER 5 ✦

As soon as he could, Jonathan returned to the battlefield. For him, it was a good place to be. His future with Eliah denied, he concentrated on the strategy of warfare. He wanted to learn how to trick his enemies and beat them at their own game. He hated to admit that his father was the best teacher for that feat; this is, if he could find him in a steady mood.

To Jonathan's disappointment, it was his father's commander Abner from whom he must learn. As one might expect, Jonathan's independent nature caused Abner much concern. When Abner reported Jonathan's obstinacy to the king, Saul described his son with harsh words, referring to him as the "'… son of a perverse and rebellious woman!'"[9] He could recognize his son's rebellious nature, but not his own. Sharing similar innate characteristics, and perhaps because of that, there was no meeting of minds between father and son, a sad commentary on their lives.

After serving his father faithfully for twenty-five years, Jonathan met a woman much younger than he was from his own tribe of Benjamin. Adina was not as lovely as Eliah, nor did his feelings for her match those he had for his first love. In any case, Jonathan wanted a son, one like "Binny" or Malki-Shua. He loved those brothers, and they often fought side by side at Abner's command. His brother Ish-Bosheth, on the other hand, always seemed to be fighting somewhere else in one of Saul's regimes.

When Jonathan was forty-three years of age, he and Adina were married and enjoyed the blessings of both families. It would not be until eleven years later that Adina would bear him the son he had looked forward to for years. The child's name would not be negotiable. He would be called Mephibosheth after Jonathan's half-brother with the meaningful name he had long admired. Unknown to him at the time, Jonathan would meet a real "exterminator of shame" called David.

—◆—

The superior, daring Philistines remained a serious thorn in Israel's side. To make matters worse, one of their warriors from the town of Gath took great pleasure in taunting any Israelite he encountered. He was over nine feet tall and wore brass armor weighing 125 pounds. His name was Goliath.

A young shepherd boy called David was sent by his father Jesse one day to check on his brothers who were engaged in Saul's army. When he found them, wild stories about the giant were circulating around the camp. What sounded like a great problem for most of the soldiers became a challenge for David who stood unmoved, watching the towering enemy across the way. To intimidate the Israelites, Goliath stepped out from the Philistine lines and shouted defiance toward the soldiers on the opposite side.

David announced aloud, "'Who is this uncircumcised Philistine that he should defy the armies of the living God?'"[10] No one had ever spoken to the mighty Philistine like that. A stunned silence prevailed.

—◆—

Later, the young shepherd boy's brash words and courageous stand were reported to King Saul. He could not believe that one so young and inexperienced had the nerve to stand up to the feared Goliath. Incredulous, he sent for David. He had to see for himself.

When David entered the king's presence, he bowed, and then filled with a confidence that only God could provide, he lifted his head and spoke.

'… Let no one lose heart on account of this Philistine; your servant will go and fight him.'[11]

Saul, not believing what he heard, admonished the young David.

'... you are not able to go out against this Philistine and fight him; you are only a boy, and he has been a fighting man from his youth.'[12]

After convincing Saul that he could conquer Goliath as he had the huge animals that often threatened his sheep, David was sent out. His arsenal consisted of only a staff, a sling, and five smooth river rocks.

As usual, Goliath was waiting. He began to deride David because of his age and size, cursing as he approached him. Speaking with a boldness far beyond his years, David challenged the giant.

'...you come against me with sword and spear and javelin, but I come against you in the name of the Lord Almighty, the God of the armies of Israel, whom you have defied.'[13]

Then, running as fast as he could toward Goliath, David flung the sling around, loaded with one of the stones, and hit the giant in the middle of his forehead. Goliath fell forward with a great crash, dead. With Goliath's own sword, David cut off his head as a warning to all the Philistine warriors who watched in shock before they fled.

One of the Israelite soldiers who commanded a division of 2,000 men looked on in awe and indescribable admiration and pride. He wanted to know more of this one who had done the impossible. He would get his answer before the day was over, for the Israelite soldier was Jonathan.

When Saul learned of David's challenge to and success over the Philistine giant, he sent for him again. When David entered, he was still holding Goliath's head. Jonathan was standing nearby. He looked again in disbelief upon the fearless, young warrior who was twenty-seven years younger than *he* was.

Saul announced to all those present that he was granting David a high position in his army. No one had ever heard of anyone so young receiving such an honor.

Also present was Abner, Saul's nephew and military commander. He pulled Jonathan aside and spoke words meant only for Jonathan's ears.

"Have you heard? The prophet Samuel has already anointed this young man to replace your father Saul. He said that God was displeased with the king, and He has chosen another. I'm sure the king has not been told or he would not be honoring him right now." Abner paused, then whispered even lower, "The shepherd boy will not be safe."

When Jonathan learned about Samuel's actions, instead of becoming jealous he vowed that he would always protect David, even if it contradicted his own father, King Saul.

Jonathan was so taken with the young David that he wanted to do something to honor him. As soon as King Saul and Abner left the room, Jonathan approached David.

"I am Jonathan, the king's oldest son. I saw you today as you defeated the great Philistine warrior, Goliath. You are the bravest young man I have ever seen. My father's commander Abner told me that you, as young as you are, have already been chosen over my father to be Israel's king. I know that Samuel is a man of God and has done this in good faith. I want you to know that I will do all I can to protect you."

David was surprised at Jonathan's remarks, especially that he would defend a mere shepherd boy over his own father. To his astonishment, he believed Jonathan.

Before David could respond, Jonathan removed his royal robe and handed it to David. Then he did the same with his tunic. David was startled, too shocked to comment. Jonathan then gave David his sword, bow, and belt, saying, "I have never seen a warrior like you. We had heard of Goliath for a long time. It is hard to believe that I am standing before his executioner."

All David could say was, "Jonathan, I will try to be worthy of your trust." David bowed before the rightful heir, the one assumed to be the next king, and said, "May we be joined in our love for Israel and our faith in the one true God." Jonathan likewise bowed to honor David, unaware that his actions were being observed by one watching close by ... his father, Saul.

In spite of what he had seen and heard, Saul decided to keep David there in Gibeah. He wanted to enlist the service of one so brave while keeping a close eye on him at the same time. In addition, he had learned that David was a musician. How pleasing it would be to have someone soothe his frayed nerves at day's end with the melodious strings of the harp.

As for Jonathan, what he had seen on the battlefield that day changed his life forever. David replaced Saul in Jonathan's allegiance.

In the following days, the two became fast friends. Jonathan promised to stand by David no matter what happened; and David, in time, would honor a promise *he* would make that would affect Jonathan's son, Mephibosheth.

CHAPTER 6

"Saul has slain his thousands, and David his tens of thousands."
1 Samuel 18:7

Word spread throughout the land about David's defeat of Goliath. When King Saul heard the women of Israel singing words praising David's victory, anger burned within him, and a deep jealousy was born. He would have no one honored above himself regardless of what the boy had accomplished. He had kept David in his service only to satisfy his own penchant for control. The more David was revered, the more Saul's irrepressible fear engulfed him. To make matters worse, seeing his own son in the presence of one who had become his enemy was more than he could endure. He decided to take action. He was sure his royal decrees would still be obeyed. So, he called in Jonathan as well as all of his officials.

It is my order that you kill the shepherd boy, David. I will make it well worth your success with a handsome reward.

The king's men went out from his presence while Jonathan remained behind to try to dissuade his father.

'Let not the king do wrong to his servant David; he has not wronged you, and what he has done has benefited you greatly... Why then would you do wrong to an innocent man like David...?'[14]

– 155 –

As a result of his son's plea, Saul said he would rescind the order. However, recalling past experiences, Jonathan doubted the sincerity of his father's hasty promise that he would not harm David. He had come to see his father in a whole new light. His reasoning proved correct, for Saul, himself, tried to kill David the following evening. Although David was able to elude the king, he realized he could no longer be alone with him.

David's feeling of safety was temporary at best, soon to be replaced by ongoing fear. After all, he was still young, and the life to which he had been exposed was much different from his days watching sheep on a peaceful hillside near Bethlehem. He needed reassurance from Jonathan. Yes, he had promised to protect David, but he was, after all, the king's son. How long would he be able to reject his father's pressure? To find out, David made contact with Jonathan, and they met in a field outside Gibeah where David expressed his misgivings.

"'Your father knows very well that I have found favor in your eyes, and ... as surely as the Lord lives and as you live, there is only a step between me and death.'"[15]

David's plaintive words voiced a concern Jonathan had not expected. He sought to reassure his friend.

> So Jonathan made a covenant with the house of David,
> saying, 'May the Lord call David's enemies to account ...
> Go in peace for we have sworn friendship with each other
> in the name of the Lord....'[16]

David left, confident that his life was safe in Jonathan's hands; but it was not long before Jonathan, himself, became as much a target for Saul's wrath as was David. The second time Jonathan tried to persuade his father not to harm David, *he* was almost killed. His father hurled a spear at him, barely missing. The event convinced Jonathan with undeniable certainty that his father was a madman. No one was safe in his presence. He was torn between a desire to maintain family ties, and the realization that his safety was in great jeopardy. He decided he must never again be alone with the king, the same conclusion David had reached; but nothing would keep him from seeing his mother, Ahinoam.

Also, during that time the Israelites under King Saul's command enjoyed a brief respite from their enemies, the Philistines. The break from war allowed Jonathan time to spend with his wife Adina and their young son Mephibosheth. Although it was a welcome diversion from troubles with his father, his constant concern remained the safety of his friend David.

———◆———

As the months turned into years, David became more and more popular as he engaged in battles outside Saul's command. His military exploits were always successful, giving rise to hundreds of followers. Even so, no matter where he went or what he accomplished, he was never free of Saul's relentless pursuits. The king who once had honored David for killing the giant Goliath now regarded him as his mortal enemy.

Jonathan wanted to encourage his friend David, but sometimes he was hard to find. The one who had been anointed the next king of Israel was constantly on the run to escape King Saul, occupying temporary residence in one stronghold after another. The last time that Jonathan saw his friend David was at Horesh in the desert of Ziph. He had learned that his father was close on David's trail, and he wanted to warn him. He wanted to give hope to David whose life was in daily turmoil. In addition, David had just returned from saving the people of Keilah against the insatiable, military appetites of the Philistines, and he was battle-weary. Jonathan's words to David were as refreshing as a soft spring rain.

> 'Don't be afraid…My father Saul will not lay a hand on you. You will be king over Israel, and I will be second to you. Even my father Saul knows this.'[17]

———◆———

In the few quiet moments that Jonathan enjoyed back home, he remembered Abner's words about David's anointing by the prophet Samuel. It puzzled him that his father Saul was still king, still fully in charge. So, he wondered, *when will David reign in Israel?* It saddened him that he might not see that in his lifetime. He soon had to put those musings to rest, for the war cry sounded again. The persistent Philistines were on the offensive, and his friend David was in hiding!

CHAPTER 7

Victory did not always come to Israel's first king. Because of Saul's disregard for God's commands, resulting in blatant disobedience, God removed His protective hand from Saul's military endeavors. This proved true at Mount Gilboa.

The Philistines, forever at war against Israel, approached the Israelites with a strength that Saul's army had never before seen. What they experienced that day was more treacherous and bloody than they could have imagined. The heavily-armed Philistines had wisely positioned themselves on the cliffs of Mt. Gilboa, awaiting their adversaries. Saul and his men, led by his commander Abner and accompanied by Jonathan and two of his brothers, assembled in the valley below in readiness to charge the Philistines that they expected to encounter at the north end of the ravine. Instead, the Israelites got a surprise!

All of a sudden, Saul's commander Abner shouted, "Look! Those Philistine pigs are posted on top of the mountain. All is lost if we do not attack them there in full force, for they have complete advantage. Come! Away! We will fight to the end."

Over the crags of the mountain they climbed with only Abner's words as encouragement. The fear of battle shone in their eyes; still they pushed forward. Finally, in order to avoid total vulnerability, Abner divided the men: his unit would attack on the north, Saul's on the west.

The heated battle began as Abner's regiment approached the peak on the northern edge. Men fell all around the stalwart commander yet he pressed on. By the time Saul and his group appeared at the top of Mt. Gilboa on the west, he had already lost many of his soldiers who were clear targets as they attempted the steep ascent. Saul's three eldest sons,

Jonathan, Abinadab, and Malki-Shua, fought alongside their father that fateful day. It never occurred to Saul to separate them to prevent total annihilation. The one son, though, not present with the king's men that day was Ish-Bosheth. He was with Abner, far to their left.

Out of nowhere, or so it seemed, appeared the fierce Philistine warriors who made an unparalleled, savage assault against Saul's men. Jonathan, recalling the extreme bravery of his friend David in his attack on the Philistine Goliath, became fueled with renewed strength and drove fearlessly into the melee. His sword struck with a vengeance greater than those of the comrades beside him. Before all was done, Jonathan alone had attacked and killed countless numbers of the enemy. As he turned to survey his success, a Philistine soldier seized the chance to stop the fury visited upon them by the enraged Israelite. With one swift move, the soldier propelled his javelin which found its target. Jonathan gasped a moan, released the grip on his sword, and fell forward to the ground with his young son's name on his lips: "Mephibosheth. My Mephibosheth."

The Israelites suffered utter defeat that day. The few men who were left fled, glad to escape with their lives. Saul's three sons who had fought with valor beside him would not return home. Saul stumbled through the carnage, tramping over body after body until he found them lying there, not yet cold, on Mt. Gilboa.

"Not my sons!" Saul cried out, flashing his sword to and fro at anything that moved in the coming darkness. Then, with one shot of the enemy's bow, Saul was hit. He plummeted to the harsh ground, critically wounded. His pride still intact, refusing to be the enemy's victim, he called to his armor-bearer, the only one left standing. "Here. Plunge your sword into my body." When the attendant refused, Saul lifted himself as high as he could above the ground to reach his sword. Leaning upon its sharp tip, he slid the sword into his already perishing flesh as far as his strength allowed, and died there on the mountain.

He and his sons lay there, lifeless spoils of war, prized plunder for the victorious Philistines.

In an act of disrespect for the Israelites and a show of great victory, the Philistines decapitated Jonathan, his brothers, and their father Saul. To further display their conquering arrogance, they hung the bodies on the city walls of Beth Shan in the territory of Issachar. Ish-Bosheth was Saul's only military son unscathed that terrible day.

⬥

When the news reached Jonathan's household that he had been slain, panic struck the city and the surrounding territory. The Israelites were without a king and their great army had been decimated. Almost everyone lost a family member and disarray was everywhere. People were running here and there, not sure where to go or what to do.

In haste, Mephibosheth's nurse grabbed a few things, swooped up the child in her arms, and ran from the home. The articles she had gathered flew in all directions. As she bent to retrieve something, she dropped the child who was much too large for her to carry, and his feet were crushed beneath him. He would be crippled for the rest of his life, testing an oath that Jonathan had asked David to take many years before:

> '...show me unfailing kindness like that of the lord as long as I live,...and do not ever cut off your kindness from my family....'[18]

CHAPTER 8

Several days passed before David received the news that Jonathan and Saul had fallen in battle. Although David had suffered countless attempts on his life by Saul for years, he respected the king because he knew he was God's appointed one. His grief following the sorrowful news of both his friend and his king gave birth to a lengthy, poignant lament. Sections of the dirge were devoted to both men whose lives, as diverse as they were, had affected David since the age of fifteen.

> 'From the blood of the slain, from the flesh of the mighty,
> the bow of Jonathan did not turn back, the sword of Saul
> did not return unsatisfied... How the mighty have fallen in
> battle! Jonathan lies slain on your heights. I grieve for you,
> Jonathan my brother; you were very dear to me.'[19]

Jonathan's request and David's promise made years before were not forgotten. After David became undenied king of Israel, following Ish-Bosheth's failed attempt to usurp the throne, he remembered his friend Jonathan.

One day he asked one of his royal officials, "'Is there anyone still left of the house of Saul to whom I can show kindness for Jonathan's sake?'"[20]

His quest for an answer revealed that Jonathan's son Mephibosheth was a cripple and had been so most of his life. Without hesitation, David sent for him. Mephibosheth arrived and humbly bowed low before King David, intimidated and fearful.

'Don't be afraid,' David said to him, 'for I will surely show you kindness for the sake of your father Jonathan. I will restore to you all the land that belonged to your grandfather Saul, and you will always eat at my table.'[21]

And Mephibosheth lived in Jerusalem, because he always ate at the king's table and he was crippled in both feet.[22]

David remembered that Jonathan expected to be his second in command. He regretted that his friend's hope was never realized. Instead, Jonathan's memory lived on through the life of his son Mephibosheth, and a promise made many years before was honored by the greatest king that Israel ever knew, King David.

The Story Of Abigail

THE STORY OF ABIGAIL
PREFACE

There are two Abigails in the Bible. One is the sister of David, Israel's greatest king. The other Abigail is the one who ultimately became one of David's wives. The latter is the one explored in this story.

So little is known about Abigail's private life except what we learn from the brief details given in I Samuel 25 and I Samuel 30. However, those concise sketches challenge one to imagine what this lovely woman's entire life might have been like. As with the other stories presented in *Reading Between the Lines,* much of the following text is purely speculation and is created to fill in the gaps where further information is not given.

Meet the beautiful, intelligent, and daring Abigail!

CHAPTER I

Around the year 1025 B.C., constant unrest was the state of being for the nation of Israel. At one time or another they were at war, "... against enemies on every side...."[1] Making matters worse, the nation had a weak, ineffectual king.

Saul, Israel's first king, was disobedient and arrogant before the Lord who had chosen him to fill that position. Displeased and regretful, God directed Samuel the prophet to anoint young David, a shepherd boy, to succeed Saul. As a result, Saul's intense jealousy drove him to pursue David relentlessly with the intent to kill him. It was at this time in Israel's history that the story of Abigail begins.

A man named Nabal lived near the town of Carmel. He was a descendant of the Judahite Caleb, the brave Israelite spy who along with Joshua had reported to Moses that the land of Canaan could be attacked and overcome while ten other spies disagreed. It was Caleb who had asked Moses for Hebron and received his "prize" in the Promised Land.[2] One would think such a noble heritage would have influenced Nabal for good. It did not.

The countryside around Carmel was perfect pastureland for raising sheep. A shrewd and often unscrupulous sheep farmer, Nabal had amassed great wealth after purchasing the best of the land surrounding Carmel and populating it with three thousand sheep, as well as a thousand goats. He became known far and wide as the most prolific producer of the finest wool available. In addition, he sold his animals for the milk, hides, and meat; nothing was wasted. No one equaled his success in that part of Judah.

As a young man, Nabal could have had his pick of beautiful and eligible young women. Instead, his business deals had occupied most of his time and left little opportunity for romantic interests. Before long he found himself a middle-aged man with great wealth and numerous servants, but no one with whom to share it all.

On occasion Nabal was approached by a father looking for the right man, especially a rich one, to take an unmarried daughter. One such man was Rael of Aphekah, near Hebron.

Rael traveled to Carmel with the pretense of buying sheep to enlarge his own flock. He took with him his lovely, oldest daughter, Abigail. He planned to explain to Nabal, if necessary, that he had brought her along because he valued her opinion. In addition to her looks, perhaps mention of her intelligence would enhance his daughter's chances, he had reasoned.

Not a man of means, Rael had borrowed from a neighbor two of his best donkeys for the trip. He loaded Abigail's animal with the choicest food items that his wife Uriella could prepare. He was careful to observe the custom of presenting gifts to one from whom you expected a favor. At the least, it would express good will.

Upon arrival at the vast expanse of farmland, what an impression Nabal's home made on the young Abigail. When she and her father dismounted in front of the wide gate that joined rows of fences to the left and right, they stood in awe. Before them stood a massive house of hewn stone larger than anything they had ever seen. They were too amazed to speak. It was windy springtime, sheep-shearing time, and the strong gusts at the high elevation lifted strands of Abigail's rich, dark hair, revealing a young girl's face of remarkable beauty. Her large, dark eyes glancing this way and that, showed a sense of curiosity as well as alertness. *How could one man own all this*, she mused as she looked to her father to guide their next move.

Soon a maid servant who looked to be in her thirties, petite and hasty of step, came out of the house to meet them. She bowed to honor the visitors before speaking.

"I am Leora. My master is away but will return soon."

Rael's face reflected his disappointment. "We have come from Aphekah near Hebron to buy some of your master's sheep. I need a few to add to my flock." Had she not been accustomed to her father's ways, Abigail would have flinched at his bending of the truth.

Leora bowed again. "Please come in out of the heat. I will bring cool water from the well."

"First," Rael said, "let me present these gifts to you for your master." He stepped back and lifted from the camel's side several containers his wife had filled. He handed them to Leora who thanked him and led them inside the gate to the house.

They entered Nabal's home, were seated, and Leora disappeared with a large jar for the water she would draw from the well outside.

Alone, Abigail and her father looked around. They had never seen such magnificence. To the two common people it was what they imagined a king's home to be. Abigail wondered if even King Saul had such a palace. It mattered not, for talk was already circulating that he was going to be replaced by one called David, a son of Jesse. In fact, it was said that the prophet Samuel had already anointed him.

The room in which Rael and Abigail were sitting was furnished with pieces only a skilled woodworker could have produced. It was appropriate that the sheep-skin covers of the cushions upon which they sat were made from Nabal's own animals. From an adjourning room arose the distinct aroma of meat boiling—*leg of lamb?* They wondered.

Soon a squeaking door announced Leora's return. They could hear her pouring water in the room from which had come the pleasant smell. Her quick steps brought them cool, refreshing drinks of the purest water Abigail had ever tasted.

It seemed an eternity before the sheep owner returned home. Interaction with the servant girl had been scant. She was behaving as she had been taught for one in her position, meekly speaking only words of necessity, especially to strangers.

An odd discomfort surrounded the young Abigail as she sat waiting. She knew the real reason they were there. She knew, too, that her father's actions were traditional among her people. The father of her best friend, Keita, had arranged *her* marriage to a man she had never met. She heard that Keita was resigned to her present life but was not happy. *Poor Keita. She will be expected to bear many children for her husband, preferably sons, though she is scarcely out of her own childhood.*

Will it be the same for me? Is it possible to be happy with a man I don't even know? Maybe he will not want me! If he does, will he be good to me? I wish I could tell Father I want to go home, yet I can't. It would be devastating to him. He wants what is best for me. All those thoughts invaded Abigail's mind as she and her father continued their wait.

Finally, heavy footsteps were heard approaching the front. The door flung open and Nabal entered. Abigail turned to look. What she beheld was not at all what she had hoped for.

CHAPTER 2

The man standing before them was tall and burly. The top of his head had skimmed the door lintel as he passed through. His dark, unkempt beard was bushy; and the striped, wool outer garment he wore, much too warm for the weather, was dusty with frayed edges along the bottom. A deep frown creased his thick forehead, and he muttered something to himself before he spoke aloud.

"I saw your donkeys. Why have you come?"

His tone reeked with suspicion and added to an already awkward situation. Rael rose to be polite as did Abigail, but Nabal held his ground, reluctant to approach his guests.

Finally, Rael stepped toward Nabal and bowed in respect to one so well-to-do.

"I am Rael and this is my daughter Abigail. I know of your vast flocks and have come from Aphekah to purchase some if you are willing to oblige."

A sudden look of surprise crossed Nabal's face! It was apparent that he noticed for the first time the lovely girl standing slightly behind her father. He was so taken with her beauty that he stuttered a bit before replying to Rael.

"Uh --- yes, yes. I sell sheep, especially the young lambs."

Rael took a step closer to Nabal to make his case.

"I am really looking to buy sheep over a year old. We need them for the mutton.[3] Is that possible?"

By time time, Nabal was impressed more with Abigail than with any business transaction. His demeanor became gentle, and he motioned for them to be seated again.

"Please stay awhile. I will have Leora and the others prepare food. It is almost mealtime."

He left the room, and the two visitors could hear him barking instructions to his servants. They heard Leora answer, "The lamb is done. The rest will be ready soon."

———◆———

When the meal was finished, Nabal said, "Come. We will go out to the pens. I will show you what I have. You can pick out the sheep you like."

The two men, followed by Abigail, walked down a slope to the sheep pens. The bleating of the fluffy animals filled the sultry air. Nabal opened a gate, and the three entered among the woolly creatures. The earlier wind had abated, and the three men working the sheep stopped now and then to wipe their brows. Nabal led them through another opening to a smaller pen that held less sheep.

"Choose from these, Rael. How many do you want?"

Rael turned to Abigail. "You choose, my daughter." Turning to Nabal, he added, "She has an eye for this kind of thing."

Nabal, for the first time showing a hint of a smile said, "Very well." He turned to face Abigail. "The choice is yours to make."

After some deliberation, Abigail settled on three of the better looking ones, then joined her father who would do the negotiating. What came next was a surprise to her.

Nabal stroked his heavy beard and made a suggestion which only the two men were meant to understand.

"I will have one of my men deliver the sheep to you in a few days. It will be easier for you because they are experienced sheep herders. Sometimes three sheep are more difficult to manage than a whole flock. They do not have a clear leader to follow and often wander off."

Abigail doubted the validity of his statement, but was not free to challenge the man with whom they were doing business. Apparently a plan was already growing in the mind of Nabal, and Rael sensed what it was. Without indicating its meaning in the slightest, both men parted, expecting to get something for themselves out of the meeting that involved much more than the lives of a few sheep. No money had changed hands.

On the way back home, Abigail's heart was troubled. First, she had misgivings about the place, Carmel. It was the town where King Saul had erected a monument on its heights to honor himself.[4] Her mother, Uriella, had said that it was an act of idolatry and that God did not honor those who glorified themselves.

Then there was the man Nabal. It was obvious that he was rich and powerful, but she was wise enough to know that wealth did not bring happiness. She was not sure what lay ahead; she only knew that whatever it was, as a good daughter, she would accept. She wondered if her mother had experienced similar doubts as a young girl. After all, she had married when she was only fourteen. Abigail shuddered. She, herself, was barely two years older.

CHAPTER 3

Back home in Aphekah, Abigail busied herself with the usual duties their home required. Being the oldest of three daughters, she was a great help to Uriella who was not a healthy woman, and Abigail often feared her mother would not last through the day. The two younger girls had come along later, Talia now twelve and Nava ten. Abigail out of necessity had become a surrogate mother to them; but it was Uriella, a devout Hebrew woman, who had versed her children in the laws of God, quoting daily the Holy Scriptures that had been passed down from her parents.

No matter how occupied Abigail was, she could not shake from her mind one stark possibility. The mere thought of Nabal pressed her to stay even busier than usual, for she was aware that the "few days" he mentioned were coming to a close. Regardless, her mind was steadfast; she would not shame her parents. She had been taught all her life to obey them in all things, and that she would do. An inclination of what was coming prompted her to train with speed Talia the twelve-year-old to take her place in the household. She did not think it unfair, for she, herself, had been trained by her wise mother at an even younger age to perform duties needed to maintain a home. What saddened her most was that she may have to leave her beloved mother who needed her now more than ever.

❖

Exactly six days after their trip to Carmel, one of Nabal's men appeared at Rael's home with the sheep. Abigail knew her father had not paid for the animals, and she suspected that they were a gift offered in exchange for her hand; it was part of a plan similar to others that had existed for generations. She was not alone.

As expected, the man called Rael outside to talk. They first led the sheep to join others of Rael's flock, then stopped and leaned against the fence. Abigail could not hear them from where she stood inside, but she was sure the talk was about her. She waited, hoping the day would last forever and she could remain at peace in the home she loved.

The men returned to the house, and Rael alone entered. His facial expression was ambiguous. His mouth, lifted at the corners, mimicked delight; yet his eyes shone a sadness that was rare for Abigail to witness. He waited until Uriella was present, as well as the other girls, before he spoke.

"Nabal's employee has come with an offer from his master." He looked directly at Abigail. "He wants you, my daughter, for his wife. As you know, he is a very rich Judahite who will be able to provide for you in a way that I never could. You will have servant girls at your disposal anytime you need them, and you will not have to work hard like your mother has all these years. You will never want for good food; there will always be a plentiful supply. Carmel is not so far. We will be able to see you when a need arises."

Abigail listened to her father's long speech, and then stoically asked, "When is this to take place, Father?"

"In a week or so. We will be informed when all the plans are finished. That will give you time to make your wedding dress. We will accompany you to Nabal's home where the festivities will take place. It will be a joyous occasion, Abigail. You will be the wealthiest woman around. How happy you will be!"

Abigail believed that her father's words were meant more to console *him* than *her*. In the few days that had passed since their return from Carmel, she had readied her mind, if not her heart, to accept what had to be; and for her family's sake, she would force herself to appear satisfied. In no way did she want to discourage her sisters who would someday face similar experiences in their lives. A pleasant memory of herself was what she wanted to leave with them all; still, long after Nabal's servant had departed with the good news for his master, Abigail in silence lamented all that had occurred. She was not at all sure what she was gaining, but she knew for certain what she was losing.

Chapter 4

The day of the couple's wedding drew near. Nabal departed from the tradition held by most Israelites that the marriage should take place at the home of the bride. Only the feast was customarily hosted at the bridegroom's home.[5] As Abigail wondered about Nabal's action, she recalled the story of Rebecca leaving her home in Haran and traveling to Canaan to wed the great patriarch, Isaac.[6] It was sad that she, like Rebecca, would not be married in her own home.

Nabal's home was awhirl. Several servant girls were preparing food for the guests while Leora was getting the house in order. The best linens and the most expensive pottery would be used; and Nabal had even hired musicians to entertain during the feast which would be held outside. Two of his male servants were busy brushing the yard surrounding the house free of debris.

In contrast, Rael's home near Aphekah was quite serene. Weak as she was, Uriella was putting the final touches on Abigail's wedding gown. She had already fashioned a crown of woven flowers to which was attached a veil that would cover Abigail's face. Talia helped her sister pack a small trunk with favorite belongings. Her eyes grew damp as she watched Abigail lovingly touch each item. Talia knew in time the precious mementos would be her sister's connection to home.

Rael had absented himself from the house in order to avoid unwanted emotion he knew would come soon enough. He had intended to prepare the crude family cart for transporting them to the wedding. Even with only two wheels, it was almost as large as a wagon. He learned it was not needed, though. Nabal had sent one of his men to say his canopy-covered wagon would come for the family. It would be pulled by horses rumored to have come all the way from Egypt. Rael was pleased. It was somewhat consoling to know that his eldest daughter would have the best life possible, including a good husband. He had observed Nabal's ill temperament once and had not considered it reason for concern.

The big day arrived on Tuesday, the third day of the week as custom dictated.[7] Uriella had made a decision the night before that she could not attend the wedding. She said she was just tired, more so than usual, and that the lengthy festivities, sometimes lasting a week, might be too much for her to bear.[8] She insisted they must go without her, vowing she would spend the time in prayer for a successful event.

Abigail almost refused to go. Something did not seem right to her anyway, and leaving her mother was breaking her heart. Uriella faked a strong front as she stood admiring her lovely daughter, a vision of unmatched beauty in the long, flowing gown she had created in such a short time. Abigail reached for her mother, and they embraced so long that Rael had to pull his daughter away, saying, "We *must* go." Abigail felt like she was going to a funeral instead of what should be the most joyful day of her life.

Off she went … to a world unlike any she had ever known, one far different from the one she was leaving.

CHAPTER 5

Although the trip to Nabal's was only ten miles long, in some ways it seemed much longer to Abigail. There was too much time to think. She felt that something strong was fighting to pull her back; still the carriage continued on. She almost wished they could hurry and get there so she could put the deep yearnings of home and Mother behind her. Her feelings were contradictory. On the one hand, she wanted to forget completely the life she left so that the pain in her heart would vanish. On the other hand, she never wanted to forget, for her roots had been solidly planted there with her father, mother, and sisters.

As the lovely canopy-covered wagon clattered along toward its destination, up the steep incline to Carmel, Abigail pressed her hand to her heart and vowed: *I am going to a strange place, but I will embrace my former life forever.*

A few friends of both families had already arrived. As the wagon pulled in front of the big gate, pleasant chatter could be heard above the whirring wind sweeping around the corners of the house. Abigail wondered if her veil would remain in place until she got inside. *Does it really matter?* she pondered. *Nabal will probably still have a dirty beard.* Had the occasion not been so serious a matter, Abigail might have giggled aloud.

Nabal's driver helped the bride down, and she was directed toward the house, followed by her father and sisters. Leora greeted them at the door; then Abigail got a big surprise. Nabal appeared, clean beard and all. His colorful, long-flowing simlah was neat, as well.[9] She suspected that Leora had taken care to be sure her master was well-groomed. *I must thank her sometime.* She smiled to herself, surprised she could think anything was funny at a time like that.

Nabal directed Rael to a small table serving as a desk upon which lay the ketubbah.[10] It was the contract that the two men must sign that would officially bind the bride and groom in the bond of marriage. It was a Hebrew custom and Abigail was glad that at least a semblance of her heritage was being observed. A detail which Rael had not discussed with his daughter was that Nabal was not a believer in the one true God. Somehow Abigail knew. It was just one of those things one senses. She could not help wondering, *How can he be a Judahite and not believe?* The stark revelation, however, had troubled her since that first day in Carmel. Still, it was not a topic a daughter could discuss with a father. It would appear as a challenge to his judgment. It was just not done.

◆

A preliminary celebration began soon after the contract was signed. The servants carried large silver patens, loaded with a variety of foods, outside to the waiting guests.[11] That was the cue for the musicians to begin. Before long people in the crowd, especially the young, began dancing to the rhythmic sounds. It was a custom that Abigail had seen before at Hebrew weddings, and she regarded *that* part as delightful. The festivities would begin again the next day and would continue for six more days, another custom she knew all about.

Abigail pretended to be happy throughout the evening. She smiled at each person and even teased her sisters from time to time. To the guests, the event was one of the biggest and most important events many of them would ever attend.

Nabal's men servants brought out his best aged wine, known to be an expensive variety by those who knew such things. Abigail had never tasted fermented drink until she sipped from one of the special chalices purchased for the bride and groom alone. She did not know much about wine. From what she had heard about its sedating effect on one's mind, she decided she might need it before the present occasion was over.

The night wore on until the wee hours of the next morning. Tired guests began leaving, many yawning as they said their goodbyes. Three little ones had fallen asleep and were carried out in their mothers' arms. Abigail was exhausted beyond anything she could remember. *I am weary of all the smiling, also standing for hours.* When she realized the alternative, her muscles tensed and she felt somewhat ill. Be that as it may, Abigail knew she would survive. She would get through it all. She was strong.

———◆———

On Wednesday morning, before the sun had cast its rays across the desert below, the chuppah, the intimate consummation of Abigail's marriage to Nabal, had taken place.[12] She had embarked on a journey that she could not have imagined, one that would take her further than she would have felt prepared for. But, God had his hand on Abigail and would fulfill His purposes for her, as well as for another she had heard stories about, a man she had never met.

CHAPTER 6

The week-long festivities finally came to a close, and Abigail began familiarizing herself with the huge house that was now her home. She was quite uncomfortable having someone ready to provide her every need, and she had not the slightest idea what to do with the five personal maids at her disposal. It seemed such a waste to her.

From the first day, she learned that Leora was in charge. She had worked for Nabal several years and was quite adept at all the intricacies of running a large household. Abigail did not resent her. Instead, she chose to learn from her. Besides, she liked her right away and believed that in time they would become close friends.

Leora began by showing Abigail where necessary items were located. First was the wine cellar. Leora, speaking before thinking, divulged that Nabal was a regular visitor to that lower part of the house. Abigail had surmised as much from observing him the evening of the wedding. She wondered if the only time Nabal could be jovial was when he was drinking, for most of the time he was stolid and preoccupied. He certainly was not one who engaged easily with others, especially his wife. Perhaps his business acquaintances were a different matter.

After explaining where and how the wine was kept, Leora directed Abigail to a large room off the kitchen where rows of wooden barrels rested along the walls. Leora removed the lid from one to reveal its contents. It was full of grain. She explained the different kinds of grain, their usages, and how to tell the difference. Abigail knew about grain, but in her humble home, there had been only barley.

Nabal's sprawling house had ten rooms not counting the storage areas. Leora's room was above the roof at the back of the house, and was accessed from a large courtyard. It was larger than those provided for the other maid servants. She explained that the eight men servants lived in the three mud-brick dwellings behind the main house. Abigail had noticed the small buildings and wondered about their use. She had not yet become comfortable enough to question her husband.

"I see a fourth one there apart from the others," she said to Leora as she pointed to the building which seemed purposely disconnected.

Leora displayed a rather strained look before she replied. Nonetheless, she concluded that Abigail was the mistress of the house. She had the right to know everything.

"My master likes to entertain his friends there. He is a hard worker and often conducts business with people from Hebron to Tekoa and sometimes further. He buys from *them*; they buy from *him*. When his business friends come, we prepare much food and ...," she hesitated, "... much wine is consumed. I think it is the master's way of settling himself down. We prepare the food in here, and take it out there. The master, alone, sees to the wine." Abigail was curious as to why Nabal did not entertain inside with such a huge house. *Perhaps out there he can drink as much as he likes and sleep it off with no interference. I know so little about this man who has become my husband!* Abigail had heard the loyalty in Leora's voice and she respected that. She wished she could feel the same about Nabal. But, she *was* grateful for what she had.

As Leora continued to show her the pottery shelves, the enclosure where the bedding was stored, and a myriad of other belongings, Abigail thought of her friend. Both she and Keita had married men they had not known; by contrast, she knew *her* life was much better. Keita's husband was of poor means, and she would never have all that Abigail surveyed.

I am blessed, she told herself at the end of the day. *I will try to be a good wife. I do not yet love my husband; in due time surely I will.* With firm determination, Abigail set her mind on doing just that.

❖

An important responsibility, one Abigail accepted as her duty, was to bear Nabal's children. Although she had helped rear her two sisters and was well-equipped for motherhood, she was not at all sure it was something she wanted. As always, her dear mother came to mind. *Did she want children when she wed my father? It's funny. I never thought about that until now. Our mother is so loving, so giving. I doubt she ever thought it could be otherwise.* Abigail tried to put that kind of thinking aside. It made her feel guilty, and it made her homesick.

CHAPTER 7

It did not take long for Abigail to realize that Nabal's wrath could be poured out on anyone he chose. Those of his household were not exempt, including his wife. She remembered how he had yelled out his demands to the servants during that first meeting several months before. She wondered if her father at that time had noticed that the man's behavior was so different from his own.

Since Abigail had promised to be a good wife to Nabal, she did everything she could to please him. It was not in her nature, anyway, to be unkind. But, in spite of her submissive attitude, life with Nabal became more and more difficult. He had begun to treat her like one of the servants, which, as it turned out, was a good thing. Abigail became one with them. It was not an act. She had come to love each of them; and they, in turn, demonstrated great respect for her. Even Leora, who provided a protective cover for Nabal, was aware of the pain Abigail endured at the hands of one who was unworthy of her.

"Do not pay attention to the Master. Sometimes his mind is all mixed up. All of us know you are a good wife to him. Please do not be sorrowful. Come. I will prepare something special for you." It was Leora's way of consoling Abigail and, at those times, the two of them would share a cup of milk, a raisin cake, and long talks together.

Abigail often wondered if Nabal had married her to add to his possessions. In the beginning he had found her attractive and enjoyed showing her off to his friends in the same way that he boasted about his pastures full of sheep and his big house filled with servants. What a contrast to her father Rael who had so little but was always kind to his wife and daughters. The marriage arrangement he had made between

Abigail and Nabal was the worst thing he had ever done. He believed at the time that he was doing the right thing for his daughter. Abigail knew that he did it for good, never expecting that it would bring heartache to the daughter he cherished. How she relished the memories of home and family! Unfortunately, warm memories could not prepare her for what she faced next in her young life.

———◆———

Abigail had not seen her father since the wedding seven months earlier. But, there Rael stood at the door, anguish etching his face. He had come to tell her that Uriella's condition was much worse and recovery was unlikely. Abigail had half-expected such news, considering her mother's declining health; still, she was not ready to hear it from her father's lips. She regretted that she had not returned home to check on her loved ones. Each time she had mentioned it to Nabal, he had blurted sharp retorts. To avoid a confrontation, she had put it aside.

Leora helped Abigail gather her things together. In addition, they packed several parcels of food for mourners who were certain to be waiting at Rael's home. When they finished, the two women embraced and exchanged caring words. To Abigail's satisfaction, Nabal was off somewhere and not expected home until later in the day.

The road trip to Aphekah that day with her father was heart-wrenching. She had hoped that when she saw her mother again, it would be a joyous reunion. Instead, it was a sad homecoming.

Uriella's eyes brightened when she saw her beloved daughter. Too weak to speak, she could only run her fingers along Abigail's outstretched hand as if to assure her things would be all right. Uriella had a way of making others feel secure and safe. Abigail needed *that*. How she would miss it!

———◆———

The burial of Rael's faithful wife of a much-too-brief twenty-two years was almost more than he could bear. In less than a year he had lost a daughter and now his wife. Talia, soon to turn thirteen, had matured much since Abigail left home; and she had become a responsible caregiver to her family. Now, duty called her to fill her mother's place as best she could.

"I will remain here for two or three days before I return to Carmel." Abigail clasped both girls' hands before continuing. "I want the two of you to come live with me. I will speak to Nabal about the matter. We have such a large house. There is plenty of room for you. I know Father will want to stay here where all of his memories are. He would never leave the farm life he loves."

Talia waited with patience until Abigail finished; then she spoke.

"Abigail, *my* memories are here, too. So are Nava's. We must stay here and take care of our father."

Abigail knew her sister was sincere. It was what Talia wanted, and she would not consider leaving; so Abigail smiled and changed the subject.

"We must each one keep something special of Mother's to remember her by. She would like that. I love the beautiful shawl that our mother wove before she married our father. If you have no objections, I will take it with me when I leave, and I will cherish it forever."

Her sisters nodded; then all three, arm in arm, wept for some time over the greatest loss they had ever experienced.

As the sun was setting, Abigail found her father outside near the animal shed. They talked for a long time before retiring for the night. The warmth of being near her loved ones should have been a consolation. To the contrary, she was unsettled knowing she must return soon to Nabal's home where no such love existed. *I am strong. I am strong,* she kept reminding herself. *Mother would want me to expect the best.*

The coolness of the evening demanded a heavier bed covering than usual. As Abigail pulled her mother's quilt up around her neck, she wished she could make her unhappiness vanish as easily as she had the cold night air.

CHAPTER 8

Rael's neighbor, the same one who had lent him the donkeys for that first trip to Carmel, took Abigail back to her home because Rael was still in mourning. On the short trip that always seemed long to Abigail, she promised herself that she would make greater effort to satisfy her husband. She knew Nabal wanted a son. He had told her that more than once. It was believed that a man had little worth if he did not have a namesake to continue the family line. Daughters were nice; a son was a necessity. Most men of the time felt that way, and Nabal was no exception. To his way of thinking, Abigail had not done her duty.

Leora, sensing Abigail's "dilemma," shared with her what she considered to be a magic formula. It consisted of the roots of a mandrake plant, as well as its fruit called dudaim.[13] These were chopped and steeped in wine to be taken internally. The mixture sounded awful to Abigail. Despite what it might taste like, she was willing to try anything. The two women kept their secret, and Abigail drank the concoction twice a day as Leora prescribed.

Weeks passed into months with no results. All the while Abigail withstood the crude remarks that Nabal heaped upon her. One of her enduring qualities, perseverance, got her through many difficult times. Greatest of all, her abiding faith in God sustained her day by day. She believed that her life was in God's hands no matter what came.

Over a period of time, Abigail released her personal maids for other services in the house; that is, except for one. Her name was Maya, whose loving presence made Abigail feel worthy and of value. Maya saw to it that her mistress took care of herself. She massaged her shoulders when she was tense and made her drink plenty of water, saying it was the miracle drink of the gods. *Oh! Keita told me she heard that the gods' food was ambrosia,* Abigail remembered, smiling to herself. Her friend Keita, a strong believer, had told her that in jest when they were young girls, probably having heard it from some pagan girl. Abigail never failed to grasp such an opportunity to remind Maya that there was only one true God, Yahweh.

One morning Abigail called Maya into her room. Something did not feel right. She was seldom sick and was surprised that she felt so ill. She thought it was probably the "magic formula," that maybe she should have left well enough alone. *Am I trying to take matters into my own hands as did Sara, the wife of the great patriarch, Abraham?*[14] *Perhaps God wants me to remain barren.*

By mid-morning Abigail was bent over in pain, holding her abdomen. Maya ran to get Leora who was older than either of them and would surely know what to do. When Leora arrived at Abigail's side, she frowned as she spoke.

"I have seen this many times before. You have not looked well for several days and I should have warned you. I think you are about to miscarry a baby in its early stage."

"No, that cannot be. I think I am sterile. Some women are, you know." Abigail grimaced as she paced back and forth across her room as if she could walk away the pain. Finally, Leora gently took her arm and guided her to the bed.

For the next two and a half hours, Leora and Maya took care of Abigail as Leora's prediction proved true. Once they had cleansed everything that was necessary after such a painful event, they turned their attention to Abigail. They covered her shaking body and stroked her arms gently to comfort her, hoping she would fall asleep.

Leora turned to Maya and said, "She will never be able to have another baby." She spoke in soft tones, but Abigail heard.

The next day Maya would not let Abigail get out of bed. "You must rest. You must get your strength back. Leora is wrong. There will be other babies. Now you must take care of yourself." She closed the door so that Abigail could have the solitude she needed to speed her recovery.

Nabal was away as usual when his wife needed him. When he did return and learned what had happened, he showed no concern, offered no words of comfort. Although Abigail was too weak then to care, what followed altered her resolve to be a compliant wife.

As soon as Abigail was able to join the others for a meal, Nabal used the occasion to belittle her.

"You cannot even carry a child for me! What kind of woman do I have? I should have known you were too young to be a *real* wife."

His words stung Abigail to the core of her being. The servants who were present turned away in shame. Abigail said not a word. From that day forward she absented herself from Nabal's presence when possible; and more importantly, she had Maya prepare another room for her sleeping quarters. She would never have believed she could do such a thing; likewise, she could never have imagined a marriage so bad. Nabal had fulfilled the meaning of his name: "fool."[15] She wondered why he had not found himself a concubine, which was not at all unusual in their culture.[16] Also, he could give her a certificate of divorce; of course, she had done nothing to warrant such action, but she knew Nabal's rules were not the same as God's.

She decided that if Nabal came to her, she would fulfill her duty. She doubted he would remove her from his house because he would have to face his many business acquaintances. They had come to admire Abigail, having witnessed many times her abiding tolerance for a pertinacious husband.

Furthermore, Abigail believed she would never be able to conceive another child just as Leora had said. There was, therefore, no way she could ever please Nabal. That reality would have left most women in despair. Not Abigail. *If it is my plight in life to remain barren, it is for a purpose. I will accept it, for God is with me.*

CHAPTER 9

Possessing a new, self-gained independence, Abigail made a decision. She would go visit her father and sisters—that day. Her plan was to stay for several days. She was sorry she had not done it before. The timing was perfect because Nabal had gone to En Gedi, located near the western edge of the Salt Sea, to secure extra workers for the upcoming sheep-shearing season. At least, she would not have to contend with his opposition.

Maya and Leora helped her prepare for the short journey. Abigail chose not to take Nabal's fine canopied wagon, an act befitting her unpretentious nature. She enlisted their youngest male servant, Chanan, to accompany her. After feeding and watering three donkeys, he loaded one of them with bags of grain, jars filled with dates and raisins, and two skins of wine. He then groomed the other two which he and Abigail would be riding. Maya was concerned that Abigail was riding too soon after her recent physical ordeal. Abigail assured her she would be fine—she must not worry. With reluctance, the two women sent them off, entreating Abigail to use caution, especially on the decline leading to the desert.

As it turned out, the rocky terrain proved more of a challenge than Abigail had anticipated. She had to stop twice, once just to walk around, the other to rest on a soft mound of grass beside the road. When she saw the anxious look on Chanan's face, she told him she would be okay; they just needed to proceed at a slower pace.

Rael saw dust rising in the distance and stopped his feeding chores. He placed the wooden bucket on the ground and raised his hand above his eyes to shade the eastern sun. He soon recognized Abigail's dark hair flouncing about as she and someone with her approached the house.

"Father!" Abigail yelled when she saw Rael coming toward them. She almost leapt from the donkey into his arms. Tears of joy erupted from father and daughter as the servant looked on.

"Oh, this is Chanan. He is a valued employee who has been a great help to me."

"Welcome," Rael said. "Welcome to our home."

By the time the three reached the door, Talia and Nava were waiting, smiles big as life. They were happy beyond expression to see their big sister. Abigail gave them both long, tight hugs.

"My, Nava! You have grown since I last saw you. You are about to pass Talia."

Not to offend the older of the two, Abigail patted Talia's shoulder. "You, Talia. You are the perfect size and still beautiful." She remembered and pointed behind her. "My traveling companion back there is Chanan." The girls smiled. It was still hard for them to believe that their sister had a servant, and that there were even more. It was too much for them to fathom.

<hr />

Toward evening, after Talia's plentiful meal, the five sat and talked. At first it was awkward for Chanan to be included with the family. After all, he was a servant and was accustomed to being in his place among other servants. As the evening progressed, he soon felt comfortable and actually joined in the conversation.

Rael prepared a place for their male guest to sleep while Nava found adequate blankets for his bed. Abigail helped Talia put the kitchen items away, basking in the warmth that was still a part of her home. The only thing missing from the scene was their beloved Uriella.

Abigail's visit lasted for four days. They were precious days, cherished days. She realized that the longer she stayed, the harder it would be to return to that other life. A constant reminder to her was that she had accepted a commitment when the ketubbah was signed by her father and Nabal the day of the wedding. She would honor it as best she could, except she would keep her private sleeping arrangement.

Before she and Chanan left, Abigal told her sisters they must visit her, that they were old enough to travel alone. If Father did not think so, she would send someone for them.

"When Father thinks he can do without us, we will go, Abigail." It was the quiet Nava who spoke this time.

Their goodbyes were not as sad as before because Abigail assured them she would not wait that long again.

She had decided before arriving not to mention to her family about her miscarriage. It was past and better not discussed. She had their love, and that, for now, was enough for her.

What God had planned for Abigail would soon place her in uncharted territory and would become the challenge of her life.

CHAPTER 10

Nabal arrived home empty-handed the day after Abigail. The workers he had hoped to procure at Tekoa had already obtained jobs elsewhere. That meant that two of his male servants who were not skilled in sheep-shearing would have to be taught quickly by the others.

When Abigail heard the news from Leora, she commented, "I, myself, could help. I often worked beside my father shearing our small flock. When I was a little girl, I was afraid that the poor sheep were being hurt. My father assured me otherwise. In time, when I was old enough to help him, I realized it was true. How amazing it was to learn how to lift the entire fleece in one piece.[17] It seemed like a miracle to me as a young girl." Abigail returned to the moment. "Leora, I don't think Nabal would approve of my doing that here." With a twinkle in her eye, she added, "It would not look appropriate in the eyes of his friends."

They both laughed. Then Leora told her mistress what to expect from the big event coming soon.

"Sheep-shearing is more than an agricultural happening. It is also a time of celebration with music, dancing, drinking, and, of course, lots of food. It can last for several days, depending upon the number of sheep and how fast the shearers work. Furthermore, it is a time for settling debts and righting wrongs." Leora displayed her usual frown. "Abigail, I must warn you. Sometimes, with the drunkenness that often occurs, tempers flare and old scores are settled. It can become a boisterous occasion, as well."[18]

Abigail admitted that she had not seen anything to match Leora's remarks. She was glad to have a friend to apprise her of things unfamiliar to her.

"Thank you, Leora, for preparing me. I will be on guard."

Abigail pondered many of the things Leora had told her. She did not know exactly what her own role was. No matter what other women of her standing did, she, as usual, would help the servants prepare and serve the food and assist them in anything that was necessary. She was not at all comfortable being a mere hostess, still she would do her best to be cordial to all who entered their home. She had been taught that hospitality was a virtue. Her mother Uriella had trained her well.

——◆——

Sheep-shearing day arrived. Men with their sheep came from various farms in that part of Israel. They came because they had no experienced shearers and knew that Nabal did.

The women brought food of all kinds, and the kitchen became crowded and stuffy. It was springtime and quite warm. The servant girls kept everyone as cool as possible with water from Nabal's three large cisterns.

Many of the families brought their musical instruments in readiness for the grand occasion. It was as Leora had said. It was more than just the shearing of sheep. It was a time of fellowship, with stories shared and the latest news from family and friends.

Many years before, Nabal had constructed a separate building for the shearing process. Some of the female servants cleaned the facility to prevent unwanted diseases during the procedure. Shearing implements were sharpened, cleaned, and set aside. Taking good care of the sheep was of utmost importance, for a great deal of money had been invested in them and ample profits were expected from the marketing of the wool.[19]

——◆——

It was the second day of shearing and feasting. Nabal imbibed even more than usual from his choicest wines. Since he did not have to participate in the work, he spent hours in rowdy revelry with the men and boys who were present. He spent much of his time boasting of his land acquisitions and pointing to his home's costly amenities; that is, when he was steady on his feet. In his drunken condition he joked too much and his laugh was too loud. Embarrassed as Abigail was to witness such a display, it was not her

– 202 –

place to correct him. As a result, she stayed out of his sight as much as she could.

Later that day, ten riders were spotted approaching Nabal's home. It was clear they were not coming for the sheep shearing since that occasion was coming to a close.

✦ CHAPTER II ✦

Several years before the prophet Samuel died, he had anointed David, son of Jesse, to replace Saul as king of Israel. However, Saul remained king for several years and became excessively jealous of David's popularity after he killed the giant Goliath. He also knew of David's anointing, a fact that increased his fears of the young man even more. As a result, he sought to kill the one he considered his enemy and pursued him throughout Israel. Strange as it might have seemed under those conditions, it was David who had the opportunity more than once to take *Saul's* life but refrained because he revered the one God had appointed as ruler.

During one of his many efforts to escape Saul's attacks, David and the six hundred men he had accrued fled to the desert, not far from Carmel. While encamped there, they saw shepherds nearby caring for their sheep, and David's men encircled them to provide them protection from robbers or wild animals. David had instructed them to do so because he knew, firsthand, how dangerous it was to care for sheep out in the open, especially such a large flock.

After having traveled here and there for days to avoid King Saul, David and his men ran short of food. They were tired and hungry. David had heard of a rich man near Carmel who was shearing sheep at that time. He decided to send ten of his young men to ask for food because he knew at such a time of celebration there would be plenty. He told them to remind the owner that they had not harmed his men in any way and had, in fact, kept them and their flock safe. David added, "Greet them in my name," for he knew by then that he was known throughout the land.

Nabal was enjoying the final hours of the sheep-shearing event when David's men arrived. He was drunk as he usually was following such an occasion.

The men delivered the message just as David had directed. Nabal, upset at the interruption, growled his reply.

> 'Who is this David? Who is this son of Jesse? … Why should I take my bread and water, and the meat I have slaughtered for my shearers, and give it to men coming from who knows where?'[20]

David's men returned to him with Nabal's answer. David became angered that the man would do such a thing. He told his men to arm themselves, and he and four hundred of them departed to pour out his revenge on Nabal and his entire household.

One of Nabal's servants had overheard the requests of David's men and reported the whole story to Abigail. She was not totally surprised. Still she wondered, *how could someone, even a man like Nabal, behave in such a way? These men were protecting his property and did them no harm.* She thought of all the servants who would pay with their lives because of the selfish decision of her husband. Somehow she felt responsible. She had to do something fast.

Nabal was sleeping off his last round of drinks and would be no obstacle. In a moment's time, she had two of the male servants helping her.

> She took two hundred loaves of bread, two skins of wine, five dressed sheep, five seahs of roasted grain, a hundred cakes of raisins and two hundred cakes of pressed figs, and loaded them on donkeys.[21]

She promptly sent the servants on ahead, while following close behind. In days past, she would have informed Nabal of such a huge decision. Not this time. He would not have agreed anyway; and besides, all their lives were in eminent danger and she had to act quickly.

As Abigail and her servants reached a ravine below the mountain, they saw David and his men riding toward them on their way to Carmel. David suddenly halted his men. Abigail wasted no time. She dismounted and fell at his feet.

'My lord, let the blame be on me alone. Please let your
servant speak to you; hear what your servant has to say.
May my lord pay no attention to that wicked man Nabal.
He is just like his name—his name is Fool … I did not see
the men my master sent.'[22]

She thanked David for not committing bloodshed and ventured beyond
what most women would have in order to give him some advice: "'Let no
wrongdoing be found in you as long as you live."'[23]

Abigail also knew of David's anointing, so she went a step further, being
careful to show great respect for the one before whom she bowed.

'When the Lord has done for my master every good thing
he promised concerning him and has appointed him leader
over Israel, my master will not have on his conscience the
staggering burden of needless bloodshed or of having
avenged himself.'[24]

Then she added, "'And when the Lord has brought my master success,
remember your servant."'[25]

Her words of wisdom impressed David, and he thanked her for
preventing him from doing wrong. He gladly accepted the food she and her
servants had brought, and he showed kindness to her as he sent her away in
peace. David knew for certain that he would not forget her.

———◆———

The following morning when Nabal went in for his meal, Abigail told
him the whole story—what she had done and David's response. Either
because of his excessive drinking or the shocking news that his wife shared,
Nabal suffered a stroke right then and there and became paralyzed. Leora
and Abigail put him to bed and cared for him night and day. He lived for
ten more days before he died. In earlier days, Abigail would have felt guilty
to entertain what she thought at that moment. She believed that God had
stricken Nabal as punishment for his wickedness.

What must I do? What will happen to all the servants? She knew she had no property rights to Nabal's house and farmland. Everything had happened so fast, and she did not have a ready answer. Without her knowledge, God's plan for her was still unfolding.

CHAPTER 12

Two weeks after Abigail had departed David, he sent several of his men out to pillage for food. They and their families were again desperate for supplies. A few days earlier those same men had plucked enough barley grain for roasting and had drawn a small measure of water from an abandoned well. Those provisions were soon depleted. Now of necessity they were again foraging for any nourishment they could find. When they came upon a field that looked promising, they spotted a worker and asked if he could help them. He agreed to assist them, but what he told them next was too important to keep. Immediately one of the men headed back to report the news. He rode fast, allowing nothing to deter him until he found David.

"That wicked man Nabal, the husband of the beautiful woman Abigail, is dead. A worker in the field told us"

David said, "'Praise be to the Lord, who has upheld my cause against Nabal for treating me with contempt.'"[26] Straightway he sent for Abigail to be his wife.

> His servants went to Carmel and said to Abigail, 'David has sent us to you to take you to become his wife.'[27]

Abigail found it hard to believe what she was hearing. She thought, *I am not worthy of such an honor.* When God spoke to her heart, she knew that it was His will. She would obey.

While David's men waited, Abigail gathered her clothes and the lovely shawl that had been her mother's, and went to each servant and said goodbye. She decided to take the five maids with her who had been assigned to her in the beginning. It was all she desired to keep from her tumultuous marriage to Nabal.

The last servant she spoke to was Leora.

"I want you to go with me if you will," she said, having already anticipated Leora's reply.

Leora said she could not go. She was not good at wandering around, and she expected that would be the case with David still running from King Saul. Abigail understood and was ready to present a positive idea to her servant and friend.

"Leora, you were always faithful to your master. You and the other servants who are left must stay here and keep the house. Nabal had no children and I know he would want you to have it. He was from the tribe of Judah, and you once told me that you were, too. My master who has sent for me is also a Judahite. In time, I will speak to him about this property, sheep and all, and ask that you be allowed to keep it within the tribe of Judah. You have been a good friend to me, and I will always hold you close to my heart."

Leora smiled at the prospect. The two women embraced and said their goodbyes. Abigail, with her five maids, accompanied David's emissaries to the desert where David was waiting.

Abigail became David's second wife. He had already married Ahinoam from Jezreel. In addition, Saul had given one of his daughters, Michal, to David years earlier, and then gave her to someone else, an act assuring Saul of his ability to control the lives of others.

———◆———

Abigail had experienced much in her young life that challenged her mental strength. She would now face tests of physical endurance, as well.

First, there was something she must do, and she would petition David with her request. She wanted to see her father and sisters before embarking on what surely would become the adventure of her lifetime.

David was willing to grant Abigail's request. He fully understood her love of family because he had once sent his own parents to the King of Moab for their safety when he was being hunted day and night by Saul and his men. David sent two of his servants with Abigail for protection and said that her maids could stay there in the desert until she returned. Abigail thanked him and said that she would be in Aphekah for only one night and would return the next day.

"God be with you and with your family," David said as he sent them off.

Rael and his daughters had already heard of Nabal's death and had determined to go to Abigail within the week. He knew she needed time for the burial and other responsibilities. What a pleasant surprise when he saw her and the others riding up to his house.

It took a while for Abigail to explain all that had happened to her. With pride she told her father and sisters that she was now David's wife and that she knew someday he would become the king of Israel because the prophet Samuel had anointed him to succeed King Saul. She believed without a doubt that God would finish what he had already ordained.

Rael was happy for his daughter because she was happy. As a caring father, he was also concerned about her safety. People knew that David was in exile, shunning Saul's murderous attempts, but what could Rael do? He loved Abigail and knew that his late wife Uriella would probably have said, "God will go with her." He must take that same position with faith.

Next day, following the morning meal, Abigail and her entourage left. She promised her father and sisters that she would see them again.

"May God bless you, my daughter," Rael whispered, feeling already a void in his heart. Abigail's sisters waved to her until she was over the hill and out of sight, heading toward the desert and a new life.

CHAPTER 13

The great prophet Samuel, who had anointed David according to God's plan, died. There was now no divinely-appointed one to whom David could turn for guidance. In order to save his own life, not to mention those of his family and followers, he had to continue running to escape Saul's relentless pursuits to kill him.

Many of David's soldiers had their wives and children with them. When Abigail returned, she joined them in the wilderness, living as they did in tents or other temporary shelters. She had pledged, without hesitation, to follow her new husband from place to place for years if necessary. Being able to settle down with him in a lovely palace in Jerusalem was an eventuality she had not even considered, for it was not important to her now.

From the desert they moved to the Philistine city of Gath, beyond Saul's search. David appealed to King Achish to provide him a city where they could live. The king complied and gave him Ziklag where David and his entire company lived for a year and four months. What a pleasure it was to be there because now they all had plenty of water to drink and for bathing. In addition, an abundance of food was available. The city was also a much needed respite from the unbearable desert heat.

The gift of Ziklag did not come without a price. Achish asked David to join forces with him against King Saul. As much as David feared Saul, he did not want to attack the one God had appointed king of Israel, yet he was bound by his commitment to the Philistine king. With great reservations, he and his soldiers left Ziklag early one morning and set out for what they expected to be a long, hard-fought battle. He left 200 of his men at the Besor Ravine to guard their supplies. As a result of their leaving, the coming event would be the most fearful experience of Abigail's life.

Before noonday, after David and the rest of his men, 400 in all, had departed, Abigail and the other inhabitants of Ziklag heard the thunder of riders approaching the city. Boisterous laughter and yelling drew closer, and sudden fear gripped the town. Abigail grabbed the young children who were playing outside, unaware of the apparent danger, and pushed them into enclosures. She instructed the others she saw to hide anywhere they could. She ran to help Ahinoam, David's other wife, who had fallen with her young son, Amnon, while trying to find safety somewhere, anywhere.

Abigail screamed, "Who are these men? Why are they here?" She soon learned Ahinoam did not know any more than *she* did.

Suddenly, both women saw men rushing here and there carrying torches. Flames began engulfing anything that would burn while utter chaos prevailed in the city. Abigail prayed for calm in order to do what she must do to ward off personal attacks that she feared would come next. To her surprise, the men in the raiding party began gathering the children and every female, young and old, onto their animals. Then she realized ... they were being captured, taken away to who knows where. One filthy, smelly, gruff renegade snatched Abigail from the ground and placed her in front of him on his restless mount. His foul breath was suffocating. One kind of fear was soon replaced by another. She had heard what happened to women who were taken alive. She wondered, *would death have been better?*

Before long, the smoldering city of Ziklag lay in ruins. The captives caught glimpses of the total destruction as they turned to look. Onward they rode, clinging to the vicious riders to avoid falling, with no idea of their destination. A great distance from the city they finally stopped for rest and food in the countryside. The women and children, afraid and bewildered, were at last free to stretch their legs and gather with their loved ones. Soon their captors' bellies were full, and they laughed and cajoled as they drank themselves into drunken stupors.

In the meantime, David on his quest to help his Philistine benefactors was having some surprises of his own. Achish's top commanders did not trust David to help them fight against Saul because he was, after all, an Israelite and had at one time been one of Saul's top-ranked soldiers. As a result of their strong objections, Achish had no choice. He told David and his men they would have to return to Ziklag—he could not use their services. Stunned and pleased, they obeyed his command.

What a shock they found upon re-entering Ziklag! It had been burned to the ground, and their wives and children were gone. The sounds of the men weeping and wailing soon filled the charred streets where they searched in vain until all strength was gone. Heartbroken, yet forced to make a quick decision, David sought the help of the priest Abiathar, who had attended them since he, too, had recently escaped Saul's wrath. The priest, using the urim and the thummim in his ephod,[28] told David to go after the perpetrators and that he *would* succeed.

After hours of searching the open countryside, they came upon an Egyptian who was an Amalekite slave and had been part of the raid on Ziklag. He agreed to lead them to the place where the raiding Amalekites were resting.

———◆———

After hours of being held captive, Abigail and some of the others heard their rescuers advancing before their captors did, for some of the men were napping while others were keeping watch, though intoxicated.

Abigail prayed. *God, let that be my master David and his men. Please do not allow more terror to be visited upon us.* Before she could finish, the attack on the hostile Amalekites began.

In haste, the women pulled the children together and found refuge out of range in the thick brush nearby.

David and his men fought their formidable opposition nearly twenty-four hours, killing most of them. A few were able to escape. The victorious Israelite warriors recovered all that the Amalekites had stolen, including their wives.

Abigail rushed to her husband ahead of Ahinoam and began to bow in deep gratitude for their miraculous rescue. David stopped her.

"No, Abigail, do not bow. What a terrible thing they did to you—to all of you." Concern crossed his weary face. "Did they violate you in any way?"

"No. Not I, your servant, nor anyone else was harmed … in that way."

"I am your husband, Abigail. You are not my servant. I will always protect you. I am not like Nabal."

Abigail smiled. How warm and secure she felt for the first time since she left her father's house. She was completely content.

— ❦ CHAPTER 14 ❦ —

Back in ran-sacked Ziklag, David learned from a messenger about the death of his beloved friend Jonathan, as well as that of Saul, the king to whom he had pledged his allegiance and protected time after time. The two had died on Mt. Gilboa during a fierce battle against the Philistines. David's sadness was overwhelming. He chose to express his deep grief in the only way he knew, by writing a lament as a tribute to them both.[29]

After fasting for seven days, David, along with his wives, journeyed to Hebron. He had already been anointed king of Israel years before by the prophet Samuel. Now that King Saul was dead, men representing David's own tribe went to Hebron to honor him by anointing him king of Judah. He was thirty-three years old and would reign for forty years.

Abigail was proud of David, and, as circumstance would have it, at that time she bore him a son whom they named Kileab.[30] It was David's second son, but Abigail's only child.

Leora told me I would never again have a child. God has surely blessed me, and I will praise Him all of my days.

Shortly thereafter, David and his men marched into Jerusalem and claimed the city. It became his residence and that of his large family. He named it the City of David, and it became the Holy City of God.[31]

> Now Hiram king of Tyre sent messengers to David, along
> with cedar logs and carpenters and stonemasons, and they
> built a palace for David.[32]

Abigail had come a long way from her humble beginnings in Aphekah to the royal seat of the Israelite nation. She remained a splendid tribute to her heritage, a devoted wife and mother, and a faithful servant of her amazing God for the rest of her life.

The Story Of King Josiah

The Story of King Josiah

Preface

How can an exceptionally good son descend from an evil father and grandfather? Josiah was the sixteenth king of Judah, the Southern Kingdom; and along with Hezekiah, was one of the only two good kings Judah ever had.

The question arises: what transpired in Josiah's life that produced such a king? We can only speculate. However, one thing is certain. God had his hand on Josiah all the way.

In chapter 1, background information is presented in order to understand the conditions that influenced Josiah, from the ungodly heritage from his father Amon and his grandfather Manasseh to the godly guidance of his mother Jedidah.

CHAPTER I

In the early 600's B.C. the Southern Kingdom experienced one of its many political upheavals. The most evil king Judah ever had was the reigning ruler. His name was Manasseh, who sacrificed his own sons to the false gods. He ruled for a whopping fifty-five years, and under his command succeeded in turning the Israelites away from God. That would have been bad enough, but he passed on his godless beliefs to Amon, a surviving son.

In the twenty-fifth year of the reign of Manasseh, his son Amon met a beautiful, intelligent young woman named Jedidah. She was from the town of Bozkath in the lowlands of Judah. She had been nurtured by strong, godly parents who lived by the Laws of Moses. Amon was immediately attracted to her. Within a year, he made her his wife and took her to Jerusalem into his mother's household.

From the beginning, Jedidah felt out of place. None of the religious observances that had been practiced in her home were honored in King Manasseh's palace. Perhaps it was because her ancestors had settled in the somewhat secluded area of Judah called the Shephelah,[1] where Bozkath was located, that they had been able to practice their stringent Jewish beliefs. Whatever the case, Jedidah refused to give up the training she had received, and in time she passed her beliefs on to her children. There were three in all, and her only son, Josiah, was the youngest. Jedidah knew of the horrible practices of sacrificing one's children, and she did all within her power to protect her own.

From the time little Josiah could speak, he questioned his mother about his Jewish heritage. It fascinated him, yet he never felt free to talk of such things in his father Amon's presence. Nevertheless, Jedidah never failed to instill truth and goodness in her offspring, in particular Josiah, who thirsted after any and all knowledge his mother could impart.

"Son, I believe that God has special plans for you. I don't know what they are. I just know that you are not an ordinary child. You ask questions beyond my understanding. I was taught that you are '... to love the Lord your God, to walk in his ways, and to keep his commands ....'[2] If you do that, my son, all will go well with you." Josiah smiled at his mother. In his heart he vowed that he would not forget. Jedidah somehow knew that her son would face a difficult road ahead even though she did not know at that moment what God had in mind.

At the death of Manasseh, Josiah's father Amon was placed on the throne. He was evil like his father Manasseh had been and continued to enforce the idolatrous beliefs of his predecessor. His own officials, disenchanted with yet another ruthless leader, assassinated Amon after he had reigned only two years. Even so, the people of Judah still wanted to maintain the Davidic dynasty, so they murdered the king's opponents and placed the deceased Amon's eight-year-old son Josiah on the throne. They had succeeded in salvaging the line of David, but had a child as their king. The year was 640 B.C.[3]

An eight-year-old as ruler of the Southern Kingdom—what could he possibly do? Smart as he was, Josiah needed advisors, good ones, to bring about the changes needed to take Israel back to God.

The Lord had his hands on the young lad and placed godly counselors around him to guide him until he could lead alone. Hilkiah, the high priest at the time, provided the maturity and wisdom necessary for the "making of a king." Jeremiah, the outstanding prophet of the day, was accessible for several years into the king's reign. Zephaniah, another prophet during Josiah's time who also prophesied in the Southern Kingdom, was instrumental in guarding and directing the new king, preventing him from falling into the depths of evil practiced by his father and grandfather. Finally, Jedidah, the Queen Mother, who was Josiah's closest confidante, was always available to guide her son's decisions.

It is remarkable to think how one so young could glean from his elders all that he needed to prepare him to become Judah's finest king since King David.

CHAPTER 2

From the time King Josiah was eight until he reached his teens, he could not, because of his position, spend his time like other boys his age. Only on special occasions were his cousins invited to the royal palace to join him in some type of recreation, often involving a series of contests. The winner was awarded fresh-baked ashishot, a special delicacy prepared by the head cook.[4] In inclement weather they remained indoors and played board games, at which time some of the female cousins were invited to participate. Those times of youthful abandon, though, were rare for the young king.

Whatever else Josiah's day may have entailed, it always included several hours of tutelage. Two of the finest teachers of language and history were enlisted to provide Josiah with a variety of subjects needed for diplomatic purposes, as well as schooling him in necessary social amenities. He was a fast learner. His teachers were amazed at his questions and on occasion were exasperated with their young scholar. He was never happy until satisfied he had complete answers to all his inquiries. Above all, Josiah was determined to discover the truth.

His favorite subject was his Jewish heritage. From his mother he learned about the patriarchs Abraham, Isaac, and Jacob; and although she taught him all she knew, he longed to know the specifics of the laws that God had given to Moses. For the past several hundred years, his people, the Israelites, had neglected the rules of the God of their fathers, and even his teachers were ill-prepared to educate him in that part of his training. The king wondered, *why?* His hunger to learn more was a constant quest. He could not understand the emptiness in his heart, and it would be several more years before he would discover what had been missing.

The young king's evenings were more relaxed. His mother made sure that he was exposed to the best musicians she could obtain. As a result, he learned to play the flute, contrary to his own desire to master the lyre. However, in his lone hours, it was the flute that provided the serenity he needed to cope with all that crowded his young life. It had been his mother's choice, and in time he was grateful for her wise decision.

There was one source of concern to Josiah: idol worship. If, as his mother had taught him, Yahweh was the Supreme God, the true God, why were false gods worshipped throughout the city of Jerusalem? Why had beautiful shrines been built to honor them? When he observed the devotion given those lifeless images, he was baffled. He could not reconcile the two vastly different beliefs.

Each year he became more concerned. By the time he was sixteen years old, King Josiah, after being under the guardianship of his elders for eight years, sought further knowledge from the one he believed could satisfy his questions. He made his way to the temple to see Hilkiah, the priest.

Hilkiah was not surprised to see his young "understudy," for he had been approached before by the eager inquisitor. This time was different. Josiah wanted to know how he could become a good king, not like his father and grandfather. He had prayed to Yahweh many times. He desired to walk in His ways, but how? He had serious questions for the priest who had become his friend.

"What was it like when you were a young man, Hilkiah? How long have our people worshipped all these false gods? The Queen Mother tells me it was not meant to be so."

Hilkiah stopped what he was doing and sat down to face the child-king. "Your mother is right, Josiah. I am sad to say that what you see around you has been this way for a long time. Not since King David have we had a godly king, one who followed the precepts of Almighty God. Your great-grandfather, King Hezekiah, came very close. Since *his* reign, however, we have unfortunately become a nation of idolaters, brazenly disobeying the laws given to the prophet Moses a long time ago." Again, King Josiah wondered, *why?*

The sadness in Josiah's heart was reflected in his expression. He hung his head as one brought low by a heavy burden. The high priest had not given him any advice, not even the answers for which he was searching. Josiah thought perhaps that was for a purpose. He must start thinking for himself. He knew that in the near future he would be called upon to make decisions affecting the whole nation. After a moment, he lifted his head and made a commitment to the spokesman of God who was seated before him.

"I know I am still quite young, but I *will* make changes. We must not worship false gods! That is where I will begin."

The young king left the temple heavy-hearted, with a determination to effect a new direction for God's people.

He walked fast, almost in a run, back to the royal palace to tell his mother what was in his heart. As always, she listened attentively to this one who was twenty-four years younger than she was. Then she had some advice for him that had been on her heart for some time. Knowing her son was impatient by nature, she got straight to the point.

"My son, you are wise to see there is much to do in our beloved Judah. Because you are still a young man...." She stopped to smile. "I should say 'young *king*,' this I must tell you. In order to prepare yourself for the tasks ahead, you must spend much time in prayer. Before supplication, remember to give Yahweh thanks and praise. A pure heart is necessary to ready you for the work the Lord has for you."

Josiah thanked his mother Jedidah for her advice and left her side intent on obeying the one who had never failed him. For the next four years, he left political matters in the hands of Shaphan his secretary, Maaseiah, the city ruler, and Hilkiah the high priest. Instead, Josiah devoted himself more than ever to study and prayer. When time allowed, he walked among the people of Judah to see first-hand all that was going on. As always, what he saw troubled him and reinforced his resolve to make God's chosen people a better nation, at least the Southern Kingdom.

CHAPTER 3

Josiah continued to grow and mature in ways that brought revered status to his kingship. He became recognized by foreign dignitaries as a force to be reckoned with. His military strength was second to none during his reign. Because of his standing, relative calm existed in the Southern Kingdom as it enjoyed peace with its neighbors for some time.

It was during that time, at the age of twenty-two, that Josiah decided to take a wife. He had availed himself of families outside Jerusalem on many occasions to seek their advice and learn of their concerns. No king in recent years had done that. It was on one of those excursions that he met a family from the tiny area of Benjamin who had a daughter named Zebidah. She was a lovely girl five years Josiah's junior who exuded the overwhelming confidence of one much older.

The courtship was brief, and soon the two were joined in marriage. It would have been better if they had known each other longer, for when Zebidah became Josiah's queen, all things regal became her foremost interests. She acquired every piece of new, fashionable royal attire she could find, the more elaborate beadwork it had, the better. She also insisted upon impeccable beauty sessions with her personal maid, after which the finest jewelry available was placed atop her perfectly coiffed hair as well as on her arms and fingers. She carried herself with aplomb and dignity, qualities far removed from her upbringing.

She treated her husband with honor in his presence as expected. When the king was away, it became obvious to those of the court that her greatest concern was herself. Therefore, it was somewhat surprising to all that she would jeopardize the beauty of her body to bear children for her husband, yet she did.

Their first son was Johanan, who was in ill health from the time of his birth. Zebidah could not bring herself to deal with him and gladly relinquished his care to a full-time nurse. When Johanan was two years old, his mother presented Josiah with a second son, Jehoikim, her last.[5] Zebidah's child-bearing ended when King Josiah took another wife as was often the custom of that time.

Hamutal's personality contrasted that of Zebidah in countless ways. Hamutal's main interests included making the palace attractive and comfortable for entertaining. She gave explicit instructions to the palace cooks concerning what foods to prepare and what drinks to serve. She was happiest when the main hall was full of important visitors so that she could display her exquisite taste. She was not as graceful of form and fashion as Zebidah, and it was apparent she spent minimal time on personal needs. The one common trait the two women shared was that of neglect, neglect of their sons. Zebidah simply did not care; Hamutal was too busy with social affairs in the palace. In that day, as in the time of King David and others, fathers did not interact often with their children. It was just that way. Therefore, it was the mothers who shouldered the full responsibility of training their offspring whose later behavior often reflected the kind of nurturing they received, good or bad, when they were young. Both women failed greatly in that respect.

Busy as she was with palace interests, Hamutal bore Josiah two sons, Jehoahaz and Zedekiah.[6] Sadly, all four of Josiah's sons would fail to walk in the upright ways of their father, and three of them would someday become kings.

CHAPTER 4

I n spite of four difficult years with two women jockeying for royal dominance, King Josiah maintained the focus of the mission he had begun six years before.

Each time that Josiah went to pray or to speak with the priest, he noticed more and more how the temple had deteriorated. He was not aware of its degraded condition so much when he was younger; but as he matured and prayed about what else he could do for God's people, his eyes were opened to the temple's approaching demise. The place where God had placed His Name was in disrepair, parts of the structure disintegrating before his eyes. Josiah got busy solving the problem.

He sent his secretary and his recorder to Hilkiah to obtain all the money that the temple doorkeepers had collected for the purpose of repairs. He gave them further instructions:

> 'Have them entrust it to the men appointed to supervise the
> work on the temple. And have these men pay the workers
> who repair the temple of the Lord....'[7]

The men did as they were told. In addition, the supervisors, mostly Levites, bought lumber and dressed stones for the carpenters and masons. In spite of the mammoth undertaking, the large assemblage of men worked with diligence and even sang with delight as they labored.

Once the work began on the temple, an amazing thing happened. In the midst of the renovations, Hilkiah the priest found the Book of the Law, the scroll containing the Laws of Moses. It had been lost or hidden for half a century, and Hilkiah could hardly believe what he held in his hands. He rushed to Shaphan, the secretary, shouting, "'I have found the Book of the Law in the temple of the Lord.'"[8] Shaphan began reading God's words recorded by Moses, and then he ran to find King Josiah to report the unbelievable, good news.

The king was on his way to inspect the temple work when Shaphan ran up to him, out of breath. "Hilkiah found this," he said, pointing to the scroll in his hands. He began to read aloud to King Josiah. After only a few words, the king became visibly shaken. For him, it was the missing link.

> When the king heard the words of the Book of the Law,
> he tore his robes.... He said, 'Great is the Lord's anger that
> is poured out on us because our fathers have not acted in
> accordance with all that is written in this book.'[9]

Hilkiah's discovery appeared to put a cap on all that Josiah had been trying to accomplish. It could have been the perfect "finishing touch;" except as usual, Josiah was not finished. He said to those standing around him, "This is only the beginning of what we must do."

He knew there was more to be done even if he was not sure just what. His mother Jedidah was ill, and his wives would be of no help in such matters. He had no idea where the prophets Jeremiah and Zephaniah were at the time. He was in most urgent need of divine direction. So, as he often did, he sought the priest.

Hilkiah and other men close to the king said that they would inquire of the prophetess Hulda who resided there in Jerusalem. King Josiah agreed.

> Tell her to inquire of the Lord what I should do now that
> the Book of the Law has been found. Tell her I know that
> God's people have not followed what is written therein.

The prophetess received the men graciously and listened to their entreaty. Then she proceeded to tell them the good news along with the bad news to deliver back to the king. Her prophetic reply was quite lengthy. The king's emissaries left her home joyful on the one hand, yet greatly distressed at the rest of what she had said.

King Josiah was waiting in his library when they returned. He rose to meet them.

"I trust you have an answer for me. What did the prophetess say?"

Hilkiah reported that great destruction was coming to the land of Judah because its people had forsaken their God and had worshipped idols instead, and that God's anger against them was so strong that it would not be turned away. At that point Hilkiah lowered his voice and offered a welcomed smile as he continued.

"On the other hand, the prophetess said that because of your humility and goodness, King Josiah, you will not see the disaster that God will pour out on this rebellious people. It will occur after your death and you are buried in your own tomb."

Anguish greater than the king had ever experienced overcame him, and he wept aloud in their presence.

"Please depart from me," he said. "I must read the entire scroll!"

CHAPTER 5

The following morning when the sun rose over the alabaster city of Jerusalem, King Josiah was still sitting with the scroll in his hand. He had not slept, for he had read every word, many parts over and over. He read of horrible punishments that would be inflicted upon God's people if they did not obey Him. Some of the atrocities described were difficult for Josiah's mind to absorb. He also learned that the Israelites would be scattered among other nations as their own nation lay in ruins, all because they would not obey the Lord. The word *obey* appeared over and over again, making it clear that God would not bless His people if they chose to ignore His commands.

What bothered him the most was the list of responsibilities designated for the king. He had, of course, never seen them before. He suddenly remembered what Hilkiah the priest had once told him: not since the time of King Hezekiah, his great-grandfather, had the chosen people of God obeyed His covenant. Now he realized they had not even read it! That included his father Amon who had never mentioned the Book of the Law. Likewise, according to Josiah's mother, his grandfather Manasseh had done no better, never obeying God's precepts. Troublesome questions raced through Josiah's mind. *Did they not know of its existence? Had it been lost all that time?*

King Josiah was so convicted in his heart that he vowed right away to uphold the explicit laws he had just read about and to right the wrongs of his people. He was aware of the immensity of the task. At the same time, his heart was fully committed. The first thing he did was to call all of the elders of Judah together at the temple. He also included the priests and the prophets. In addition, he wanted all within hearing distance to listen.

Once the people were assembled, he positioned himself by one of the bronze pillars in the portico of the temple and began. He read, for all to hear, every word from the scroll he held reverently in his hands. When he finished, he made a personal commitment:

> ...to follow the Lord and keep his commands, regulations, and decrees with all his heart and all his soul, and to obey the words of the covenant written in this book.[10]

To the king's surprise, the large crowd that gathered that day pledged to do the same, and joy flowed as never before throughout the city of Jerusalem.

———◆———

King Josiah's next order of business was a big one! Though unusual for one of royalty, he removed his scarlet robe and donned peasant-like clothing, for he had much work, hard work, to do throughout the land. He gathered the most robust men he could find to accompany him.

The clean-up began. King Josiah "...began to purge Judah and Jerusalem of high places, Asherah poles, carved idols and cast images."[11] He had enlisted the help of the citizens of Jerusalem he knew to be worshipers of the one true God. They tore down Baal's altars and diminished them to ashes. In an act of "righteous defiance," he and his men threw the ashes upon the graves of the ones who had made sacrifices to the false gods. He also did something he could not have done at a younger age: he burned the bones of all the evil priests on their altars as predicted by a prophet years before:

> 'A son named Josiah will be born to the house of David. On you he will sacrifice the priests of the high places who now make offerings here, and human bones will be burned on you.'[12]

When the priests had removed all the items that represented idol worship, King Josiah took them to the Kidron Valley and burned them. He took the ashes to Bethel just inside what previously had been the lower part of the Northern Kingdom of Israel and left them there. It was significant because Bethel was the place where Israel's first ruler of the Northern Kingdom, Jeroboam, had made two golden calves for the people to worship.[13] As part of his wide-spread purging, Josiah desecrated the evil spot where so many idolatrous sacrifices had been made.

His next act was to get rid of all the pagan priests and destroy the shrines of the male prostitutes. In addition, the women who had honored the goddess Asherah with their fancy weaving would no longer have a place in which to practice their idolatry.

Furthermore, King Josiah went out to the place called Topheth, where children were sacrificed to Molech, and he desecrated it so that it could no longer be used. He smashed the altars he found that were erected to false gods. When mediums or spiritists were pointed out to him, he rid the land of them, as well.

His work took weeks to accomplish. King Josiah was intent on disposing of anything and anyone who lured the people away from God. When he stepped back to survey the damage, he was confident he had purged the city and all of Judah of the evil embedded within its borders. But, he was never satisfied. With all he had accomplished, he believed there was still much to do.

When Jeremiah the prophet returned to Judah from a trip to the Northern Kingdom, he was amazed at what had occurred in his absence. How refreshing it was to see the land free of idols that had defamed the hills and disgraced the huge, spreading trees. For once, there was a sweet aroma in the air, surely pleasing to the God of all creation.

When the fourteenth day of the first month arrived, King Josiah ordered that the religious celebration, the Passover, be observed. What a sight it was to behold, for the people had never participated in such an event. Actually, no one had observed the Passover since the time of the prophet Samuel. King Josiah had to refer to the ancient covenant from time to time to carry out the celebration as it was intended.

The Levites, whose duties from the beginning had been assigned to the service of the temple, learned anew exactly what they were to do. The king also appointed two of the priests to find the ark that had been stored in a home there in Jerusalem, and to place it in the restored temple where it belonged.

King Josiah continued his religious renewal. Specific instructions for the slaughtering of the Passover lambs were given and followed. The king gave 30,000 of his own sheep and goats for the Passover meal. Others contributed, as well, and there was plenty of food for all the people. Voluntary offerings were collected while the musicians, all descendants of David's music director, Asaph, performed with lyres and harps and singing. The celebration lasted for seven days. Joy spread throughout Judah, for the Israelites knew, for the first time, that they were following the will of their Creator, the one Holy God.

At the end of the restoration period which lasted for months, King Josiah breathed easier. The mundane, day to day activities in his life had become secondary to his mission of re-establishing God's law in the land. He took no credit for himself, yet a heavy burden was lifted from his shoulders. He could look out across the land of Judah, as far as the eye could see, and know that the land was pure again and that he and all the people had become what the Covenant of God directed them to be.

CHAPTER 6

When King Josiah was thirty-nine years old and Judah had been at peace for some time, finally obeying God's laws as taught to them, an incident occurred that changed the political landscape in Judah forever.

Pharaoh Neco of Egypt set out with his army to assist Assyria in their ongoing struggles with the Babylonians. On his way to Carchemish near the Euphrates River, he took his men through the pass at Megiddo which was north of Judah, too close for King Josiah's comfort. At that time, Judah was not any happier with Assyria than they were with Egypt. Fearing that Neco's intentions were directed against Judah as much as against the Babylonians, King Josiah, in his royal chariot accompanied by his military men, left Jerusalem to attack Neco in Megiddo. In that way he had hoped to prevent possible danger to Judah in the coming days.

When Neco heard that King Josiah was on his way, he sent word for him to go back, that his quarrel was not with *him*. However, Josiah did not trust Neco. Ignoring the Egyptian king's warning, Josiah decided to engage the pharaoh of Egypt in battle anyway—a fatal decision. Even a man of God like Josiah was capable of making a grave error in judgment.

Though he disguised himself to hide his identity and increase his chance of a surprise attach, it did no good. An enemy archer recognized him and released his deadly shot, mortally wounding king Josiah of Judah. The year was 609 B. C. Josiah had ruled for thirty-one years and died while still a young man.

King Josiah's men took his body back to his home of Jerusalem where he was buried in his own tomb as foretold by Hulda, the prophetess. All of Judah mourned his death for many days. The great prophet Jeremiah composed a fitting lament for his fallen king:

'He did what was right and just, so all went well with him.
He defended the cause of the poor and needy, and so all
went well.'[14]

After the death of their best leader since King David, the people of
Judah knew not what awaited them. Had they known, they might have
mourned him even longer.

Four evil kings followed King Josiah. Three of them were his sons:
Jehoahaz, Jehoiakim, and Zedekiah. They chose to rule as they pleased,
defying the laws of God. Then, as the prophetess Hulda had also predicted,
the Lord remembered His anger against Judah's people and their evil ways.
In just twelve short years they were invaded by King Nebuchadnezzar of
the Babylonian Empire, a tool of God's righteous discipline. Deported to
a strange land, the people of Judah spent seventy years there in captivity.[15]
As also foretold, King Josiah had been spared the pain of seeing the decline
and devastation of his beloved land of Judah.

Neither before nor after Josiah was there a king like him
who turned to the Lord as he did—with all his heart and
with all his soul and with all his strength, in accordance
with all the Law of Moses.[16]

In Hebrew, the name *Josiah* means"Jehovah will support."[17] Fittingly,
with God's help, Josiah had done his best to heal the land of Judah. Over five
centuries later, Matthew, in his book of the Gospel, thought it important to
list Josiah in the genealogy of Jesus.[18]

The sixteenth king of Judah had served his country well, turning the
people back to Almighty God. "This he did to fulfill the requirements of
the law written in the book that Hilkiah the priest had discovered in the
temple of the Lord."[19] He would be remembered as the last godly leader in
a long list of Israelite kings.

The Story Of Esther

THE STORY OF ESTHER

PREFACE

Esther is an important character in the Bible, for one of its books bears her name. Even so, nothing is known of Esther's younger years. Though she later became queen of a vast empire and was instrumental in saving her fellow Jews in Persia, she nonetheless must have possessed the same desires and faced the same problems that any young girl would have at that time.

So, we will explore the Jewish girl Esther in her entirety.

─ ❊ CHAPTER I ❊ ─

"At that time the officers of Nebuchadnezzar King of
Babylon advanced on Jerusalem and laid siege to it."
2 Kings 24:10

"Mother! Mother! Where is my mother?" The young girl's wails rose above the clamor of the crowd. Throughout Jerusalem, people were rushing here and there to evade the inevitable. Horsemen wearing elaborate uniforms pulled their charges this way and that to corral the crowds while others directed their captives toward the edge of the city, the thundering gallop of their horses deafening. Chaos was everywhere.

The small girl, her long, brown curls dancing about her shoulders, ran toward her home, weaving in and out among the crowds. Smoke had begun to engulf the city, its stench stifling her tender nostrils. Close on her heels was Avishag, her nurse.

"Wait, Elisheva! Please wait," she yelled, but her words were lost in the uproar. *Oh, why did I take her to the market with me today?* The turmoil all around her made Avishag run even faster.

In spite of the pushing and shoving, little Elisheva reached her home only to find their kind neighbor, Nissim, standing in the doorway, arms stretched wide, his large hands firm against the door posts barring entrance. The child charged forward and pushed against him with all her might. It was useless. She slipped to the ground screaming. Tears drenched her fearful face.

"Where is my mother? Where is Father?"

Nissim tried to hide the grief gripping him. He reached down and lifted the child in his arms, cradling her head against his shoulder.

"They are gone," he said, his tender words barely audible as he struggled to control his own emotions. "Please trust me, little one. I will take care of you." He stepped away from the door, for he knew what was inside.

At that moment Avishag reached them, out of breath from the chase. The neighbor's demeanor told her not to go inside. Before she could question him, a decorated soldier, his sword flashing in the spring sunlight, motioned them down the street. Without resistance, they followed the rushed march of humanity onward to the east. Nebuchadnezzar, King of Babylon, had seized Jerusalem, set fire to it, plundered the Lord's temple, and taken prisoner Judah's king, Jehoichin.[1]

> He carried into exile to Babylon the remnant who escaped
> from the sword and they became servants to him and his
> sons until the kingdom of Persia came to power.[2]

CHAPTER 2

The massive deportations of Jews to Babylon began in 597 B.C. and continued for years.[3] Only the poor were left behind. Because of blatant disobedience to God's laws, Judah's punishment was just and inescapable as foretold by the prophet Jeremiah:

> 'This whole country will become a desolate wasteland, and these nations will serve the king of Babylon for seventy years.'[4]

For obvious reasons, most of the ones taken captive died there. Only those who were young during the deportations had any hopes of returning to the land of their birth. Characteristic of warring nations during that time, a momentous shift in power occurred in that part of the world which, over time, staged the events that would fulfill God's promise to His chosen people.

In the year 539 B.C., Cyrus, king of Persia, conquered Babylon, and conditions began to change for the Jews living there. King Cyrus allowed the Jews to return to their homeland, as did his successor, Darius I, at a later date.[5] Many of the Jews, especially those born in what became part of the extended Persian Empire, chose to remain there. Ties to their national heritage, though, stayed strong for many. Men like Ezekiel, Daniel, Ezra, and Nehemiah, who were deportees to Babylon, had maintained their devotion to God and passed on the Holy Scriptures they had protected.

During the reign of King Darius I of Persia, a Jewish woman named Hadar gave birth to a baby girl in the city of Susa, one of the Empire's four capitals. She named her Hadassah, whose Persian name became Esther, meaning "star."[6] Past the safe age for childbearing, Hadar died two days later. Equally sad was that within a month, her husband, Abihail, died of an accident sustained at a nearby quarry. Perhaps a coincidence, but young Esther, like her great-great-grandmother Elisheva a century earlier, lost both of her parents at an early age.

Esther's only living relative was Mordecai, a Jewish cousin of the child many years her senior. A short, somewhat portly man, Mordecai's dark beard covered most of his face, yet the hair on his head showed signs of thinning. When he spoke, his eyes twinkled below his heavy brows, and his broad smile was contagious, evidence of a sincere compassion for those in need. He was a devout Jew from the tribe of Benjamin. His parents and grandparents, though aliens in a strange land, had kept strong their faith in the true God, the One who had delivered the Israelites from bondage in Egypt, parted the waters of the Red Sea, and led them into the land promised to Abraham's descendants.[7] They had instilled in Mordecai the laws of Moses from the days of his youth, and he had not departed from them.

Without hesitation Mordecai agreed to take the child Esther into his own care. A man of sufficient means, he was fortunate to find a nursemaid to help him in the child's early years. She was a young Persian girl named Aniseh. In addition to her responsibility of caring for the infant, she also became the cook. She was pleased to be employed by Mordecai, for he was known to be a kind man of impeccable reputation.

The day that Mordecai brought Baby Esther into his home, Aniseh was waiting. She had already secured a small bed for the little one and had gathered a few infant items of clothing that her niece had outgrown. Soon after, Mordecai sought a well-known worker in silk and embroidery there in Susa to create clothing for his adopted child. He wanted her to have the best that he could afford.

Since a baby required full-time care, it was necessary for Aniseh to reside in Mordecai's home where she remained for several years. The arrangement continued until Esther reached twelve years of age. That year, Aniseh's widowed mother became unable to care for herself, and she needed the aid of her unmarried daughter. Though Aniseh moved back into her mother's home, she still returned to Mordecai's each evening and prepared a meal for the two people she had come to love like family.

——◆——

Esther became a mature young lady. She readily accepted responsibilities presented to her and learned early to be accountable for her actions. Alone during the day, she tended the house, maintained a small garden outside, and completed the studies that Mordecai had assigned her the day before. Her passion was the great outdoors, to which she escaped whenever possible. One fact, though, was always in her mind. She was a Jew, and Mordecai never failed to remind her of her heritage.

Rather unusual for that time, Mordecai had been an only child. His parents died after he was grown, working, and on his own. He never married, and he had no relatives; he had only his work. As a result, Esther became his life. He watched over her as a mother hen her chicks, providing her the best that his earnings as one of the scribes in the king's court would allow. She was aware that she had far more advantages than her Jewish counterparts in Judah, the home of her ancestors. Growing up, Mordecai had often told her stories about the sufferings there; and with each telling, her heart melted with pity for them.

"Esther, you have such a good heart; still, you must not grieve for those times and those people," Mordecai often told her. "God has promised complete restoration for the nation of Israel, and I believe it will come."[8]

His words pacified her only a little. She loved Mordecai deeply, but at times like that she longed for a mother, or even a grandmother, with whom she could discuss the feelings in a girl's heart. She was thankful she had friends with whom to share interests, and she determined in her young heart never to take them for granted. She vowed, as well, never to discard the ties to her roots. In spite of the luxuries of Persian life, she would always be a Jew. She would not let the beautiful city of Susa, which for good reason had become the winter home for the great kings,[9] turn her heart from her origins. The lovely hanging gardens throughout the city, which simulated those of the city of Babylon,[10] displayed the most elegant blossoms one could imagine, yet they represented only a hint of the immense attraction of the glorious city she loved. Regardless, she knew, even at a young age, that its alluring splendor would not deter her from helping her fellow Jews someday. The desire was always in her heart even though she had no idea how she would accomplish it.

The source of her strength and sense of direction was Mordecai, whose abiding Jewish convictions and gentle guidance proved to be lasting influences in his adopted daughter's life. When Mordecai was not busy with work in the court, he often sought the company of a man they called Shabtai, a staunch follower of the Lord who knew Ezra, the priest. Mordecai loved to hear him tell how Ezra wanted to return to Jerusalem to rebuild the temple of the Lord, and about Nehemiah, another man of God, who planned to restore the great wall there that was destroyed during Nebuchadnezzar's siege.[11] Shabtai spoke of things Mordecai had never seen, like the great festivals, the elaborate priestly rituals, and the daily sacrifices that the Jews had once observed in Judah. It saddened him that none of those could be practiced in the great Persian Empire, his home.

CHAPTER 3

Mordecai watched with mixed feelings his Esther grow into a beautiful young woman, lovely in form and disposition. As a young teen, without her intention, she became a temptation to each young boy she passed as she lifted her long, dark lashes to acknowledge his presence. For the most part, potential young suitors were wary of Mordecai, for he was a watchful guardian. He kept a tight rein, knowing all the while that someday he must relinquish his beloved Esther one way or another. The only time she challenged his watchfulness was when the weather turned warm. At those times, she, herself, loosened the reins to take in all that nature had to offer.

Esther's rich, full locks lightened here and there by the sun were signs of her love of the outdoors. Her complexion, which in the colder months resembled fine, polished porcelain, was in the warm months kissed with a light tan glow. The minute she was finished with her studies, off she would go searching for less trodden paths of adventure. Sometimes a friend joined her; if not, she was content being alone to breathe in the fragrance of the season, touching with gentle hands each leaf and petal along the way.

One sunny afternoon, Esther's friend Dorsa joined her on one of her frequent walks. Both of the young girls loved poetry and recited their favorite verses to each other as they took in the sun-rays of late spring streaking through the date palms.

"I wonder what it would be like to be Queen of Persia," Dorsa said, as she reached up to claim an errant blossom draped over an ornamental fence along the path. "It must be glorious having anything you want and giving orders to one servant after another. Don't you think so, Esther?"

"No, I don't," she replied. "I think I would be bored having to live like that day after day, always having to fulfill someone's expectations. I'd rather be free to explore this beautiful world, sing when I want to, and...," she laughed, "recite poetry!"

"Oh, Esther. You are so...so usual, so predictable. I'd like to ride in the royal carriage and have maids looking for ways to please me. Is that wrong, Esther?"

"I don't think it's wrong, Dorsa. It's just not for me. Oh, look! See the brook there in the distance. I've never noticed it before. Come. Let's see." Esther pulled her friend down the hill to get a better look.

By the time Esther arrived back home just before dark, Mordecai was waiting for her, somewhat worried. Sometimes her walks went beyond the allotted time, and he wanted her safely home.

It was Mordecai's custom, after the evening meal, to avail Esther of as much education as he could pass on to her. He had been fortunate to have parents who did the same for him, and he wanted Esther to enjoy those benefits, as well.

Mordecai's job as a scribe afforded him material that otherwise he would never have possessed. He copied anything he could find of use to fill his apt student's mind. He schooled Esther in mathematics, history, language, and the Holy Scriptures. She was lucky to be exposed to those kinds of learning. If she had been a boy, she might be learning horsemanship, archery, spear throwing, hunting, and other masculine activities. Those were not for Mordecai's child.

He sometimes wondered why he felt compelled to follow that regimen. It was as if he were working out a plan of some kind, one he knew not. For Esther, the lessons were a pleasure. She was a willing student and absorbed all the information he shared with her. She never questioned his motives, for she was almost as interested in learning facts as she was in observing nature. Her mentor was amazed at the breadth of her interests. He could not possibly know what the future held for his Esther. Lately, his chest tightened with some unknown worry that shortened his sleep at night.

Mordecai had noticed only one deficit in Esther's personality: she had no culinary inclinations. He once said to her in the presence of his cook, "It is good we have Aniseh, or we would surely starve I am convinced." He grinned and winked because it did not bother him in the least that Esther cared not for cooking skills. She was smart, even clever, and could discuss almost any topic with him. He relished that far more than a well-roasted duckling with all the trimmings.

CHAPTER 4

In 486 B.C. Xerxes, son of King Darius, became king of Persia.[12] Though he did not impose harsh standards upon the large population of Jews in his country, he lacked the self-discipline of his predecessors, often relying on the whims of his court officials. His reign was different from that of his father, Darius. Xerxes prided himself more in the grand banquets he held than in keeping the Jews happy in Persia or in Judah. He used his elaborate parties as a means to display his majesty and wealth. When Mordecai observed such opulence that was used to enlarge one's own image, it reminded him of his parents' stories of another great king called Solomon. A once-wise king of all of Israel, he had allowed his wealth and power, not to mention his hundreds of wives, to tarnish his loyalty to God, leaving him to lament, "'Meaningless, meaningless... Everything is meaningless.'"[13]

In the third year of Xerxes' reign, he decided to give a banquet to top all banquets. It was to last for six months, extravagant even for Solomon's time. The palace and gardens were decorated with gold and silver and the finest linen hangings that could be found. His choicest wines flowed like water among his guests who represented all stations in life.

Vashti, his Queen, was not one to be outdone. She decided to give her own banquet, a decision that, not surprising, did not please her husband. He was, after all, the king, and nothing was done without his sovereign approval. The two did not share a close relationship, and it was common knowledge of those close to the king that he had been drawn to Vashti's beauty and that alone. They lived in different compartments of the palace and were seldom seen together. He called for her only at times that benefited his ego as well as his sensual pleasures.

During the first week of Xerxes' lavish feast, he sent for Vashti in order to display her beauty to all his guests. When the messenger arrived at her door, she curtly replied, "I will not go." Vashti was aware, as was the entire land, that when one is summoned by the king, whether queen or vassal, one must go. It was the law of the Persians which she willfully chose to ignore. When her response was reported to Xerxes, he rose from his chair, stamped his foot, and slammed his fist on the table hard enough to upset the utensils.

"What do you mean she will not come?"

The messenger lowered his eyes. He had no reply. Xerxes became inflamed. Refusal to abide by his request had never occurred before. Never once had his father King Darius mentioned such a thing. He thumped his temple hard, not quite sure what to do. In haste, he consulted those schooled in Persian law who agreed that Queen Vashti was in error to make such a decision. In addition, they feared she would influence other women of the kingdom to act likewise. So, they devised a plan.

'...if it pleases the king, let him issue a royal decree and let it be written in the laws of Persia and Media, which cannot be repealed, that Vashti is never again to enter the presence of King Xerxes. Also let the king give her royal position to someone else who is better than she.'[14]

Hardly blinking an eye, King Xerxes accepted his advisors' solution, and a proclamation was sent throughout the region describing in detail his decree. Before the king was able to look for a new Queen, he encountered political issues with his adversary, Greece, which called for his sustained military presence.

For the next several years the Persians engaged the Greeks soundly in one battle after another, yet finally being defeated with only a peace treaty for their efforts.[15] Xerxes' military exploits ended, and he returned home. He was still king, but the country did not have a queen. After taking a much-needed respite from his rigorous campaigns, King Xerxes ordered that a suitable companion be found to share his throne. His requirements were extensive.

CHAPTER 5

"[Xerxes]…remembered Vashti and what she
had done and what he had decreed about her."
Esther 2:1

The search for a new queen began. Xerxes' weakness for beauty dictated the nature of the hunt. The contenders must be virgins, perfect in form, and obvious stand-outs among their peers. Once several girls were found meeting those requirements, they were to be put into the care of the harem's eunuch, Hegai, who would pamper them with expensive beauty treatments and delightful delicacies provided by the palace baker. Nothing would be spared.

The news spread fast, especially among potentially eligible young girls. Dorsa ran fast to catch up with Esther who had already begun her walk. Almost breathless, she yelled her announcement before reaching Esther's side.

"Did you hear, Esther? The king has returned, and a search will be made throughout the kingdom for a new queen. What could Queen Vashti have done that was bad enough to cause her dethronement?" She waited, expecting Esther's reply of shock.

"I don't know, Dorsa. It doesn't concern us. Something is always going on in the government of the land. That's what Mordecai says. Come. It's a beautiful day!"

The two friends began walking along the same rocky path they had taken many times before. Esther made a sudden stop and looked upward.

"Listen! The Rose Finches are singing. They're just happy to be alive. Look! One just lit on that limb there." She pointed to a prolific pomegranate tree, its tubular-shaped, coral blossoms soon to be replaced by luscious fruit. "Dorsa, even if circumstances are bad in the government, for us life is good."

Dorsa was surprised at Esther's lack of interest in the day's news, and she would not be deterred.

"Esther, you don't understand. All the beautiful girls will be taken to the king's harem, and the prettiest one will be selected and crowned the new Queen. Don't you think that's exciting! Oh, I wish *I* were beautiful."

"You *are* beautiful, Dorsa. Your name even means 'like a pearl.'[16] That's what you told me." Esther patted her friend on the shoulder. "I want things to continue as they are now. You wouldn't want to be locked up inside those palace walls!" She seated herself on a large, smooth rock in the shade of a spreading Myrtle tree, its glossy leaves glistening in the sunlight.

"Sit here," she said, handing her friend a small bag of fresh almonds that Aniseh had given her the night before. "I want to tell you what Mordecai taught me last night."

Dorsa calmed down somewhat and began munching on a handful of the nuts. She squeezed in beside Esther to listen. She felt like a student of Mordecai's, herself, because Esther shared so many stories with her, things none of the other girls knew.

"Did you know, Dorsa, what happened to this beautiful city over 300 years ago?"

"No. Tell me." Dorsa's eyes widened. She was ready for any tidbit she had not heard before.

"Well, it was completely destroyed by the Assyrians.[17] You wouldn't know it to look at it now, would you? And, did you know that King Cyrus the Great nearly a hundred years ago was killed in battle because he always fought alongside his soldiers, never sending them into battle alone? Mordecai read to me that he was also a king who was respectful of all cultures, even of all religions."

While Dorsa was mulling over this latest piece of her education, Esther was wishing that their present ruler, King Xerxes, was as generous. Mordecai had also told her that King Cyrus had allowed many of the Jews who were taken captive during Nebuchadnezzar's reign to return to their homeland.[18] Although the subject was close to her heart, Esther did not discuss her Jewish heritage with others. She was, after all, Persian by birth.

The girls' time together came to a close. How Esther enjoyed basking in the warm sunshine, discussing history and science with one so attentive. She and Dorsa embraced in friendship as they always did after one of their meetings, and they each returned home.

❖

When Mordecai heard of the king's search for a queen, he was inclined to hide Esther. He knew she fit the qualifications, but she was so young, barely into her teens. The fact that she had developed beyond her years made her more appealing for what Mordecai considered a vicious trap. He was aware of the selection process and winced in distaste at how Esther's innocence would be blemished. At the same time, he knew there was nothing either of them could do to prevent her summons if, indeed, it arrived. More sleepless nights.

❖

As feared, Hegai's emissaries arrived early one evening at Mordecai's door and the command was issued. Esther was to be escorted to the royal palace the following morning where she would be added to the group of eligible virgins to be preened for twelve months before the selection of a new queen would be made.

Mordecai dismissed Aniseh earlier than usual so that he and Esther could be alone. Esther was in a state of confusion, knowing that she was unprepared for what lay ahead. She wanted to run to some secluded, safe place in the countryside; yet she realized that her real place of comfort was there with the one who cared more about her than anyone else. Mordecai assured her that if there was anything he could do, he would. All the same, he reminded her that the king was not one given to compromise or negotiations. When Mordecai saw the sadness on her delicate face, he tried his best to comfort her. He told her he would always be close by and would check on her daily. His words seemed to soothe Esther's fears somewhat, but she could not prevent the tears that fell upon her cheeks.

"Mordecai, you have been so good to me. I never knew my mother and father; you have been my only family. How will I be able to live apart from you?"

Using words that bruised his own heart, yet words needed to protect her, he spoke.

"Hadassah, you who have become my daughter, I have loved you from your birth and always will." He paused to guarantee her complete attention. "This advice I must give you." His brow furrowed as he spoke rather sternly, uncharacteristic in his treatment of Esther. "Never reveal your Jewish heritage. That will make things better for you. As I have told you before, our race is not regarded in high esteem by some of the Persians. No one yet knows *I* am a Jew. It will be difficult, but I repeat, you must not reveal your identity. Do you understand?" Esther waited a moment, then nodded. She wondered why he had addressed her by her Jewish name. *Does he think it is the last time he will ever be able to do so?* She also wondered about what Mordecai had just said. *Surely the king knows he is a Jew. After all, Mordecai is a scribe in the court. Somehow, I think the king knows everything.* She decided to put those thoughts aside. There were more important things to worry about.

Mordecai was satisfied that he had given Esther good advice; beyond that, he did not know what else he could do. He placed the dilemma in God's hands. The two embraced, not knowing when they would see each other again.

The next morning Esther, too soon, was gone.

CHAPTER 6

E sther had never seen anything to parallel the king's harem. She had heard tales about it, but being a part of it was quite different.

Fourteen girls were brought in from all parts of Persia. Most of them were strangers, only one did she recognize. One thing they all had in common was beauty. As for herself, she had never considered herself impeccable in looks. Sure, Mordecai referred to her as his lovely daughter. *That* was Mordecai. How could she match the incomparable loveliness surrounding her? Really, she did not want to. All she wanted was to return home and for her life to continue as it was before.

In spite of her feelings, Esther realized she had been placed there for some reason, and that being strong of will, she would survive. She told herself that at least by the end of twelve months she would be released and life would return to normal. Still, a year was a long time in the life of a young girl. She had no control over the length of time or the elaborate plans explained by Hegai, the harem eunuch in charge. Since she had no voice in the matter, she resigned herself to make the most of it.

At the beginning of the year-long period, Esther had to admit it was interesting. She and the others were given countless beauty treatments, elegant apparel, and the finest of foods. In addition, they were exercised daily; and when the weather was good, activities were held outdoors in the courtyard. Those days were her favorites, not only because of her love of nature, but also because she often saw Mordecai walking near the courtyard fence. She knew he was keeping his promise to check on her well-being. His kind face and loving smile always provided the comfort she needed, for her nights were often lonely and her tears fell plentiful upon the soft, silk pillows where she slept.

Esther discovered rather soon that jealousies ran rampant among the girls of the harem. One morning as they were all dressing, assisted by several aides bustling about fitting this one or that, one of the girls, the one issued in from the East, deliberately turned over a bottle of costly perfume on another girl's cream-colored, embroidered gown, ruining it. The two had quarreled the night before when one had called the other a bad name and the score was being evened. The two were removed fast, not to be seen again. Esther avoided such conflict and, as a result, was shunned by some, yet secretly admired by others.

———◆———

In the eleventh month, it was Esther's time to be taken to the king's chamber for approval. She felt prettier than she ever had before while noticeably lacking the extravagant appearance of her peers. The other girls, before being summoned by the king, had dressed elegantly from head to toe. Glorious jewels hung from their necks and wrists, sparkling combs adorned their up-swept hair, and their hands were laden with bejeweled rings on their smooth, slender fingers. What a picture of royalty they presented!

How she dreaded her turn. Her chaste upbringing loomed prominent in her mind as she readied herself to be given to the king. It was not her desire. It just had to be.

When Esther was called, she wore a modest, simple—yet lovely— flowing white gown with a single-strand pearl necklace. On her arm was a gold bracelet, no jewels. Her rich dark hair, lush as always, was twisted and pulled back, secured with an unpretentious comb.

Esther was ready to be presented to King Xerxes in his exhaustive search for a Queen. She was escorted by Hegai down the long hall to the king's chambers. Soon Esther's reluctant, rigid body stood before the dubious door, behind which awaited an event that could change her life forever. She seized the moment to bow her head. Hegai, standing at her side, glimpsed the quiet movement of her lips. He waited a minute, then knocked. The door opened wide, and Esther entered, head held high.

Now the king was attracted to Esther more than any of
the other women and she won his favor and approval more

than any of the other virgins. So he set a royal crown on her head and made her Queen instead of Vashti.[19]

———◆———

As one might expect, deposed Queen Vashti never forgot the treatment she had received from King Xerxes and had been biding her time until his return from the wars. She engineered her revenge by hiring a virgin to finagle her way into the king's harem to secure information for her concerning the king's whereabouts at all times. In addition, she sought the help of Teresh, one of the king's officials who she knew was displeased at not receiving special favors from the court anymore. Vashi and Teresh, along with another disgruntled official, Bigthana, put a plan into motion: if the king were assassinated, Vashi's young son Artexerxes would inherit the throne, she would become the Queen Mother, and the two conspirators would be awarded special places of honor.

One day as Mordecai sat at the king's gate, he overheard the brother-in-law of Bigthana telling a friend about the assassination plot. Mordecai knew there was nothing he could do. Perhaps Esther could. The next afternoon he saw Esther walking in the courtyard outside the palace and spoke with her through the opening in the fence, sharing in detail the information he had learned. Esther said she would straightway inform the king.

Immediately she reported the names of the conspirators to her husband as well as naming her cousin, Mordecai, as the informant. Without hesitation, King Xerxes called the men in and had them severely questioned. Their guilt was revealed and he set their execution for the following day. Vashti's plan for the time being was thwarted.

CHAPTER 7

"What is all the commotion about?" Esther asked her personal maid, Jaleh, who was fashioning the Queen's long, sable hair into braids which she wove into a spiral from the nape of Esther's neck to the top of her head. "It sounds like my husband the king is planning some kind of celebration. Perhaps he is celebrating the anniversary of the impalement of the two who planned to kill him. I would rather it be a ceremony to reward my cousin Mordecai for uncovering the conspiracy."

Jaleh replied, "Your highness, I believe it means he is elevating that evil man Haman to a higher position than he already enjoys. Please do not share my feelings. I cannot help it; I do not trust that man."

"You have nothing to worry about, Jaleh. Your private thoughts are always safe with me. When I am called into the king's chamber again, I will ask him about Haman. I am afraid it may not be soon. Our king seems to be preoccupied with other business these days. I learned yesterday that a new group of virgins have been brought into the king's harem. Do you suppose that's what occupies him now?" She smiled at her maid as though she were joking, while in her heart she wondered if she might be losing favor in Xerxes' eyes.

Jaleh's answer came soft and tender to her mistress' ears. "Oh, no, Your Highness. Your beauty and kindness outweigh all the others."

The noise did, indeed, represent Haman's promotion. Special foods were brought into the banquet hall, and the best musicians were employed for the evening gala. Queen Esther, who attended the festivities, as well, found it hard to behave as a gracious hostess. Xerxes was not aware, as *she* was, that Haman was descended from the Amalekites who were among the Jews' greatest enemies, spurned by God for their attack on His people at Rephidim near Mount Sinai before they entered the Promised Land.[20] Mordecai had told her all about it. He had also told her that her own relative, Israel's King Saul, at one time had been at great odds with the Amalekites and decimated them.[21] So, the words of praise she heard that evening concerning Haman fell heavy on her mind.

Every occupant throughout the city soon learned that Haman's latest acquired position carried certain requirements which he imposed upon the citizenry. One was that everyone must bow in his presence. Everyone. No exceptions. When one of the king's officials chided Mordecai for not bowing to Haman, in anger and without thinking, he blurted out, "I am a Jew. I will bow before no one except my God."

His cutting reply traveled fast. When Haman was told that Mordecai, a Jew, refused to honor him, he became furious. He decided it would not be enough to have Mordecai, alone, killed. He would find some way to kill all the Jews in the entire kingdom. He met with his staff, and they decided on a day that the event would take place. First, he needed the king's approval.

Haman requested and received an audience with King Xerxes and presented his plan, which was peppered with lies, before the king.

"As part of my job, Your Majesty, I have learned that a certain group of people throughout the land refuse to obey your laws. They are disrespectful of Your Kingship and cannot be trusted. I fear they will bring serious trouble to the throne if measures are not taken to stop them. They must be killed."

Haman's words disturbed Xerxes; and without investigating the matter, he gave Haman permission to do as he pleased. Soon orders were dispatched throughout all the providences to kill the Jews wherever they were found and take their property. Age mattered not. Kill them all!

> When Mordecai learned all that had been done, he tore his clothes…and went out into the city, wailing loudly and bitterly.[22]

When Esther heard that Mordecai had left the palace and was going around the city dressed in sackcloth and ashes, her heart sank. *What will the king do when he hears this about one of his scribes?* Her thoughts ran rampant. With haste, she sent fresh clothes for him to wear. When he refused them, she sent another one of the servants to find out what was wrong with her cousin to cause him to behave in such a manner.

The servant's message was devastating to Esther: all the Jews were to be annihilated. The servant even presented her with an official copy of the king's edict. Furthermore, he said that Mordecai wanted the Queen, his Esther, to plead with her husband to rescind the order.

Unlike her usual, calm demeanor, Esther paced back and forth in her chamber. *What can I do? I haven't been called into the king's presence in many days. I must do something. If he doesn't extend his scepter to me, I could be killed. But I am a Jew through and through, and if the edict is fulfilled, I will be killed anyway when they find out.* She sent words of her concern to Mordecai. His urgent reply stung her to the core of her being:

> 'And who knows but that you have come to royal position
> for such a time as this?'[23]

Come what may, Esther knew she must go before the king. First, she sent word to Mordecai to fast for three days and have other Jews do likewise. She and her maids would fast, as well.

CHAPTER 8

Esther dressed in her best royal attire and stood waiting before the King's hall. His throne was at the end, and he caught sight of his beautiful Queen, her appearance a vision of graceful grandeur. Sheer pleasure swept over him at the mere sight of her. He was sorry he had not called her into his chambers in quite some time. He extended his scepter toward her.

With sure steps and confident determination, Esther approached the King and stopped before the throne.

"What can I do for you, Queen Esther?" he asked.

Having earlier conceived a safe plan, she told him she was giving a banquet that evening and requested that he and his official, Haman, attend. Xerxes was pleased with her invitation, and enthralled anew with her beauty; so he did as she asked.

At the banquet, the musicians Queen Esther had secured performed until midnight. Haman had never attended such a glorious banquet, not even the one honoring his recent promotion. He leaned over and whispered to a fellow nobleman, "I believe the Queen has gone to this much trouble for me, me alone. I have noticed the special attention she has paid me lately."

"Perhaps," his table companion said. "*She* is a delight, not at all like the former Queen." The two men's laughter was lost in the frivolity of the evening, for it appeared to be a joyous occasion for all who attended.

Before the King excused himself for the night, Queen Esther said she would be giving another banquet the following evening and again requested that he and Haman attend. Somewhat surprising to Esther, the king again accepted.

Haman could not have been happier. The Queen, herself, had singled him out to accompany the king to two of her banquets. He was certain that great things were in store for him. The only drawback to his joy was that the Jew Mordecai still refused to bow down to him. With the encouragement of his wife and friends, Haman erected a gallows on which Mordecai would be hanged the next morning. He was sure that the king would sanction the plan.

That night, Esther's sleep was scant, for she was unsure of what step to take next. For hours she tossed and turned. Finally, before daybreak, she arose from her bed and draped a shawl over her head. She went to her window, kneeled, and prayed: *God, please help me save my people. I know not what I must do. Please show me the way.*

Little did Esther know that across the palace, the king, himself, was having trouble sleeping. He called his servant to read the royal diary of current events to him. The writings contained information about Mordecai having exposed the plot to assassinate the king.

"What have we done to honor that man?" the king asked his servant.

"Nothing, Your Majesty," the servant replied.

———◆———

When morning came, Haman arrived to get his wish granted concerning the hanging of Mordecai. Before he could speak, the king, not knowing Haman's devious intentions, asked him what should be done to honor someone the king highly esteemed.

Thinking that the king was referring to *him*, Haman replied:

> '... For the man the king delights to honor, have them
> bring a royal robe the king has worn and a horse the king
> has ridden ...and lead him on the horse through the city
> streets, proclaiming before him, "This is what is done for
> the man the king delights to honor."'[24]

Satisfied with Haman's suggestion, King Xerxes rose from his royal throne and gave the command:

> 'Go at once...Get the robe and the horse just as you have
> suggested for Mordecai the Jew...Do not neglect anything
> you have recommended.'[25]

Haman's eyebrows lifted; his eyes bulged. He was too shocked to speak. He could not believe what he had just heard. It was clear. The King had given the order. Now he, the newly acclaimed high official in the king's court, must comply. What Haman had intended for Mordecai was *far* from glory and honor. *How can this be?* Puzzled and confused, he bowed grudgingly before the king and scurried from his presence. *I have no choice. I must do the unthinkable.*

◆

Queen Esther's second banquet commenced according to her plan. The King and Haman were again present. During the lavish meal, King Xerxes, as was his custom, asked his queen what he could do for her.

Esther swallowed hard to gain courage. She had never revealed her Jewish identity and was unsure how the King would respond. She knew, however, that the survival of her fellow Jews in Persia was dependent upon her petition. It might mean her death. At that moment, the words Mordecai had sent to her marched through her brain. Perhaps she *was* Queen of Persia now for this very reason. She would first appeal to the king's weakness for her beauty. Then she would expand her request.

She faced the king, smiled with the greatest respect, and spoke in a quiet, gentle voice.

> '... If I have found favor with you, O king, and if it pleases your majesty, grant me my life—this is my petition. And spare my people—this is my request. For I and my people have been sold for destruction and slaughter and annihilation.'[26]

To her relief, Esther's revelation of her Jewish heritage did not surprise the king. What bothered him was that someone would plan such a thing against his Queen. When Esther continued her humble entreaty by implicating Haman as the instigator, the king was filled with rage. Without warning, he dashed from the banquet hall and entered the palace garden. The sweet, fragrant scent of hyacinth filled the night air, a poignant reminder of his times alone with Esther. His thoughts darted here and there as he tried to recall his past meetings with Haman.

Yes! I gave the scoundrel permission to kill all those he said were a danger to the kingdom. That deceiving lackey did not mention the Jews. I knew that Queen Esther was a Jew, as well as my faithful scribe Mordecai, her cousin. I would never have ordained such a plan. Now I learn that an official from my royal court has tricked me. He is the one who must die!

King Xerxes returned to the banquet hall just in time to see Haman on Esther's couch pleading for mercy. He mistook Haman's actions as a sexual assault.

"Guards! Guards! Grab him! Take him away!" he yelled, pointing to Haman. His orders were immediately carried out. King Xerxes had already made his decision and announced that the execution would take place right away.

————◆————

So they hanged Haman on the gallows he had prepared for
Mordecai...That same day King Xerxes gave Queen Esther
the estate of Haman...The king took off his signet ring...
and presented it to Mordecai. And Esther appointed him
over Haman's estate.[27]

Immediately, the king rescinded the order he had given concerning the Jews. Instead, he drafted another edict granting all Jews full protection and the authority to destroy any and all who did them harm. The decree became law on the thirteenth day in the month of Adar, a date which would be remembered by the Jews for centuries to come. It would be called *Purim* from the word *Pur*, meaning "lot."[28] Haman and his friends had cast lots and set that day for the annihilation of the Jews. Their plan had failed, and the Jews in Persia were granted freedom from their enemies.

At last, Esther could proclaim her Jewish blood to everyone and announce with pride that Mordecai, her cousin, was a Jew, as well.

CHAPTER 9

The Jews in all of the provinces of Persia began to carry out the new edict with courage. They were led by Mordecai who had become second in command to the king and supplied with royal garments and a golden crown.

Having acquired a confident stance in the king's presence, Queen Esther went before him yet again to offer a request. She had difficulty believing that she, of such a tender heart, would ask a hideous thing of the king. On the other hand, she felt that the action might serve as a deterrent to others seeking to harm her people. She asked that the bodies of Haman's ten sons whom the Jews had killed after the king's edict be hanged on public display. Without reservations, the king granted her request and it was done. The action engendered such fear of the Jews in some people of other nationalities that they began claiming that they were of Jewish heritage themselves. It was an occurrence that amused many of the Jews.

In the following days, the Jews killed thousands of their enemies; and although the king had instructed them to take the plunder from those they attacked, they did not. Mordecai remembered something his parents had told him about King Saul of old, Israel's first king. Against the Lord's directions, King Saul had seized the plunder of the Amalekites he fought against.[29] As a result, it became one of the reasons he lost the kingship. Mordecai's advice to his fellow-Jews was not to make that mistake. He did not want to tempt the Lord, his God.

After months of executions carried out by the Jews, they enjoyed a period of peace. On a cool, fall evening Queen Esther called Mordecai into her royal chamber. They embraced as they had on the night before she left his home for the king's harem. She directed her cousin to join her by the warm fire her servant had prepared in advance.

"Mordecai, I have never strayed from my strong upbringing. Because of you, I have accomplished feats for our people that I never could have imagined, and who would have expected all this?" She waved her arms around the room. "I'm the Queen of a great empire! Your trust in me shown by your words, 'for such a time as this,' gave me encouragement to risk our lives for a greater cause. The king has also been kind to you. Look at you—a Jew, second only to the king of Persia. Thank you, Mordecai. You have been a friend, a teacher, and a parent to me." She reached for his hand, holding it like she would never let go.

Mordecai's eyes became damp with emotion. Yes, the two of them had come far, and their people had been saved.

"Remember, I am a scribe, Esther. I will record everything so that we and others will never forget. Now, come with me. We will celebrate. I have sent letters throughout the land that this occasion must be celebrated by our people each year for three days and passed on from one generation to the next."[30]

"Why, Mordecai, that's the number of days that I asked you to fast before I went before the king on our people's behalf. It now takes on an added meaning." They both smiled.

The two left her room, hand in hand, to join other Jews in the citadel of Susa, knowing that *Purim* would be observed for years to come. It was a grand day indeed!

> Mordecai the Jew was…preeminent among the Jews, and held in high esteem by his many fellow Jews, because he worked for the good of his people and spoke up for the welfare of all the Jews.[31]

Beautiful Queen Esther served the rest of her days with poise, wisdom, and dignity, a lasting tribute to the king, the empire of Persia, and her fellow Jews throughout the land.

Epilogue

We do not know for sure what Leah's daily life was like in Haran; how Aaron received God's call to assist Moses; or how Naomi journeyed from Bethlehem to Moab. Likewise, we cannot be sure whom Jonathan married or when; what Abigail's daily relationship with Nabal was like; nor what kind of personalities King Josiah's two wives possessed. Finally, Esther's young years with her guardian Mordecai are unknown.

The stories presented here, besides the actual biblical accounts, include mere speculation built upon information that we do have. Hopefully, my attempt to acquaint you better with these characters, by making them appear completely human, has at least heightened your interest to explore them further. Herein, we have been merely <u>Reading Between the Lines</u>.

NOTES

INTRODUCTION

1. "The Meaning of Numbers in the Bible: The Number 7." *The Bible Study Site.* biblestudy.org. www.biblestudy.org/bibleref/meaning-of-numbers-in-bible/7. html. Accessed April 29, 2017.

ABRAHAM'S FAMILY TREE

2. "Image for Abraham's Family Tree." *Abraham's Family Tree-Wikipedia.* Wikipedia. org. https://en.wikipedia.org/wiki:/abraham%27 family tree. Accessed April 28, 2016.

THE STORY OF LEAH

1. Exodus 2:1, 10; Matthew 1:1-16.
2. Douglas, J.D. and Tenney, Merrill C. "Haran, Charran." NIV Compact Dictionary of the Bible, Zondervan Publishing House, Grand Rapids, Michigan, 1989. p. 238.
3. The Editors of Encyclopedia Britannica. "Ishtar." *Ishtar/Mesopotamian goddess/.* britannica.com. Posted: December 14, 2000. www.britannica.com/topic/ishtar-mesopotamian-goddess. Accessed April 4, 2016.
4. Genesis 29:31.
5. The NIV Study Bible, The Zondervan Corporation, Grand Rapids, Michigan, 1985. Study note: Genesis 30:14, pp. 50-51.
6. Genesis 27:41.
7. NIV Study Bible, Text note: Genesis 25:25(1), p.43.

8. Genesis 27:6-10.
9. Genesis 26:34; 27:46.
10. NIV Study Bible, Text note: Genesis 35:18(s), p. 59.
11. Proverbs 15:13.
12. Genesis 37:10b.

THE STORY OF AARON

1. Exodus 4:10.
2. Genesis 45:17-18; 46:28-29.
3. "Clothing in the Ancient World." Ancient Israelite Clothing, Israelite man, 3.1.2. Outer garments: simlah.Wikipedia.org. https//en.wikipedia.org/wiki/ Clothing_in_the_ancient_ world. Accessed May 2, 2017.
4. "Men's Galabeya." *Nile River Connections*, nile-river-connections.com. http://nile-river-connections.com/2017/04/11/mens-galabeya/. Accessed: June 13, 2017.
5. "Egyptian Gods: Mafdet." *Egyptian Gods and Goddesses*. egyptian-gods.org. https://egyptian-gods-mafdet/. Accessed: May 2, 2017.
6. "New Evidence for Thutmose 111 as Exodus Pharaoh in 1446. B.C." bible.ca. www. bible.ca./archeology/bible-archeology-date-1440 b.c.htm. Accessed: April 10, 2017.
7. Exodus 5:1.
8. Mark, Joshua J. "Nile: (section 3) Importance to Egypt," *Nile-Ancient History Encyclopedia*. ancient. eu. published September 2, 2009. www.ancient.eu/egypt. Accessed: March 5, 2017.
9. Exodus 8:1-3.
10. "Ancient Egyptian Gods; Heqet." www.ancientegyptonline.com. Accessed: July 26, 2017.
11. The NIV Study Bible, The Zondervan Corporation, Grand Rapids, Michigan, 1985. Study note: Exodus 8:2, p. 96.
12. Exodus 8:8.
13. NIV Study Bible, Study note: Exodus 12:2, p. 101.
14. Exodus 12:29-30.
15. Ibid., 7:5.
16. NIV Study Bible, Study note: Exodus: 12:2, p. 101.
17. Exodus 16:3.
18. Douglas, J.D. and Tenney, Merrill C. "Manna," (next to last sentence), p. 364, 2 Edras 2:1; Wisd.16:20. NIV Compact Dictionary of the Bible, Zondervan Publishing House, 1989.
19. Exodus 16:33.
20. Ibid., 32:22-24.
21. Numbers 12:2.

22. Ibid., 12:9.
23. Ibid., 18:7.
24. Deuteronomy 28:1.
25. Numbers 20:12.

The Story of Naomi

1. "Reformed Musings: Preaching on Barley." blogspot.com. Posted on March 12, 2009. jasonffoster.blog.spot.com2009/03preachingonbarley.html. Accessed: April 29, 2017.
2. Genesis 12:7; 17:8.
3. Joshua 24:15b.
4. "Barley Cakes." *Barley cakes-Cedar Ring* Mama-*WordPress.com.* wordpress.com. Posted April 10, 2012. https://cedarringmama.wordpress.com. Accessed: May 9, 2017.
5. "What they wore, how they lived: fabrics." *Ancient Clothes, Houses.* womeninthe. bible.net. www.womeninthebible.net/bible-extras/clothes-houses/. Accessed May 10, 2017.
6. "History of Fullers Earth," *HRP Industries.* fullersearth.com. www.fullersearth. com/about_fullers_earth/. Accessed May 4, 2017.
7. Douglas, J.D. and Tenney, Merrill C. "Feasts." NIV Compact Dictionary of the Bible, Zondervan Publishing house, Academic and Professional Books,1989. p. 201.
8. "Kinsman-redeemers," NIV Study Bible, The Zondervan Corporation, Grand Rapids, Michigan, 1985. Study note: Ruth 2:20, p. 367.
9. Douglas and Tenney. "Arnon." NIV Compact Dictionary of the Bible, pp. 49-50.
10. Ruth 1:1.
11. Deuteronomy 29:5.
12. Douglas and Tenney. "Moab." NIV Compact Dictionary, pp. 388-389.
13. "Clothing in the Ancient World." Ancient Israelite Clothing 3.1.2. wikipedia. org. https://en.wikipedia.org, Biblicalclothing#outer_garments. Accessed July 10, 2016.
14. NIV Study Bible, Study note: Joshua 14:12, p. 312.
15. "Zered." NIV Compact Dictionary, p. 640.
16. "Clothing in the Ancient World." Ancient Israelite Clothing, under-garments 3.1.1. Same as #13 above.
17. "Kir Hareseth," NIV Compact Dictionary, p. 334.
18. Isaiah 38:21.
19. "Threshing Floors." NIV Compact Dictionary, p. 593.
20. Deuteronomy 23:3-4, 6.
21. Numbers 21:29a; 2 Kings 23:13.

22. Ruth 1:4a.
23. Ibid., 4b.
24. Ibid., 1:16.
25. "Aten." Wikipedia.org. https://enwikipedia.org./wiki/Aten. Accessed May 5, 2017.
26. Exodus 16:4, 31.
27. "Batah." *Hebrew Words for Faith. The Word Internet Bible College.* internetbible college.net. Posted February 15, 2006. internetbiblecollege.net/lessons/hebrew% 20words%20for%20faith.htm. Accessed June 6, 2017.
28. "Tekoa." NIV Compact Dictionary, pp. 581-582.
29. Ruth 2:1.
30. Ibid., 3:4.
31. Ibid., 4:1.
32. 1 Samuel 13:14.
33. Ruth 4:21b-22.

THE STORY OF JONATHAN

1. "The Psychotic king who drove himself mad." *Saul Becomes King. Timeline, maps, chronology, sermons.* bible.ca. www.bible.ca/.../bible-archeology-maps-timeline-chronology-1 Samuel-16-20-Saul-jon. Accessed April 2, 2017.
2. "Carob: the new, ancient ingredient." *Aglaia's Table on Kea Cyclades.* aglaiakremezi. com. Posted June 9, 2015. www.aglaiakremezi.com/en/carob-the-new-ancient-ingredient. Accessed April 5, 2017.
3. "Mephibosheth." *Mephibosheth Definition and Meaning.*biblestudytools.com. www.biblestudytools.com/dictionary. Accessed July 6, 2016.
4. Numbers 1:3.
5. 1 Samuel 13:13-14.
6. Ibid., 14:1, 6-7.
7. *Saul Becomes King. Timeline, maps, chronology, sermons.* bible.ca. accessed April 2, 2017.
8. Witcombe, Christopher L.C.E."Sacred Places: Trees and the Sacred." sbc.edu. witcombe.sbc.edu/sacredplaces/trees.html. Accessed May 8, 2017.
9. 1 Samuel 20:30a.
10. Ibid., 17:26b.
11. Ibid., 17:32.
12. Ibid., 17:33.
13. Ibid., 17:45.
14. Ibid., 19:4-5.
15. Ibid., 20:3.
16. Ibid., 20: 16, 42.

17. Ibid., 23:17.
18. Ibid., 20:14-15.
19. 2 Samuel 1:22, 25-26a.
20. Ibid., 9:1.
21. Ibid., 9:7.
22. Ibid., 9:13.

THE STORY OF ABIGAIL

1. 1 Samuel 14:47.
2. Numbers 13:6, 30; Judges 1:20.
3. "Lambs, hogget, and Mutton." *Lamb and Mutton-Wikipedia*. Wikipedia.org. https://en.wikipedia.org/wiki/Lamb_and_mutton. Accessed February 8, 2017.
4. 1 Samuel 15:12.
5. "The Three Stage Ritual of Biblical Marriages." (stage 3ci), bible.ca. www.bible.ca/marriage/ancient-jewish-three-stage-weddings-and-marriage-customs-ce. Accessed November 5, 2016.
6. Genesis 24:61.
7. Kadden, Barbara Binder. "Time and Place for a Jewish Wedding." *My Jewish Learning.* myjewishlearning.com. Accessed May 10, 2016.
8. "The Jewish Wedding Analogy." *The Jewish Wedding Analogy Commentary.* biblestudytools.com. www.biblestudy/tools.com/commentaries/revelation/the-jewish-wedding-analogy.hm. Accessed May 5, 2017.
9. "Clothing in the Ancient World." *Ancient Israelite Clothing 3.1.2.* wikipedia.org. Biblical Clothing # outer garments. Accessed July 10, 2016.
10. "Ketubah." wikipedia.org. https://en.wikipedia.org/wiki/ketubah. Accessed July 6, 2016.
11. "Paten." *Paten-Wikipedia.* wikipedia.org. https://en.wikipedia.org/wiki/Paten. Accessed: May 5, 2017.
12. "The Three Stage Ritual of Biblical Marriages," (3b:stage2). bible.ca.
13. Bracha, Rebbetzin Chana. "The Secret of the Dudaim Deal." *Women on the Land.* blogspot.com. Posted November 26, 2014. rebbetzinchanabracha.blogspot.com/2014/11/the-secret-of-dudaim-deal. html. Accessed May 5, 2017.
14. Genesis 16:1-4.
15. NIV Study Bible, The Zondervan Corporation, Grand Rapids, Michigan, 1985. Study note: 1 Samuel 25:25, p. 412.
16. Douglas, J.D. and Tenney, Merrill C. "Concubine." NIV Compact Dictionary of the Bible, Zondervan Publishing House, Academic and Professional Books, Grand Rapids, Michign, pp. 128-129.
17. "Sheep Shearing: 2.3 Rooing." wikipedia.org. https://en.wikipedia.org/wiki/sheep_shearing. Accessed May 5, 2017.

18. Geoghegan, Jeffrey C. "Sheep Shearing and David's Rise to Power." Vol. 87, 2006, 55-63. bsw.org. https://www.bsw.org/biblical/vol-87-2006/Israelite-sheepshearing-and-David's rise to power. Accessed November 5, 2016.

19. "Shearing Devices." Contents 3.1. *Sheep Shearing-Wikipedia.*

20. 1 Samuel 25:10-11.

21. Ibid., 25:18.

22. Ibid., 25:24-25.

23. Ibid., 25: 28b.

24. Ibid., 25: 30-31a.

25. Ibid., 25: 31b.

26. Ibid., 25: 39a.

27. Ibid., 25: 40.

28. Waltke, Bruce. "How Did the Urim and the thummim Function?" bible. org. Posted January 1, 2001. https://bible.org/question/how-did-urim-and-thummim-function. Accessed May 5, 2017.

29. 2 Samuel 1:17-27.

30. Ibid., 3:3.

31. Ibid., 5:7, 9.

32. Ibid., 5:11.

The Story of King Josiah

1. Douglas, J.D. and Tenney, Merrill.C. "The Shephelah." NIV Compact Dictionary of the Bible, Zondervan Publishing House, Academic and Professional Books, 1989. p. 547.

2. Deuteronomy 30:16.

3. The NIV Study Bible, The Zondervan Corporation, Grand Rapids, Michigan, 1985. Study note: 2 Kings 22:1, p. 566.

4. Vamosh, Miriam Feinberg. "Ancient Hebrew Sweet You Could Make Today: Ashishot." haaretz.com. March 12, 2014. www.haaretz.com>JewishWorld>Archeology. Accessed January 5, 2017.

5. 2 Kings 23:36.

6. Ibid., 23:31; 24:18.

7. Ibid., 22:5.

8. Ibid., 22:8.

9. 2 Chronicles 34:19, 21b.

10. Ibid., 34:31.

11. Ibid., 34:3b.

12. 1 Kings 13:2.

13. Ibid., 12:28.

14. Jeremiah 22:15c-16.

15. 2 Chronicles 36:21.
16. 2 Kings 23:25.
17. Easton, M.G. "Josiah." *Easton's 1897 Bible Dictionary.* ccel.org. www.ccel.org/e/ easton/ebd/ebd3.html. Accessed April 5, 2017.
18. Matthew 1:11.
19. 2 Kings 23:24b.

The Story of Esther

1. 2 Kings 24:10, 12b; 25:9.
2. 2 Chronicles 36:20.
3. The NIV Study Bible, The Zondervan Corporation, Grand Rapids, Michigan, 1985. Study note: Jeremiah 52:28, p. 1213.
4. Jeremiah 25:11.
5. "The Commandment to Restore and to Build Jerusalem." 1. The Decree of Cyrus, 2. The Decree of Darius 1. patmospapers.com.www.patmospapers.com/ daniel/457.htm. Accessed May 5, 2017.
6. NIV Study Bible, Study note: Esther 2:7, p. 721.
7. Genesis 12:7.
8. Jeremiah 33:7.
9. "The Ancient city of Susa in Iran is a worldwide treasure." (par. 2). ancient-origins.net. Posted July 11, 2015. www.ancient-origins.net/news.../.ancient-city-susa-iran-worldwide-treasure03399. Accessed May 12, 2017.
10. "The Seven Wonders-Hanging Gardens of Babylon." *unmuseum.org.* www. unmuseum.org/hanging.htm. Accessed November 9, 2016.
11. Jeremiah 39:8.
12. "Xerxes 1." *wikipedia.org.* https://enwikipedia.org/wiki/xerxes. Accessed September 3, 2016.
13. Ecclesiastes 12:8.
14. Esther 1:19.
15. Huot, Jean-Louis. "Xerxes 1, King of Persia." *britannica.com.* www.britannica. com/biography/xerxes-1. Accessed May 2, 2017.
16. "Persian Girl Names: Dorsa." Farshid Farhats' Google Site. google.com. https:// sites.google.com/site/farshidfarhat/girl-names. Accessed July 6, 2016.
17. "Susa." *Ancient History Encyclopedia.* ancient.eu. www.ancient.eu/susa. Accessed July 6, 2016.
18. "Biography of Cyrus the Great." *Ancient Mesopotamia: Biography of Cyrus the Great-Ducksters.* ducksters.com. www.ducksters.com>History>Biography. Accessed July 6, 2016.
19. Esther 2:17.
20. Exodus 17:8-16; 1 Samuel 14:47-48.

21. 1 Samuel 15: 3-5.
22. Esther 4:1.
23. Ibid., 4:14b.
24. Ibid., 6:7-9.
25. Ibid., 6:10.
26. Ibid., 7:3-4a.
27. Ibid., 7:10-8:2.
28. NIV Study Bible, Study note: Esther 3:7, p. 723.
29. 1 Samuel 15:17-19.
30. NIV Study Bible, Study note: Esther 9:31, p. 729.
31. Esther 10:3.

Printed in the United States
By Bookmasters